Nellie and Mrs. W

— A NOVEL —

Michael DiSchiavi

Copyright © 2018 Michael DiSchiavi
All rights reserved
First Edition

PAGE PUBLISHING, INC.
New York, NY

First originally published by Page Publishing, Inc. 2018

ISBN 978-1-64350-847-4 (Paperback)
ISBN 978-1-64350-848-1 (Digital)

Printed in the United States of America

In loving memory of Clifton James Turner, for inspiring me to write this book and for believing that I could.

In loving memory of Brian Elliott Menendez-DiSchiavi, for everything. I miss you every minute of every day.

With love and gratitude always to you both.

To Bruce,
   Thank you for being the best brother/brother-in-law ever. I don't know what I'd do without you.
      Love,
      Michael
      February 6, 2019

A Note on Spelling

Nellie Boxall spelled her first name *N-e-l-l-i-e* on all her official papers. The same spelling is found on her birth certificate. Despite this, the many times Virginia Woolf wrote her cook's name (in letters, diaries, etc.), she consistently spelled it *N-e-l-l-y*. The reasons for the discrepancy are unclear.

If I were reading this diary, if it were a book that came my way, I think I should seize with greed on the portrait of Nelly, and make a story—perhaps make the whole story revolve around that—it would amuse me. Her character—our efforts to get rid of her—our reconciliations.

Diary of Virginia Woolf,
December 1929.

Prologue

London
May 1955

I ain't nobody special. I never did break any records, cure any disease, or do anything else worthwhile. All I had done in my whole life was cook meals and clean house in other people's houses. In fact, until I left service, I never did have a place to call my own. I was always a "live in." The pay was less, but they provided room and board. Seeing as the difference in pay was a lot less than the rent on an average flat, I always figured I came out ahead that way. As I said, I was just a worker woman, nobody special.

I was real surprised when that gentleman rang me up. It was a Tuesday. I remember that specifically because that's the day I played cards with the girls. I was standing over the sink in my flat, making tuna salad. I almost didn't bother answering the telly, but figured I should in case it was Adelaide, my next door neighbor and best friend. I thought she might be in trouble. At our age, anything's possible. I was panting a little when I answered it; I had to go into the living room. The phone was sitting on a card table next to the ugly orange sofa I had then.

"Hello, might this be the home of Nellie Boxall?" It was a male voice I didn't recognize.

"It sure is. And who might I be havin' the pleasure of speaking to?" I answered.

"Ahem. My name is ——" I forgot his name for a minute, but it's big. He called himself a stretching out the word like it made him the prime minister. Sorry, but I ain't any good with names. Anyways, the biographer continued.

"May I please speak to her?"

"You already are. I'm Nellie Boxall, sure as I'm standing here talking to you."

"The Nellie Boxall who worked for Virginia and Leonard Woolf?" The pitch of his voice got higher with expectation.

"Yes, the one and the same. Nobody else with my name that I know of."

"At last. How marvelous! I've been trying to track you down for so long, to finally have located you."

And there you have it. I spent all those years chopping vegetables and cleaning the loo for the most brilliant mind in this century, and now some biographer wanted to talk to me. I had no idea why.

"Mrs. Boxall, I would like—"

"No missus, sir, it's *miss*."

"Well, then, Ms. Boxall"—he emphasized the *miss*—"what I was going to say was that, if you happen to be free next week, I'd like to invite you on Monday to come stay at the Ritz in Mayfair. You'd be staying for a week." He paused for a moment, allowing me to absorb his words, then added, "At my expense, of course."

Well, he could have knocked me over right then and there! Some stranger was asking me to stay at a fancy hotel like the Ritz. I'd never dreamed of even *cleaning* a room at the Ritz, much less staying in one.

"It is possible I'd be able to come," I said, trying to play it cool. "May I ask why you want me there?"

The man's voice grew real serious, businesslike. "Everyone knows Virginia Woolf, the writer, they've read the books, the [edited] diaries and letters. I want to know about Virginia Woolf the *person*. What she was like to live with, work for, what she ate for breakfast, what she loved, who she hated. In short, Ms. Boxall, I'm looking for the things the books can't tell me. You're the only person who can tell me those things."

I took down the biographer's number and told him I needed some time to think about what he said and check my schedule. No sooner did I hang up the receiver than I ran (or what passes as running at my age) to Adelaide's place. She lived in the flat right next door, so I didn't have to even get dressed or comb my hair to go see her. So there I was, rapping at her door loud enough to wake the dead, my hair standing straight up, and me, in general, looking like a madwoman. I saw an eye sweep over the peephole, and the locks quickly being turned as Adelaide opened the door.

"Lord, Nellie, why didn't you use your key if it's so important? What's the matter, you have to use the loo or something?" I kissed her hello and walked right in, muttering that I had something unbelievable to tell her. Wagner was playing on the phonograph, filling the entire room.

"For Christ's sake, Adelaide, lower that thing!" My friend did as I requested, though with a bit of a huff. She hated the fact that I didn't appreciate her opera collection. It was more like an obsession, if you ask me. Wagner, Mozart, Salieri, it didn't matter who, the sounds of opera flooded her flat at any hour of the day until she went to bed at night. A bit of an uppity hobby for the widow of a shopkeeper, if you ask me, but who was I to talk? I was a former house servant with a bare-bones education who read books faster than the library could stock them. I could get into about how her mamma was an opera singer 'til she met her father and … but that would take too long now. The point was we're both peculiar, that's for sure. Maybe that's why we got on so well.

Within a few minutes, the music was lowered to a tolerable volume, and there was a cup of boiling hot tea in front of me, a lemon wedge left thoughtfully on the side. I sat in the recliner in her living room, and she was in the rocking chair on the left side of it. She couldn't contain herself anymore.

"What's going on? What's so important that I had to interrupt my whole day?" she asked.

After I told the story, Adelaide sat in her recliner openmouthed.

"Well, you just have to take him up on this, Nellie. It is just too marvelous to pass up. The Ritz! My lord, when else is someone like us going to get that chance again."

"But what if he is some kind of nut?" I protested. "I don't want to get involved with a nut who is going to try to hold me prisoner or something." Adelaide covered her mouth. "Don't laugh," I scolded, "I read the *Daily Mall*, I see what happens to unsuspecting women. Even old bags like me"—I didn't wait to be rude by saying *us*—"have to watch out. These young hoodlums ... who *knows* what they're after half the time."

"I'm—I'm sorry, Nellie, I really don't mean to laugh, but—" At this point, she had to force down another fit of laughter threatening to come up. "Your fears are exaggerated. At your age, that someone should mess with you. What are they going to be after, do you suppose? Your bus pass, arthritis cream, or your body?"

Point taken.

"Okay, so maybe I am being silly. But honestly, do you think I should go into business with a total stranger who looked me up in a phone book or whatever he did to find me?"

"He didn't ask you for any money, from what you told me. And if he does, no, you shouldn't give it to him. But leaving that aside, it sounds like he just wants you to talk about Virginia Woolf. No harm in that."

"That's another thing. I'd feel kind of disloyal, I think, talking about Mrs. W behind her back like that."

"Gracious, Nellie, you talk about that woman like she is on a shopping trip at Harrods. She has been dead for years now. You can't talk about her behind her back, she doesn't have one!"

I thought that last comment was a bit cruel, but I didn't get mad. That's my Adelaide. She had no tact but wouldn't hurt a fly, and her heart was made of 24-karat gold.

She must have sensed what I was feeling since she said something else.

"Besides, you've spoken to me of her a million times, and that was just the first two weeks we knew each other." Now we both laughed.

"But that was different, it was you. We're friends, and when I talk to you about *anything*, I know you're not taking notes then going home and pounding out stories about it on your typewriter."

*****

Turned out, I accepted his offer, even though I didn't go around accepting offers from strangers, particularly men—particularly men I had never even met, only spoken to over the telly. But I accepted his terms for a good reason. He said he needed my help if he was going to accomplish the work he wanted to do. When I stopped to think about it, I realized he was right.

Chapter One

Hogarth House
Richmond
6 March 1916

The appointment was for noon. Nellie got off the omnibus and began the ten-block walk, cursing under her breath that there was no stop closer to her destination. She was early, in any case, so she stopped into a shop nearby for a cup of coffee. Coffee always seemed to steady her nerves. As she reached into her coin purse to pay, she laid the book that was tucked under her arm onto the counter. Coffee in hand, she replaced the book underneath her left arm and took her coffee and a couple of napkins to an empty table next to the window. She sat for a while, drinking leisurely and looking over several parts of the book. She had already read it twice. The title was *The Voyage Out*, and the author was the lady she was going to be interviewing with, Virginia Woolf. While she sipped from the steaming cup, Nellie stared out the window at the people outside hurrying to and fro.

She wondered … what would Virginia Woolf be like? One knew her only from her novel, a brilliant if disturbing work of literature. What would it be like to meet the woman behind the story, the flesh and blood authoress? She glanced at her watch and gasped. If she did not hurry, she might miss her chance to find out. She gulped down the rest of the beverage, wiping the white foam of the coffee from her mouth. She stood up from the table, straightened her hat, and smoothed out her dress. She left the shop and began to walk toward her destination. She was going to get the position as cook; she could feel it in her bones.

Nellie found the Woolf's residence easily enough, and she quickly mounted the two small steps leading to the front door. She rang the doorbell, admiring the azalea plants on either side of the door.

She was greeted by the maid, a short stout woman who appeared to be in her late twenties to early thirties, with puffy cheeks, large eyes, and a crooked smile. As Nellie would later learn, the maid's name was Lottie. She was new to the house; she had only been with the Woolfs for three weeks.

Once inside the house, she was led to a small sitting room with bookshelves. The shelves were overloaded with volumes of all shapes, sizes, and genres. There were novels, biographies, histories, and atlases. Books were vital here, as one might expect in a home of writers. The air contained a faint smell of tobacco. She sat in a leather-bound chair that was situated by the window, facing the entryway, waiting for her interviewer.

Mrs. Woolf crept downstairs and walked into the sitting room, shoulders slightly hunched. Nellie stood up. "You must be Nellie. I'm Virginia Woolf."

Nellie extended her hand, only to have it dangling in midair. Virginia smiled. "I'm terribly sorry, but as you can see," she held up her right hand, stained blue, "I've been writing rather intensely this morning." Nellie withdrew her hand.

"Quite understandable, ma'am. I'm sure it is an occupational hazard." She chuckled quietly.

Virginia sat down on the sofa to the left of Nellie and took a small notepad and pen out of her housecoat pocket. "So tell me what experience you have, Nelly?"

"Well, my only *paid* experience cooking is for Roger Fry. I've been with him for the past four years. But then, you know that already, since he's the one who suggested me to you. But that's not my only experience, no, ma'am, Mrs. Woolf. I'm one of ten children, you see, and I was an orphan by the time I was twelve, so I've cooked plenty of meals, you can be sure." She paused. "Is there anything else you'd like to know? I have references if you'd care to read them." She received no answer. "Mrs. Woolf?"

Virginia was looking at one of the bookshelves. "Yes, I think Effie should marry, after all."

"I'm sorry," Nellie asked, puzzled.

Virginia made no answer.

"Mrs. Woolf ..." Nellie probed, "you were saying something about someone named Effie?"

Virginia blushed. "Sorry, I was thinking out loud about a character in my new book."

Nellie decided to be bold. "Speaking of your books, Mrs. Woolf, I was wondering if you would sign this." She handed her would-be employer the book she brought with her.

Mrs. Woolf took the book in her left hand, turned over the title page, and pressed her left hand on the page. She took the pen firmly in her right hand and wrote carefully, deliberately.

> To Nelly,
> With great affection and appreciation
> Virginia Woolf

No sooner did its creator return the book to the reader than they heard the front door open. A man walked in, medium height, wearing a brown suit that seemed well-worn. He wore thin rimmed glasses. The man walked briskly, but not hurriedly, passing the two women but not stopping. It seemed as though he did not notice them.

"Leonard, darling, come here for a moment." The man stopped in his tracks with a jolt, as if suddenly awakened from a dream. Mrs. Woolf held out her hand for her husband. He grasped it and held it briefly. "Meet Nelly Boxall. She is interviewing to be our cook. Nellie, my husband, Mr. Leonard Woolf."

"Mr. Woolf, it's a pleasure to meet you."

Leonard mumbled, almost unintelligibly. "Likewise, I'm sure." His voice became more distinct. "Well now, if you ladies will excuse me, I am really quite busy. Virginia, I leave the matter of the job to your good judgment. Good day, miss." He had not bothered to even try to remember the name he had heard only a minute ago.

Embarrassed at the slight, Virginia switched the conversation back to her book.

"Did you enjoy my book, Nellie?" Virginia worried incessantly over people's opinions of her novel. It was the nature of the novelist, she supposed.

"Well," Nellie hesitated, unsure of how candid she should be with this woman who was in a position to give her a job, "not exactly, no, ma'am."

Virginia stiffened. "I see. Then what may I ask did you think of my work, exactly?"

Nellie rushed to explain. "Don't misunderstand me, ma'am, I think it is brilliant work. I've never seen anything like it, and I read all the time. But it's just that … Mrs. Woolf, I've never seen a book where the heroine dies instead of marrying. It seems, oh, I don't know, not right, not normal."

Virginia smiled. "You are quite right when you say that it is not 'normal,' because it goes against literary tradition. That is exactly the point. I desire to go against tradition. I want to reshape the whole concept of the novel, make it different than it has been in the past. I will create new traditions."

"But marriage is something sacred, ma'am. Surely, it should be respected."

Virginia tossed her head to the side. "Hogwash! Marriage as an institution is rubbish. It imprisons women." She laughed. "I know that is an odd statement coming from a married woman, but you must understand, Leonard and I are different. We respect each other, it is not merely one-sided. Of course, the fact that I bring in some income does help the matter."

Nellie was undeterred. "All the same, I do think you should have had Rachel marry him at the end. Otherwise, you send the message to young girls that marriage is worthless—even death is better."

Virginia scoffed. "That is the most ridiculous thing I've ever heard."

"I don't know, Mrs. Woolf, it seems to me—"

"Are you an early riser?"

"Pardon?"

"I was asking if you were an early riser. I prefer to have breakfast by seven thirty or eight. I take walks after that. Would that be a problem for you?"

"No, not at all, Mrs. Woolf."

"Fine. You may move in by the end of the week. When you come back, I shall give you your key."

"Thank you, Mrs. Woolf. You won't be sorry." She got up to leave, grabbing her book like a precious treasure.

In her vast excitement, Nellie forgot to ask about the salary.

Chapter Two

*Richmond
Hogarth House
February 1917*

Mrs. Woolf said she would like lamb for dinner. Nellie was overjoyed. It would require yet another trip into London (she had already shopped for the day and had not bought lamb), but so what? Nellie was too happy about the request to mind any inconvenience. Under normal circumstances, Mrs. Woolf could at best be described as being blasé about food; at worst, she hated food altogether, often requiring forced feeding. Such a specific, definitive request, such as lamb for dinner, was nothing short of a miracle. Nellie could not wait to inform Mr. Woolf of the request.

Less experienced servants might have been put out by such a last-minute request for a menu item, but not Nellie. She had been in charge of a kitchen for a long time and was not fazed by impromptu meal requests. She knew how she would proceed. She would take the noon train into London, get the best lamb the butcher had, then be back by a quarter to two. With the help of Lottie, the maid, she could have dinner on the table by seven at the latest.

As she was riding into London on the train, Nellie made mental notes about the rest of the meal preparations. She would roast the lamb with cloves of garlic. She would serve baked potatoes on the side, smothered with freshly churned butter (Mr. Woolf loved butter). She would make some asparagus, marinated with lemon, and a salad of farm ripe tomatoes, radishes, and cucumbers in an oil-and-vinegar dressing. Her stomach began to growl as she thought of it. She would get a chocolate mousse from the bakery in town for dessert. Mr. Woolf hated chocolate, but the missus adored it. Nellie would go to America to do the grocery shopping if it meant the lady of the house would eat more regularly. The poor dear was looking so frightfully frail and malnourished these days.

Nellie got off the train, bought the lamb and the trimmings, and stopped to pick up some fresh flowers for the dining room table from a street vendor standing outside the gates of the British Library.

Nellie had grown very fond of her mistress, even if Virginia did refuse to spell Nellie's name correctly in her many notes. Nellie recalled the first time she had brought the misspelling to the lady's attention. It was shortly after she moved in, the Monday after the interview. Mrs. Woolf was in the study. Mr. Woolf was out. He had said he'd be gone for most of the day. Nellie wanted to get the matter of her name squared away. She had asked Lottie's advice about it, and Lottie had told her to speak to Mrs. Woolf directly, and at once. She said that the missus was the one to speak to since she wrote all the checks. Nellie knocked tentatively at the wide open door of the study, waiting to be invited in. When Mrs. Woolf did not pick up her head, the new cook knocked again, slightly louder. Still, no response came.

It was the clearing of her throat that got the writer's attention. She jolted her head upward, more annoyed than she let show (the woman was new, after all).

"What do you need, Nellie?" She looked at Nellie with such an intense gaze that it unnerved the already-jumpy cook. She edged only slightly closer, standing in the entryway of the study.

"My name, ma'am. That is, I need to correct it." She felt her cheeks getting flushed, and she spoke more rapidly, growing more uncomfortable by the second.

"When you signed my book, you spelled my name "*N-e-l-l-y*. I spell it *N-e-l-l-i-e*. I'd just like it to be right, ma'am, so that I have no trouble at the bank, ma'am." The last *ma'am* was added from nervous energy.

"Leonard writes the checks, Nellie. You'll have to take it up with him. As for me, I'll take it under advisement. Thank you for telling me."

"Yes, ma'am. I'll be getting to my work." She ran out of the room.

Nellie didn't know what "I'll take it under advisement" meant and, frankly, did not care. The experience had frightened the wits out of her. She never pursued the matter further.

Nellie's employers may have frightened the dickens out of her, but Lottie did not. The day continued without incident, the two women working separately when warranted and side by side, when needed. That night, after the last pot had been scrubbed and the dishes dried and put away, Nellie followed Lottie downstairs to their quarters rather than going for a walk in the green fields near Hogarth House, as she had done the past few nights. Once downstairs, she closed the door behind her.

"Why did you do it?" Nellie demanded. Her volume and tone indicated that she meant business.

Lottie made an abrupt bout face, her cheeks slightly flushed. "Why did I do what?" She struggled to keep her voice steady to conceal her rising fear.

"You know bloody well what I'm talking about. Don't pretend you don't."

"I don't—"

Nellie was furious. "That's a bloody crock, and you know it. You set me up. You damned well knew that *Mr. Woolf* writes the checks, yet you sent me to talk to Mrs. Woolf. What were you trying to do?"

"Nothing, I didn't realize that Mr. Woolf writes the checks. She makes the money, so I naturally assumed—"

"You're a fucking liar!" Nellie lurched forward toward the maid as though she would strike her. Lottie cowered. "You've been here for weeks, don't tell me you haven't been paid yet. Now, you tell me why you did it, damn you! Why are you trying to get me the sack, after only a few days? What have I done to you?"

"You're bloody here, damn it! That's what you've done." Lottie's voice now matched Nellie's. The tears began to trickle down her face.

"You're here to replace me, why don't you just admit it. I can't get another job. I don't have the experience you have. I need *this one*."

Lottie slumped into the secondhand armchair with the gray slipcover over it. Nellie crouched next to her, anger quickly turning into sympathy.

"Oh, Lottie, honey, I'm not after your job. I only know how to do my job, cooking. I don't clean and serve like you do, I could never. I could never do what you do, not in a million years." She took a tissue out of her apron pocket and wiped the tear from Lottie's cheek. Lottie stared silently at the new cook for several minutes. Her words sounded sincere, but could she be trusted?

Lottie chose trust over suspicion. For the moment, she had no reason to disbelieve, and Nellie seemed sincere.

Lottie nodded her head. "Thank you, luv. And I'm sorry about what I did, and I'm sorry that I misjudged you."

"It's all right, Lottie. We have to work and live together. I hope we can be friends."

Lottie smiled brightly and stroked the cook's right cheek. "We can be friends, and we will be, I'm sure of it. In fact," she added while running her right hand through Nellie's hair, "I'd wager that before long, we'll be the very best of friends." Lottie gave a bright smile, which was reciprocated.

As days turned into weeks and weeks into months, the women grew closer, to both women's delight. In spite of their duplicitous beginnings, they began to trust each other. A bond was formed, deeper than that formed of necessity by strangers who find themselves thrown together in difficult and close circumstances. This was the start of a life lived together, a bond that would last a lifetime.

The issue of the check proved moot. Leonard spelled her name correctly from the first. Virginia never corrected herself. Nellie could never surmise whether her employer's error was because she simply could not remember or did not think it important enough to care about.

*****

In the Woolfs' study were two desks, situated several meters apart, facing each other. Leonard's desk was solid oak, with several drawers full of papers he needed, bills he had to pay, and correspondence that needed to be responded to or saved for future reference. Everything was neatly organized within manila folders, clearly labeled for content. And dates! Every piece of paper had a date on it, in order to keep track of when he received something or worked on it last. If it was a would-be author's manuscript, Leonard would make notes and corrections carefully, signing and dating the bottom before either giving it to Virginia for further review or stuffing it into the provided self-addressed stamped envelope to be sent back to the author with a terse note of rejection. On his ink blotter sat whatever manuscript he was working on at the time. The center drawer contained only a few blue pens and some sharpened and unsharpened pencils and a roll of postage stamps.

In contrast, Virginia's desk was pine. The two bottom drawers were chock-full of articles she was writing, whatever manuscript or proofs she happened to be working on, and plastic wrappings containing small snacks that she had hidden away from Leonard's and Nellie's prying eyes. Atop the desk were several mounds of letters wrapped in thick rubber bands. During the course of any given week, she might receive upward of a hundred letters from other authors, fans, publishers, anyone at all. She prided herself on responding to each and every one of them, giving preference, of course, to those from people whom she knew personally or those with enclosed checks. Loose stamps littered her center drawer. Letters that were complete, addressed, and stamped were stacked haphazardly on the corner of the desk, waiting for the post. At one in the afternoon, when she had finished writing for the day, she would leave whatever she had been working on sitting sloppily atop her desk (often more than one item, as she liked to exercise different sections of her brain by writing different genres on the same day).

Virginia loved to tease Leonard about the disparity of quality of their desks as indicative to their tastes in general. She, who had been raised with the privilege that comes with money, had quite simple taste in things. He, who had been raised in financial struggle, envious of what others had, preferred the finer things in life. How ironic that it should be so. Or was it?

As Virginia sat at her desk, her eyes occasionally glancing toward Leonard scratching away with his pen at some item, she reflected on her writing process for *The Voyage Out*. She took down her author's copy of the book, which sat on a long cherry wood shelf behind her, next to her volumes of thick diaries, and opened it gingerly, as though it were a baby with a pram that needed changing. Stumbling onto a particular scene, she was mentally transported to herself back to the time when she was writing that scene. At that time, the book was titled *Melymbrosia* until her publisher convinced her to change it.

Virginia was deep in thought. Rachel, her heroine, simply had to kiss Richard Dalloway. There had to be an attraction between them. But he was a married man. Virginia did not want her readers to dismiss Rachel as a wanton whore. What could she do to redeem Rachel? Thinking about her dilemma, sprawled out on the sofa in her sitting room, she nibbled on the tip of her pen in between scribbling notes on a legal pad that she used to solidify her ideas. She bit too hard; the pen broke, the ink spilling all over her yellow dress.

"Damn it!" Virginia shouted, for no one to hear. The ink spread unchecked across her chest, but she did not move. Cleaning her dress would have meant taking her attention away from her work. That was not an option.

Distractions always bothered Virginia. Lately, she demanded total privacy when she wrote. She could abide Leonard being in the room if he must, but that was the exception. Even Leonard's presence tested her patience. Agatha, the day maid, was not permitted to dust, polish, or clean in the room until Mrs. Woolf was out of it since her movements distracted the writer. Virginia had once made a costly error. She was writing a review of a famous novelist's latest work. She brought her writing pad into the kitchen and wrote at the table. Just at the moment that a crucial sentence was about to emerge, Agatha decided to start chopping blocks of ice. The sound sent shivers up Virginia's spine. The sentence was irrevocably lost, and Virginia retreated from the room in a huff. She said not an unkind word to the servant since she was merely doing her job and in her "territory" as it were. Since that fateful day, the authoress confined her writing to either her bedroom, study, or the sitting room. For note-taking, she liked to go to Hyde Park, her favorite park in all of London, or on the steps of the British Museum, sipping herbal tea. She had a small notebook that slipped easily into her purse. She carried it with her everywhere and would frequently take it out when inspiration struck, a sentence came to her, or she had overheard (for she was forever eavesdropping on the conversations of strangers) a particular phrase or comment that struck a chord with her. Virginia loved taking long walks, socializing with friends, gossiping about friends, reading anything she could get her hands on, and a million other things.

But how was she to solve the problem of Rachel? She still was unsure of how she wanted to handle this character. There had to be something about her that would attract the reader. The reader must want to hug her, not slap her. And yet she should be human as well, with human weaknesses. Virginia listed possible resolutions on her pad; none of them seemed to work for her. She even tried sketching a scene in pencil, a last resort since she considered herself a dreadful artist. Nothing was right. She let out a deep sigh, looked at her watch, and began to put her things away. It was one o'clock; Rachel's problems could wait another day.

The snapping of the pen point snapped Virginia back to the present. As the ink splattered, she instinctively shoved the book forward, to shield it from the mess. Her efforts were unnecessary; the ink was on her only, dripping down her yellow dress. As she got up to go to her bedroom, Leonard took notice of her.

"Had an accident, did we, Genia?" he asked, using her family nickname.

"No, *we* did not have an accident at all. *I* had an accident. Now, if you'll excuse me, I must change and have Lottie wash this at once." She was almost of the study when Leonard's voice stopped her in her tracks. She turned to face him.

"I've told you time and time again you mustn't nibble so on your pens. Aside from being grossly unsanitary, this is the result." He pointed to her dress.

She rolled her eyes; she hated it when his voice had that dreadful, pedantic tone to it. She opened her mouth to say something. She would point out that her biting had nothing to do with this accident. She changed her mind. "Indeed" was her curt retort as walked out of the room, closing the door none too gently behind her.

In her bedroom, she changed into a pale-blue dress, neatly folding the soiled one for Lottie to wash. Handing it off to her maid, Virginia went back downstairs to try to resume her writing. She could not; the rhythm was broken. She could not retrieve it. That was how it was with her work. Her writing was like the beatings of an aged, failing heart. It would flow as long as the oxygen kept pumping, but deprive it of the oxygen long enough, and the heart would stop. Under ordinary circumstances, the authoress would not have moved from her spot, ink-stained dress notwithstanding. It was only her sudden lack of a pen that caused her to get up. She settled down for a rest on the sofa in the living room when she heard the servants' entrance squeak open. *Leonard really must get someone to look at that door*, she thought to herself. Almost instantly, footsteps climbed the stairs and halted behind her.

"Excuse me, ma'am, but I'm back from the market now."

"Yes, Nellie, I can see quite well that you are back. What of it?" Virginia quipped, annoyed at yet another distraction.

"Well, ma'am, I was wondering if you were feeling up to some dessert after dinner. I bought some chocolate mousse, but I'll put it in the icebox if you don't think you'll be able to have it this evening."

Virginia smiled, Nellie's thoughtfulness not going unnoticed. She was sorry she had been sharp with her a moment ago. But she would not apologize.

"Yes, Nellie, I think the chocolate will be lovely. Although I'm not sure Leonard will agree."

Nellie chuckled. "Aye. Mr. Woolf will not be likin' it much now. Never mind, I'll pick him some fresh strawberries and cream for lunch tomorrow." With a nod from Virginia, Nellie left the room and went about her business.

Something puzzled Nellie for a moment. Whenever Mrs. Woolf spoke to her of her sister, it was always Mrs. Bell, her brother-in-law was Mr. Bell, then there was Mrs. Mansfield, Mr. Duckworth, etc. Yet when the writer spoke of the master of the house, he was Leonard. Nellie wondered if it had anything to do with the fact that Leonard Woolf was a Jew. Her employer's antipathy toward Jews was well-known. Nellie once accidentally found an old letter Virginia had written to a friend in which she declared her intention to marry Leonard Woolf, "the penniless Jew." Nellie suspected that the bias was felt most keenly by Leonard's family. This might account for their infrequent visits. Never mind, Nellie had better things to do than worry about the first names and family ties of her betters. It was the luxury of the privileged to spend hours on end worrying about things that at the end of the day were totally meaningless. Nellie had no such luxury. And why would she give a damn anyway? She had dinner to prepare.

Interlude

I got to the Ritz around two on Monday afternoon. The biographer had told me he'd be waiting for me in the lobby. He said he'd gotten my photo from somewhere, so he knew what I looked like. I told him it had been some time since anyone had taken my photograph, but he said not to worry; he'd recognize me. Sure enough, as soon as I pushed through the mahogany double doors, I saw a middle-aged man in a business suit sitting on a love seat reading a newspaper. He glanced up the moment I opened the door, as if on cue. He rose to his feet, putting his newspaper off to the side, and walked toward me. He held out his right arm in greeting and grinned.

"Ms. Boxall," a flash of recognition glimmered in his eyes, "it was so wonderful of you to come." He smiled his brightest smile. I smiled in turn, appreciating his efforts to put me at ease. "It was so good of you to come. Welcome to the Ritz," he said, as if he owned it.

I shook his hand politely, still feeling a bit uncomfortable with the niceties. I was not used to being treated like a lady. I answered him sheepishly, having a hard time looking at him directly in the eye for too long.

"It wasn't any trouble. Lord knows, my social calendar has been blank for longer than I can remember." I let out a chuckle. The biographer smiled, the way you smile at a child who's just used the loo for the first time.

"Well, Ms. Boxall, let's get you checked in, and then we can get down to business." He motioned to take my arm in his. "Shall we?" He winked.

"Just a second. I wanted to ask you for a favor." His arm dropped to his side. His facial muscles tensed up instantly. I was certain he was expecting me to ask for cash.

"What is it?" His voice turned cold, businesslike.

"It's about my name. I prefer being called by my first name. I'm not used to being called Miss, and not sure that I like it. So if you wouldn't mind …"

"Of course not." He extended his arm again and broke out into a smile, his chest letting out a small puff of air. "Nellie it is! And of course, you will call me Thomas." The friendliness had returned to his mannerisms. This was going to be an interesting experience. I put my arm in his, and we walked together to the queue for the reservations counter.

Standing in queue, I was a little self-conscious. All the other women had white gloves covering their hands. I was the only one whose skin showed (and it wasn't much to look at either). When we got to the marble counter, I was about to open my mouth, but the biographer did the talking for me. All I had to do was show my passport (I never did get a driver's license). The lady behind the desk gave me a room key with a tag attached to it with the number 828 etched into it. Walking toward the lift she directed me to, the biographer told me to go on ahead.

"You should go up to your room alone. Give you a chance to settle in, in private. I have your room number and will ring you up in about an hour. I'll meet you by the lift, and we'll go for tea. We have a reservation." With that, I went up to the eighth floor and found my way to my room.

Imagine my surprise when I saw the room, *my* room. It was a *suite*. Imagine that. I entered a small foyer and plopped my suitcase down. Then I walked into the living room. The rug was real soft, expensive-like. There was a leather couch in the middle of the room with an end table on each side. One of the tables had a real nice-looking lamp on it. It looked like one of those Tiffany lamps I'd seen in fancy store windows. I had no way of knowing if it was real, but in a fancy place like this, I'll bet it was. There was a bar tucked away in the side of the room and a telly opposite the sofa. The bedroom was even nicer. A king-size bed, what I was going to do with such a big bed, I didn't know; and all the furniture were cherry wood, even the headboard. I would have given up my flat in a second to be able to live in that suite. In my entire life, I never experienced anything like it.

A maid knocked on the door to ask if I needed anything; I didn't. I put the "do not disturb" sign on the doorknob, locked the door, and sat down on the plush armchair by the bedroom window, thinking about unpacking my suitcase, which was still in the foyer.

The ringing phone startled me. I had nodded off for about half an hour. It was Thomas, asking me if I was ready. I supposed I was as ready as I'd ever be. So I said yes, left my suitcase where it was, and went downstairs for my first ever tea at the Ritz. He was waiting for me downstairs outside the restaurant and escorted me to our table. They had already seated him.

The waiter brought our tea and a plate of finger sandwiches. As we began nibbling, I felt obligated to start talking (that was after all why Thomas was paying for me). I tried to sound causal.

"Mrs. Woolf hated food, you know," I said matter-of-factly. The biographer stopped chewing and was looking at me now like he was waiting for a reading from the gospel.

"You don't say. I'd love to hear more about it." He raised his eyebrows.

I continued, slightly uneasy. "Mrs. Woolf did not like to eat at all. She had to be cajoled into it," I lowered my voice a bit, "sometimes by force."

The biographer was intrigued. "It is quite rare, I imagine, for a woman to have that strong of an aversion to food. I cannot imagine."

"Well, there was a reason for that, or at least Mrs. Woolf thought so," I continued. Now I lowered my voice real quiet so as no one would overhear. "Her half-brother, Gerald Duckworth, from her mother's first marriage, he used to touch her, you know." I pointed toward my lap so he would understand my meaning. "She was six."

He put his hand over his mouth, and I thought for a minute he was going to retch right there on the floor. I was wrong. He just gave me a funny look and then asked another question.

"That's awful, but what does that have to do with …?"

He didn't need to finish the question. I could see why he wouldn't understand. I needed to elaborate.

"He would do it to her in the dining room, on top of the china cabinet. There was a full-length mirror facing the cabinet. She could see her reflection in it as he fondled her." I spoke *sotto voce*, barely able to keep the tremor out of my voice. I continued. "As an adult, Mrs. Woolf hated food and mirrors. She never liked to see her reflection."

The newly formed lump in Thomas's throat told me that he grasped the enormity of what I just told him. He seemed even more uncomfortable than I was with the information. When you stop to think about it, knowledge is a cruel mistress. Once she beds you, she never lets go, she becomes a permanent fixture in your life, whether or not you want her there.

We continued eating, mostly in silence. Thomas seemed to want time to absorb what I said. That suited me just fine seeing as how I was hungry and never did have tea in so fancy a place before. There was a lot of food in front of us, and I wasn't planning on wasting it. Anyways, I was, all of a sudden, feeling kinda disloyal to Mrs. Woolf, having said something so personal about her life now, the first time I talked to this man. But I figured if he was going to write a biography, it was important to know, to understand some things about her. I had spoken enough for our first meeting. I would say more later.

Chapter Three

March 1918

Virginia needed to go to the doctor. Leonard, as usual, was at a meeting. Virginia never knew what meeting or with whom. It did not matter. Lord so and so, the bishop of somewhere, the vice chancellor of whatever; it was all the same to her. A thought occurred to her, suddenly, out of the blue. Perhaps Leonard had a mistress. No, she brushed the thought aside as soon as it entered her mind. Not Leonard, he wasn't the type. Not that it was outside the range of possibilities (since their wedding night, they had used their bedroom for nothing more than reading and sleeping). Although she did not feel it was entirely her fault. No matter. The thought was rubbish.

Nellie went with her because Leonard was unavailable. They took the ten o'clock train, got off at Piccadilly, and walked the rest of the way to the doctor's office. Dr. Savage—Virginia often thought that some people's names suited them. Dr. Savage was such a person. Leonard, of course, thought he was wonderful. Virginia secretly suspected that it was the doctor's low fees her husband adored rather than his expertise. But no matter; off she went, Nellie at her right side and a manuscript tucked under her left arm. In her left hand was her favorite pen, the only one she used, blue ink. Once, when she thought she had lost it, she was sick at heart and unable to write for two days until she found it (it had accidentally been put away with the folded laundry). None in the household were at peace until the pen was found. Leonard often teased her that she would sooner part with her money than her pen.

The appointment was for eleven, totally disrupting her workday (for she wrote daily from ten in the morning until one in the afternoon). The doctor was notoriously slow; he got in his office late in the morning, making him run behind from the onset, then had to have his pot of tea and something to eat, usually a scrambled egg with bacon on a biscuit. Since she knew it would be a while, and since topics of conversation with Nellie usually ran quite short, she decided to bring her proofs to correct. They had come in the previous day's post, which was late as usual. She had torn open the package eagerly, while being careful not to damage the contents. The first thing she noticed was a handwritten note from her publisher, commending her on such a fine piece of authorship. He had fond hopes for this novel and its sales should ... blah blah blah. Virginia secretly despised editors, a fact she kept secret for all the obvious reasons.

The women arrived at the doctor's office at a quarter to eleven. Virginia scribbled her name on the register and handed Nellie her coat to hang up while she took a seat in the waiting room. She covered an empty chair next to her with an outdated magazine she found on the rectangular table in the center of the waiting room. Nellie would sit there.

Nellie took her seat and let out a deep sigh, expecting a long wait. If the mistress felt at all hungry after the visit, perhaps they would have some mutton pie in Hyde Park or some French pastry in Bloomsbury. As she sat there, thumbing through the magazine that had thoughtfully been left on her chair, Nellie considered her mistress with awe. Virtually, the instant she sat down, Virginia had opened up her proofs and began reading intently, her shoulders hunched over, the rim of her glasses petering on the edge of her nose. Her pen moved slowly, meticulously over each page, marking a misplaced comma here, a misspelled word there, etc. Not a semicolon went unnoticed. She wrote slowly and deliberately, making an extra effort to be neat and tidy in her notes (for her penmanship tended to be small and barely legible). After she had finished with a page, she blew gently on it so that the ink would not smudge. She was a perfectionist in every detail; a smudged paper could signal catastrophe.

It was nearly a quarter after twelve when she finally was called into the doctor's office. She sat on the examination table in the plain white cotton gown, the white paper covering the exam table crackling under her restless bottom. Nellie stood next to her.

Dr. Savage entered without knocking a few minutes later. He was of medium height, a hard face, more suited for a laborer than a physician she had always felt, covered with a beard that was mostly gray and an overgrown mustache. He did not say hello.

"Well, Virginia, have you been eating regularly?" He tilted his head sideways as if expecting a lie.

"Yes, mostly. Nelly here takes extra effort to please my palette."

"Is that true, Nellie?"

Nellie hesitated. "I certainly try, Doctor. And the missus, she does eat more lately than she has in the past. Whether or not it's enough, I can't say, seeing as I'm no doctor."

"Hmm." The doctor scribbled something in her chart, which he cradled in his arm rather than place on the counter next to exam table, for fear that Virginia might be tempted to read it. "How about your rest? Are you getting enough sleep? Have you heard any voices since our last visit? Imaginary ones that is," he qualified.

Virginia could have slapped him across the face. Who was he to speak of what was real or unreal? How arrogant to assume he knew the inner workings of her mind, and her soul! She would address that issue in a book someday, but for now, the doctor required an answer.

"No, there are no voices, Doctor. Just ideas, forever rushing through my brain."

"What kind of ideas?"

"Literary ones. Sentences for reviews I am writing pop into my head unannounced, as do scenes from novels I want to write. A routine trip to the grocery store can send whole scenes spilling through my mind. I pull my notebook and pen from my purse and stand there in the middle of the aisle, scribbling notes." She laughed. "I cannot tell you how many dirty looks I have gotten from provincial housewives annoyed that I've blocked their access to some bloody cleaning product.

"Then why do you write the ideas down just then? Surely you can take notes at a more appropriate time, when you are not in the middle of a supermarket, for example," the doctor suggested.

"Yes, but you see, then the idea would be lost. My memory is fleeting. An idea unrecorded is gone forever from my brain. That very lost idea may well have shaped a novel, and what a travesty that would be!"

The doctor stared dumbly. He could find no fault with his patient's reasoning. He was also hungry. He wanted to end the visit and get to his lunch.

"Very well, then. I shall be giving Leonard a good report. We shall see you in two weeks for some blood."

Virginia began to protest. "Doctor, I have to finish the proofs for my book." She held out the MS so he could see it. "Then there is the meeting with my publisher. I really won't have time to—"

"Two weeks, Virginia." His tone was cold, unemotional. And so it was settled.

They returned to the waiting room to gather their coats. No payment was required. Her visits were so frequent, Leonard had made an arrangement with the doctor. A bill was mailed to him toward the end of each month. He in turn would mail a check at the beginning of the following month. Virginia did not ever have to worry about writing checks, although Leonard did not hide their finances from her (indeed, she earned most of the money). A shrewd, frugal woman, she could account for every penny she spent. While she totally trusted Leonard with their money, knowing he would always do the right thing, still she yearned for money of her own, in her own name, separate from Leonard. She felt every woman needed that. She wanted to write about it sometime, but for now, she had enough on her plate at present. Walking leisurely, taking in all the sights and sounds, Nellie dared to bring up what had been said in the office.

"You know, ma'am, I did not feel quite right in there. I felt like we lied to the doctor."

Virginia was stoic. "In what way did we lie, Nellie?"

"Well, first off, we said you were eating regular, and we both know that ain't exactly so. And then there was the question about the voices …" The cook hesitated. "Just the other day, I came into the parlor to announce tea and found you talking excitedly. I figured Mr. Woolf was home, and I'd best set another place for tea, but," she paused," there was no one there. You were talking to yourself."

"That was different. I was thinking. Has it ever occurred to you that I sometimes think? And sometimes, it helps me if I think out loud," she replied with more irritation in her voice than she had intended.

Nellie dropped the subject.

As Nellie had suspected, they did go for a walk through Hyde Park, an airing, as Virginia called it, as though Victoria were still on the throne. They ordered meat pies and lemonade. They sat on a large bench opposite the beautiful fountain built in honor of King George IV. Nellie ate her pie hungrily; Virginia picked at hers, mostly to placate Nellie. They ate wordlessly for a while, the strain of their previous conversation weighing heavily between them.

It was Nellie who broke the icy silence. "You know, missus, I didn't mean to accuse you of nothin' there with the doctor. It's just that I worry about you, we all do, carrying on the way you do with that schedule of yours. All those things you're always writing, it's a wonder you can keep them straight in your head. I surely meant no harm."

Virginia pivoted toward her cook, her heart melted at the penitent tone of her voice. She patted her hands with her own. "Of course, I understand, Nellie. You were only looking after me, you always are." Virginia exhaled deeply. "But can't you see, that is just the problem. Everyone *looks after* me, like I am some old lighthouse in dire straits that needs a keeper. I grow sick of it, sick to the death."

In fact, she thought but dared not voice, sometimes after all the fuss was made, she'd rather *be dead*.

They returned home after four, having browsed through a couple of bookstores in London before boarding the train that would take them back. When they arrived home, Leonard was waiting for them. They needn't tell him how it went at the doctor; he informed them. Dr. Savage had telephone him a short while ago.

"My darling," Leonard stood directly in front of his wife, firmly grasping her hands in his, as if fearing she might break free from his hold and run into the road screaming, "I cannot tell you how pleased

I was to hear a good report. We are making excellent progress, our plans are working perfectly. And now with your book soon to come out, why, there isn't anything we shan't be able to do. So long as you keep being a good girl, like you have been."

Virginia made a weak attempt at a smile. She was not a religious person, per se, but she believed that condescending to someone was the one unforgivable sin.

Not wanting to start a row, she aborted the discussion. "I'd like to freshen up before dinner. I feel quite grimy after being out all day. I pray you excuse me." Leonard stood up as she made her exit and firmly grasped her arm as though she were too feeble to get up or sit down by herself. She withdrew her hands from his and retreated to their bedroom, closing the door softly behind her. She breathed a sigh of relief.

*****

"Nelly, I have an important question to ask you." The cook was busy chopping onions for that night's beef stew. She laid the knife on the cutting board, wiped the onion peels off her left hand, and pivoted toward her employer.

"Yes, ma'am. What is it you wanted to know?"

Virginia looked thoughtful. "What you said the day we met, about marriage, did you mean it?"

"You mean about how important it is? Yes, absolutely. I think it defines a woman in most cases. It certainly gives her an imperative, it centers her." While she was talking, the cook alternated between making eye contact with Mrs. Woolf and checking on the meat browning in the pot to make sure it didn't burn.

"But what if she desires autonomy, independence? Ralph wants to possess her. What if she does not desire to be possessed?"

"But that is her duty. If he chooses to honor her with a proposal of marriage, Katherine should accept."

Virginia could not help but reflect on the irony of the conversation: an unmarried woman describing the necessity of marriage to the married woman, arguing against it. She chose to keep her observations to herself. She changed the subject.

"I have almost completed the outline for my book. All that remains is whether or not she will marry him. Perhaps she will kill herself instead," Virginia added, to goad her cook into a reaction, remembering how she objected to Rachel's death. Nellie did not take the bait.

"I am sure you will work it out, Mrs. Woolf. You certainly have the brains for it. Any fool can see that."

Virginia grunted. She was not particularly receptive to compliments, especially about her talent, which was constantly called into question and considered to be feeble at best. She peered into the pot that Nellie was attending.

Nellie was a bit uncomfortable. She did not like anyone leering, infringing on her space. "Yes, well, if you'll excuse me, ma'am, I have quite a bit of work to do to get dinner on the table. And if I let this meat burn, Mr. Woolf will give me the sack for sure."

"Yes, of course. Do get back to your work. I'll leave you be." She walked out of the kitchen and returned to her study. She looked at a portrait of her parents, encased in a silver frame, and ran her fingers across it. She tried to imagine what her mother was thinking when she posed for that portrait. Her mother, Julia Stephen, had died when Virginia was very young. Sometimes she felt as though she were forgetting her. What would her mother have said about the institute of marriage that day in the artist's studio? If Julia Stephen had been able to relive her life, with all opportunity open to her, what—if anything—would she have done differently? Would she still have married and had a family when she did, or would she have waited, perhaps attending university first? Maybe she could have gone into the professions, forestalling the idea of marriage temporarily, if not permanently, and children, possibly permanently. Would she have been happier? Was Julia Stephen, the mother whom Virginia so longed for, happy in her life, or did she gladly greet Death? *If it twere now to die, it would be most happy.* The sentence appeared in her mind. Was it true of her mother? She wondered … and the wondering tormented her.

Chapter Four

June 1920

Virginia decided to take a drive into London. As usual, Nellie went with her. Leonard had dismissed the part-time chauffer, they used the car so rarely, and Nellie did not have a driver's license, so Virginia herself drove. Virginia drove to about a half mile away from the bank of the Thames, parked the car, and bade Nellie to wait for her inside it.

Nellie was ill at ease. She respected her mistress's eccentricities, the price of her genius, but she did not like to leave her alone, especially when there was water nearby. Just thinking about the last time Mrs. Woolf had gone off alone near water sent chills down Nellie's spine. It had not been that long ago, a year at most, and the memory of the experience was fresh. On an impulse, Mrs. Woolf had decided to dive head first into the water, forgetting (or perhaps not caring) that she could not swim. It would have been certain death. Luckily, Nellie and Mr. Woolf had been nearby, observing surreptitiously. They leaped into action the moment her face hit the water, yanking her out and wrestling her to the ground. The rest cure that followed that incident lasted for two months.

Virginia was deep in thought. She was thinking about Rachel Vinrace. She thought of resurrecting her in another book, perhaps as a spirit guiding a loved one from the other side. On the other hand, just because Rachel died in the last book didn't mean she could not come alive in a different book. No, it did not work. She put the thought away.

When she returned to the car, she was suddenly struck with an idea. She got into the driver's seat and turned back to look at Nellie, sitting in the seat directly behind her. Virginia spoke barely above a whisper.

"Richard Dalloway, how do you feel about him, Nelly?"

"You mean that older man Rachel kissed in *The Voyage Out*? I thought him kindly enough but rather flat … boring, actually."

Virginia pressed her right index finger firmly against the bottom of her chin, a telltale sign that she was working something out in her mind.

"I see what you mean. I hadn't thought of that." Her voice trailed off into the distance.

"What about Clarissa?" The pitch of her voice was suddenly so high that her cook flinched.

"Now, *she* was interesting. I would love to see her in another story, possibly centered around her."

It seemed to Virginia an unexplainable phenomenon, how women who lived together, regardless of what the relationship was between them, began to intuitively read each other's thoughts. It was effortless. This intuition developed very early, unlike the relationships between husbands and wives, where it formed much later, if at all.

"Yes, that is exactly what is forming in my mind. I'm envisioning a novel, with Clarissa Dalloway as its heroine. But what could it be about?"

"Well, I don't know about that, ma'am, but if you'll forgive me, the hour is getting late, and I don't have all day to put dinner on the table. Otherwise, Mr. Woolf will be lookin' to sack me for sure."

"Yes, Nelly, very well, you are quite right. We should get going." She put the car into drive and had just pulled out of her spot and onto the road. She was driving not even five minutes when she slammed on the brakes. The car jerked to a halt. Nellie instinctively thrust her hand forward on the front seat. Virginia's straw hat fell atop the ridge of her nose.

"That is it! Thank you so much, Nelly. You have done it."

Nellie tried to keep her composure after her scare. "Done what, ma'am?"

Virginia laughed. Her habit of talking in riddles amused herself, especially since it irritated everyone else.

"You said that the hour is getting late."

"And so it is, ma'am." She was confused.

"Exactly! And that is to be the title of my book. *The Hours*. It will be a grand book, more so because it will be different. It will about Clarissa Dalloway, her entire life, in one day. The *hours* of that day. Oh, it will be marvelous!"

"How will that be, an entire life and only one day? It doesn't make sense to me, ma'am, if you'll pardon me for saying so."

Virginia smiled. "Of course, it doesn't make sense, because it has never been done before. But I will do it, and I will do it so well that everyone will want to do it. And all their efforts will be compared to mine. I must take notes right away." She reached into her handbag and dug out the small notebook and sharpened pencil she always kept inside. Scribbling the date on the top of a fresh page, she began jotting down her ideas and drafting a vague outline of the book. They were stopped in the middle of the road. Angry motorists yelled out vulgar remarks as they had to maneuver their vehicles around hers. Virginia was oblivious.

Nellie cleared her throat. "Dinner, Mrs. Woolf?" she suggested tentatively.

Virginia shoved down her pad and pencil. "Dinner can go to the deuce!" Born into the Victorian era, she still held onto some of the expressions.

"But Mr. Woolf—"

"Mr. Woolf will understand. And if he does not, I will take all of the blame. You need not worry."

"Easy for you to say. You're not the one in the kitchen every day, listening to his rants and threatening the sack," Nellie muttered under her breath just loudly enough for Virginia to hear.

Virginia did not say anything, but she restarted the car and proceeded home. Dinner was late that night, and Leonard did complain, as Nellie expected. Virginia didn't care. To her it was worth it.

Though Nellie would never have admitted it, she felt the same way. She had begun to care a great deal about Mrs. Woolf. Writing kept the lady going. It gave her a purpose. Nellie would not interfere with that; not for all the on time dinners in the world. Nellie only wished that Mrs. Woolf's moments of inspiration came at more convenient times. But then who was she to question the timing of genius? If her own inconvenience was the price to be paid for her employer's literary genius, then so be it.

Chapter Five

The night terrors continued, with increasing intensity. It got to the point where Virginia could not sleep for more than three hours without waking up in a cold sweat, shivering and shrieking obscenities at some unknown figure. In their bedroom, Leonard would often wake up with a start at her cries. Her outbursts filled the sparsely decorated room, and her cries seemed to reverberate off both double-size mattresses.

When this happened, Leonard would get up from his own bed and go to sit at the edge of hers. He would tap her shoulder gently and murmur, "It's okay, you're safe." That would usually do the trick for an hour or two, after which a new terror would undoubtedly take hold.

After the last rest cure, the night terrors grew worse than ever before. Virginia would soak herself and the bed all the way through to the mattress. She would sometimes change nightgowns twice in one night. Often the bedsheets were so drenched that Lottie had to change them anywhere from four to six times a week. The laundry mounted as high as Gibraltar.

Leonard was at his wit's end. He had a printing press to run, and he found himself falling asleep at his desk while copyediting typescript. Even his occasional naps during the day did not compensate for the restful sleep he was not getting at night. He pitied his wife's state but could not go on earning a living half asleep. Something had to be done.

Leonard moved down the hall, into one of the guest bedrooms.

At long last, Virginia had a room of her own. At first, there was no concern about the safety of the new arrangement. Leonard was only down the hall, after all, and the walls were paper-thin. Surely he would hear her if she were in some dire distress. In its execution, the plan was an abysmal failure. Leonard's body simply would not relinquish its newfound tranquility. Once asleep, he did not budge, no matter what noise befell his ears. One of the night terrors had been so bad that it caused the still sleeping Virginia to run down the stairs and out the front door, ranting and raving like a lunatic as she ran down the length of the driveway into the garden barefoot, clad only in her favorite white nightgown. The situation was precarious. Once again, something had to be done. But Leonard could not bear nocturnal life as it had been before. There had to be another answer.

The solution, when it came to them, seemed obvious. Nellie would, for a time anyway, move into the Woolfs' bedroom, occupying the bed that had been in the guest room before Leonard's relocation. Nellie was a light sleeper. If Virginia needed any attending to, Nellie would be right there. Lottie, they assumed, would be overjoyed with the idea. It was a chance to have an entire room to herself at night, if only for a short time.

The first night of the new arrangement, Virginia suffered terribly. She had had trouble falling asleep (she was always in bed with the lights out by eleven), and when she finally did fall asleep around two, she was almost immediately engulfed in a terrible dream about death. Half her body was burning, while at the same time, half her body was drowning. She was helpless to do anything to stop either. All she could do was scream.

And scream she did.

Nellie awoke at the first sign of distress. Seeing her employer's state, she instinctively propelled herself to the bed and plopped down in the middle of it. She began to shake her mistress awake, gently at first, then more forcefully.

"Mrs. Woolf, Mrs. Woolf, wake up, ma'am."

Virginia turned on her back and opened her eyes halfway. Seeing her cook, she let out a small cry.

"Oh, Nelly, thank goodness you're here. It was dreadful, just dreadful. I was burning and drowning, both at the same time. I kept calling out, but no one heard me. It was awful, just too awful for words."

Nellie spoke calmly, reassuringly. "There, there now. You're perfectly fine now, ma'am. There is nothing here that can hurt you." Nellie patted Virginia's right shoulder three times. The pats turned into a gentle rub. Virginia started cooing. Soon, the relaxed sounds gave way to a gentle snore. Nellie dared not move until her mistress was in a deeper sleep. After a few minutes, she ceased rubbing the shoulder and instead draped her arm around Virginia's upper torso, just below her neckline. The writer slept on. At one point, she turned over, facing Nellie, and clung to Nellie's arm as one might hold onto a life preserver. Afraid to move and potentially disrupt Mrs. Woolf's fragile tranquility, Nellie scooted herself down in her employer's bed, held fast to her arm, closed her eyes and went to sleep.

They remained that way for the rest of the night. When Virginia awoke the next morning, she was both surprised and embarrassed to discover her cook next to her. Had she slept just an hour more, her usual seven, Virginia would have never noticed the unorthodox arrangement. She would have thought she had slept uneventfully. But Virginia awakened at six, just as Nellie was about to disentangle herself from the author. Nellie spoke first.

"Oh, Mrs. Woolf, forgive me, ma'am." Her words were rushed. "This may seem mighty awkward, but you see, ma'am, you were having one of your fits again. I calmed you down by sitting on the edge of the bed and rubbing your shoulder. I was going to get up again, truly I was, but you latched onto my arm, and I thought I'd best not disturb you by moving. That's the reason we're like this. You'll forgive me, I hope, for it being improper."

Virginia was stunned into momentary silence. Shaking her head vigorously, as if trying to expel water from her ears after swimming, she cleared her throat and responded in slow, halting speech.

"Forgive you? My God, Nelly, I can find no fault to be forgiven. I cannot recall when last I have slept as soundly as I did last night. I may write about it in my diary."

Nellie exhaled sharply. "Glad you see it that way. I was planning to be up and about my work before you woke up this morning, but you surprised me, waking up early as you did. Now I best be getting to my work." She walked toward the door and was halfway out into the hallway when she turned and stuck her head back inside the doorframe.

"Will you be wantin' scrambled eggs and toast this morning, ma'am?"

Virginia smiled. "Yes, Nelly, please. And I think I'll try some orange juice. I feel I may be able to keep it down."

"Right away, ma'am." And she went to her work.

Virginia always showered as soon as she got out of bed in the morning, sometimes again before she went to bed at night. After her morning shower, if she were feeling well, she dressed fully. If she were not, she threw on some house coat or one of Nessa's old painter's smocks which she renamed for herself a "writer's robe." This morning, she dressed fully. She even put on some jewelry: a couple of old bracelets of her mother's and a ring Leonard had given her with her birthstone. Then she went down to breakfast.

Leonard was already at the table reading the day's newspaper when she came down. The table was set. Nellie was placing a jug of orange juice in the center of the table as Virginia pulled back her chair.

The scraping of the chair on the linoleum made Leonard pick up his head from his paper.

"Good morning, Virginia, did you sleep well?" Leonard inquired.

"Yes, quite. I feel fully energized this morning for some strange reason." She caught Nellie's eye and gave her a sly wink. Nellie grinned. "I feel as if I could write half of my new novel before dinner."

"Well good. Lord knows we could use the revenue," Leonard responded, the sarcastic edge of his voice ever present. His attention returned to his paper.

"A funny thing," Leonard observed, talking more to the paper than to her, "since the war ended, there seems to be less money to go around than before. You would think that in peace, especially a peace as hard won as this one was, money would be plentiful."

"Yes, war does seem to create money, as dreadful of a reality as it is," Virginia responded.

"I suppose that's why they done have them so often," Nellie quipped from her place by the stove. The glaring looks she received from both of her employers silenced her. With her head bowed and faced reddened, she brought breakfast to the table and served it on each of their plates. They ate in silence. Leonard had learned early in their marriage that silence was best at meals in which Virginia was present. Given her natural aversion to food, any conversation while food was on her plate would be taken as an opportunity to distract herself into not eating.

When they were finished and had left the kitchen (the kitchen was large, and they ate breakfast at a breakfast nook in the corner, far enough away from the sink and stove as to not be bothered by their mechanisms), Nellie called for Lottie to come up. The two of them sat down at the stools by the counter and devoured their breakfast (which basically consisted of whatever the Woolfs did not finish), talking animatedly all the while. When it was over and not a scrap of food was left, Nellie retired to the room she shared with Lottie in the basement (for she was only *sleeping* in Virginia's room; she *lived* in the basement with Lottie) for an hour's leisure. Meanwhile, Lottie cleaned the kitchen, eradicating all traces of breakfast.

Interlude

"You mean you actually slept in the bed with her that night?" Thomas asked with eyes widened and eyebrows arched. We were having dinner at a small restaurant down the block from the hotel. I can't remember the name of it, but you'd know it if you saw it. There was a giant red awning with George III's coat of arms painted in the center. That's when it had been built. When you first walked into the restaurant, there was a small room that served coffee, tea, and several flavors of soft drinks. A glass enclosed countertop near the till housed thin slices of cheesecake, along with assorted cookies and pastries. Opposite the counter were six small tables, suitable for couples having dessert or just stopping in for a snack and quiet conversation. After you passed that room, there was a fair-sized dining room. It was pretty elegant, if you ask me, but Thomas said it was nothing special. Pretty easy to say when you are used to having only the best. That was never me. Although, staying at the Ritz as I have been these past few days, I could change pretty quickly.

"Yes, I slept in the bed with her that night, and many nights after." He almost spit out the tea he was sipping. I continued. "After I had been so successful that night in getting her to sleep by simply being there, and her feeling so well and all when she woke up, the next night, Mrs. W asked me to sleep with her again."

Thomas shook his head. "The greatest female writer this country has produced in the past one hundred years, and you, her cook, slept in a bed with her. Is that what you are trying to tell me?"

Now I was getting hot. I liked the fancy hotel and meals just fine, but *nobody* calls me a liar.

"That ain't what I am trying to tell you, sir. I'm not selling you a bill of goods. It is the God's honest truth, exactly as it happened.

The biographer changed his tune in no time. "Oh, no, please don't misunderstand me, Nellie. I don't for one minute doubt you. It's just incredible, that's all."

That was better. I could deal with that.

"Yes, I guess to someone who wasn't there, who didn't live it, it would sound kinda strange," I admitted. But then, when I thought about it, what part of life in that house *wasn't* strange?

Thomas shifted in his seat and his face blushed. I had a fair idea of what was coming out of his mouth next.

"I wasn't going to ask this until a more appropriate time, Nellie, but …" He hesitated, inhaling slightly. "But I cannot imagine when an appropriate time would be for this question. What I want to know is …"

He hesitated again. This time, I finished the thought for him. "You wanted to know about sex in the house," I said with such ease that I thought I set him off guard. He turned redder than a pubescent with his first crush, a tad ridiculous I thought for someone his age. He had to be forty, if he was a day, too old to be this squeamish about sex.

"Well, yes," he agreed. "That is to say that I was wondering if there *was* any sex happening in the house?"

"Yes and no." I immediately clarified my response. "The Woolfs never had sex with each other, as you probably know. An educated man like yourself, I'm sure you've read *The Wise Virgins*." His nods of recognition told me that he had.

"Yes, that is the book Leonard wrote on his honeymoon, I believe. The heroine, Camilla, was rumored to be based on Virginia."

I chuckled. "Lordy, that's no rumor. That's the Gospel truth of it. And her sister, Camilla's that is, is based on Mrs. Bell Grant. The book may have been published as fiction, but I must say, the ladies are portrayed very closely to who they were in real life."

"Some have called the book a 'revenge narrative.' They say that Leonard wrote it to 'get back' at Virginia for what history has called her 'sexual frigidity.' Do you think so, Nellie?"

"Well, I don't know about that, but I do know that he wrote most of it on his honeymoon. And she was working on something as well. That should give you some idea as to the kind of marriage they had. Although I ain't one to judge proper, since I've never been married myself."

"And yet you have lived with women your entire life. After you left service, you lived in the house you are in now with Lottie Hope, just the two of you, alone. When you were working for the Woolfs, you shared the basement together. That must have been a pretty intense friendship?"

Now it was my turn to feel uncomfortable. "Well, yes, I sure did love Lottie, that's for sure, just as sure as I did love Mrs. W, as I began to call her, as long as Mr. Woolf was not around. *Lord*, he was a stickler for formality. And Lottie and I loved each other, to be sure." It took a concerted effort not to blush. "But in those days, nobody took mind of women in that way, not really.

"What about Mrs. Woolf? How did she really feel about marriage?"

I thought about it. "Well, she was married and stayed that way until she killed herself, but I've always thought she felt a bit trapped by it. She found the whole concept of marriage repugnant to the freedom of women, but she and Mr. Woolf didn't have the typical marriage, so I'm not sure she minded so much personally." I had stopped talking for a minute. Thomas was about to open his mouth when an additional thought popped into my head. I spoke it before I'd forget.

"But she sure did love her women. She once said to me in idle conversation one afternoon as I was preparing dinner, 'women alone stir my imagination.' After she said it, she said she was going to write it in her journal. I don't know if she did, as I've never read the journals and don't think anyone else should either."

She dearly loved Violet Dickinson, Vita Sackville-West, and some others, including her sister. What you judge that to mean, well, that's up to you now.

We ended the conversation by silent mutual agreement. I was getting uncomfortable, and Thomas looked as if he might jump out of his chair at any moment. We finished dinner, he paid the bill (this time, I insisted on leaving the tip, on account of him being so generous, even if I was helping him), and he walked me back to my hotel.

In bed that night, I dreamed I was making love to a mysterious woman, a woman of my imagination. It was a sweet, wonderful dream. When I woke up, I was wet between my legs for the first time in years.

Chapter Six

As Mrs. Woolf and the cook grew closer, the maid grew jealous. Lottie began muttering to herself around the house, giving Nellie dirty looks and making faces at the mistress whenever her back was turned. Tension in the house grew between the women. As for Leonard, he was far too busy with his copyediting and running off to meetings of this or that to notice petty resentments between women.

But the tension in the house grew nonetheless. Nellie and Lottie were hardly speaking after a while, with Lottie convinced she was being summarily replaced, and Nellie too tired from her day's work and sleepless nights to bother defending herself against Lottie's wild imagination. In the basement where the servants lived, there was a frigidity in the air that had nothing to do with temperature. A row was bound to happen soon.

The first one happened two weeks after Nellie began spending her nights in Mrs. Woolf's bedroom (more often than not, in her bed, not that Lottie knew that). It was a Sunday. Dinner being eaten early on Sunday and lunch forgone, the servants were usually finished with their duties by five thirty, leaving the rest of the evening for their leisure. Wages were paid on Monday morning (as a Jew, Leonard felt residual shame at handling money on a Friday afternoon; therefore he would not settle accounts until Monday), thus affording little opportunity for taking in the cinema or anything other than a stroll through the park. Nellie usually prepared a pork pie in their kitchen, not nearly as well-furnished as the one she worked in upstairs, but adequate enough, and they would share a bottle of red wine.

On this particular day, however, Lottie had prepared a surprise. She managed to keep Nellie from the basement for most of the day, and she herself snuck down there every chance she got to work on the surprise. On a morning trip to the florist (Mrs. Woolf loved flowers; there were Chinese vases throughout the house, fresh flowers of every variety adorning them all), Lottie had purchased a batch of daisies (she would have preferred roses, but one's taste must be tempered by one's purse) and put them in an old vase stashed away in the cupboard. She brought them downstairs to their table. On either side of the vase, she placed long stem candles in silver candlestick holders that she had "borrowed" from the china closet and spent close to an hour polishing. After the table was set, she began work on the major surprise of the evening. Lottie was going to cook.

She decided on lamb pie. Lamb was a bit pricey for her budget, but after some haggling (and, truth be told, flirting) with the butcher, she had managed it. She prepared the lamb feverishly, her fingers sore from chopping the celery and pounding the meat. She had to change aprons so as to conceal the telltale signs of flour spattered about. Finally, everything was perfect. When it was time for Nellie to come down for the evening, Lottie was all prepared with the surprise. She made the last-minute touches in the kitchen happily, humming as she worked. The bottle of wine was uncorked.

Nellie was a half-hour late coming down. Lottie was unconcerned, assuming that some last-minute detail kept her, usually going over the week's shopping list with Mrs. Woolf. When Nellie did get downstairs, the smile was soon off Lottie's face. Instead of going into the kitchen straightaway, as was her wont, she instead plopped herself on the old sofa in the living room, spreading herself eagle.

"Oh, Lottie, I am too exhausted to start dinner just yet. Give me a few moments, and I'll whip you up something."

Lottie was so excited that she failed to notice the "you" in the preceding sentence was not an "us."

"I'm only going to make a half a pork pie. I'm not hungry. I ate some finger sandwiches an hour or so ago with Mrs. Woolf." Nellie called out to Lottie, who was in the kitchen washing a glass.

The sound of glass shattering told Nellie she was in trouble. She did not understand.

Lottie ran into the living room, her face flushed, her eyeglasses falling to the tip of her nose, and the suds of dish soap dripping off her hands.

"You did what?" Lottie bellowed.

Nellie gave a confused look. "I ate sandwiches with Mrs. Woolf. She hadn't really eaten anything at lunch today, so she asked for tea. She asked me to join her and, well, you know how Mr. Woolf fusses about her appetite. I wanted her to eat, so I said yes." She paused, seeing the red flames on Lottie's face creep down her neck. For a brief second, she feared Lottie might physically attack her.

"What are you so upset about, honey?" She asked in the most conciliatory tone she could muster. Lottie exploded.

"What am I upset about, honey?" Lottie asked in a loud voice, emphasizing the last word. "I'll *show you* what I'm upset about. Come with me." She reached for Nellie's arm, but Nellie pulled back quickly, preferring instead to get up and follow on her own power. They ended up in the kitchen. Seeing the decorated table and the pie, now cooling on top of the stove, Nellie now grasped what was the matter.

"Oh, Lottie, I'm sorry. I had no idea. Look at how nice you made everything." She bent her head over the pie and inhaled its aroma. "Lamb, what a delicious treat! I'd love to have a small piece later and a larger one for lunch tomorrow." She walked over to the table. "And such gorgeous flowers, I love them."

Lottie walked to the table where Nellie stood and, in one quick sweep, knocked the vase full of flowers onto the floor. By some miracle, the vase did not shatter.

Nellie jumped back. "What on earth? What was that for?"

Lottie exploded. "You spend all your nights with that woman, sleeping in her fucking room, wiping her arse, taking away her nightmares, and doing God only knows what else for her. And I don't say anything, I live with it, even though it means I sleep alone. But, Sunday, Sunday is the one day we are supposed to have together. And what do you do, you go off and eat with your writer, while I've been busting my arse all day long like a fool."

Nellie edged closer to the maid, putting a conciliatory arm around her shoulder. Lottie brushed it away. Nellie spoke softly.

"Honey, I am so sorry I hurt you. But there is no way I could have known what you were planning."

Lottie considered for a moment and realized it was true. As if anticipating what she would say next, Nellie continued.

"As for my spending so much time with Mrs. Woolf, you know that can't be helped. They asked me to sleep in her room because of the night terrors. I couldn't very well say no now, could I?" She gave Lottie a minute to think. "Besides, luv, she needs me, poor thing."

"It is exactly that last point that angers me," Lottie responded with a pronounced huff. "I also need you. Where are you for *me*?"

"I'm here, now. And more importantly, I'll always be here for you, luv. Mrs. Woolf, she can give me the sack tomorrow, tonight yet, but you and me," Nellie cupped Lottie's face in her hands, "we're forever."

The maid was for the moment appeased. The women sat down together, the tension slowly abating.

Chapter Seven

The arrangement continued for months. It seemed that Virginia could not sleep a wink without Nellie being there. Lottie tried to be patient, for Nellie's sake, but she was reaching her limit.

Virginia saw nothing wrong. She was sleeping well and eating much better lately. Her writing sessions were more productive than they had been in quite some time. As far as she was concerned, there was no problem.

She had come into the kitchen for a glass of orange juice because she was feeling faint. As soon as she walked into the room, she had the unsettling feeling of having just stumbled onto an argument. Lottie was by the sink, her face and neck enflamed in red blotches. Lottie looked up at the mistress, pointed to her, and glared back at Nellie.

"Well, here's your chance, Ms. Nellie. Tell the missus what we've been talking about." Lottie's voice had a certain edge to it, one that Nellie seldom heard.

"What is it, Nelly?" Virginia stood by the icebox door, holding her now half-empty glass of orange juice in her left hand. She gave a quizzical look.

"Nothing. Really, missus, its nothing at all important."

Mrs. Woolf huffed. "Now, Nelly, I, am really quite busy. Something must be wrong, or Lottie wouldn't look as though she wants to bash your head in with the nearest blunt object. I have a lot of work to do and cannot spend the day discussing this. So tell me at once what the issue is so we can discuss it."

Nellie fidgeted by the sink. She grabbed the dishtowel on the countertop and began twisting it in her hands. "Well, missus, it's like this. You see, Lottie has been getting lonely all alone in the basement at night, what with me sleeping in your room and all. She kinda would like me to go back."

Virginia scowled at her maid then redirected her attention to the cook. "And *you*, Nelly, what would *you* like?"

Nellie blushed. "I, uh, I would like to move back to the basement, too. Don't get me wrong, I love being in your room, missus, but it's not home for me, you know. I prefer sleeping in my own bed, in the basement."

Virginia bit her lower lip softly. "Very well then. I have a solution that will satisfy everyone. Nellie, you will report to my room at bedtime, as you have been doing for these few weeks—"

"Months more like," Lottie mumbled half-unintelligibly.

"I'm sorry, Lottie, did you say something?" Virginia glared at her.

"No, missus, sorry," Lottie responded, shamefaced.

"Then, as I was saying," she pivoted toward Nellie, ignoring Lottie, "you will come to my room, as you have been. But you will not stay. You will return to the basement as soon as I am asleep." She paused. "Have I come up with a fair solution?"

"Yes, ma'am," Nellie responded. Lottie simply nodded in the affirmative, too ashamed to speak.

Virginia smiled coyly. "Then I believe I have made everyone happy." She put the now-empty glass down on the counter. "You may get on with your work." She left the room at once. The matter was settled.

Interlude

"So how did the new arrangement work out?" Thomas and I were having breakfast at a local café a few blocks from the hotel. We just had simple egg sandwiches. He offered to take me to someplace nicer, but I said no, thank you. You have to understand, I'm a real simple person. I don't need rich foods and fancy service all the time (not that they aren't nice). But I was getting a bit tired of all the fuss and muss. Simple was better sometimes.

"Well, it worked okay for a while, though I suspected that the missus was upset with the idea even though she suggested it."

Thomas nodded. "Yes, I can see where she would. It must have been hard for her to let go. I understand that she was quite self-centered."

I held up a finger, wanting desperately to interject but not wishing to talk with a mouthful of food. I chewed hurriedly, swallowed, and then continued.

"Whoever told you that? That is simply untrue. She was very generous. If she wasn't, she wouldn't have offered for me to go back downstairs. She only did it to make my life easier, so Lottie would be happy. There was nothing Mrs. W wouldn't do to make someone she cared about happy."

Thomas seemed impressed with my self-confidence. I don't think he thought I had it in me. Little did he know how strongly I felt about things.

"The history books all seem to say that she only cared for her writing. People did not really matter to her."

"Fah! That is rubbish. She was a gifted novelist. Her books were about people, how could she possibly write so well about people if she didn't know them well enough to care about them?"

Thomas looked at me funny all of a sudden. He spoke softly. "I see your point, actually. I also see something else. Obviously, you loved her as well, or you wouldn't be so defensive of her reputation."

"Well, yes, of course, I loved her." I felt myself beginning to blush. "You don't work for someone for so long without developing feelings."

Thomas jolted his head up, as if an electric shock had just passed through him. "Speaking of, what about Leonard?

I gave him a dumb look. "What about Mr. Woolf?" Even now, I could not bring myself to refer to him by his first name.

"You worked for Leonard for just as long, Nellie. Yet I haven't noticed any strong attachment to him, in the time we've been talking."

"It was different with Mr. Woolf. He was … the best way I can describe it is *absent*. I mean, he lived in the house and was there a lot of the time, but was different. As I said, he was absent, mentally that is, from the life of the house. I think he felt that the home was the sphere of women, a sphere he wanted no part of whatsoever. As a woman who was part of that sphere, I was not someone in whom he had even a fleeting interest. I even wondered for a while whether … Never mind."

I thought maybe I was babbling (Mrs. W used to tell me I babbled a lot) because Thomas seemed to be half-listening. But he was actually deep in thought. Something I had said set him off thinking. I wondered what it was.

"I think it's time I settle up with the waiter." He rose from the table, his shoulders slightly hunched from sitting too long. "Excuse me for a moment."

When he walked away, I had the inexplicable feeling that something had changed, though I could not name it.

Chapter Eight

Everything seemed fine. Weeks had passed. Virginia was doing well with Nellie just being there until she fell asleep. Nellie was glad to be sleeping in her own bed again, even if she did miss having a genius hold on to her while she slept. Lottie seemed content, now that Nellie was back in the basement with her again at night. There was peace on earth.

The peace did not last long. Lottie started grumbling again. She would talk to herself as she scrubbed the green and white tiles of the loo and mumble angry epithets as she dusted the furniture. Her repressed anger served the furniture well. The wood glowed and the faucets sparkled. As much as things had changed was as much as they had remained the same. Nellie was still spending all her waking time with Mrs. Woolf. Lottie only got her in the middle of the night when she would creep surreptitiously back to the basement, half-asleep. They would get to spend a few hours together before Nellie had to be up to prepare breakfast.

Outwardly, Lottie was smiles and pleasantries. Inwardly, she was seething. She and Nellie sorely needed their jobs. Even though the pay was less than most earned, the working environment was pretty fair, and most importantly, they were together. So Lottie didn't have too much to complain about, not that she let that stop her.

The explosion came after breakfast one morning. Rather than retire to the basement for her much-needed break after breakfast was done, Nellie began clearing the table and wiping it down. This allowed Lottie to start washing the pans and the stove right away. Nellie carefully laid the dirty dishes into the sink. As Lottie washed, Nellie stood by her side, drying the dishes and putting them away in the cupboard. Lottie smiled, grateful for the show of concern for her, all the more touching since this was Nellie's break time. As they worked, Lottie spoke.

"You really shouldn't be helping me with the dishes, Nellie dear, but I do appreciate it."

"It's nothing. I need to get an early start on lunch today, I'm making quite a fuss of it, so I need to have the kitchen cleared up as soon as I can."

"Are we expecting guests for lunch?" Lottie inquired, immediately assuming that Mrs. Bell was coming with the children (nasty little critters they were).

"No, at least not that I know of, anyway. It's just that Mrs. Woolf hasn't been eating again. Did you notice, she hardly touched anything on her plate?"

"No, but then I don't make as careful study of her as you do."

Nellie ignored the remark and continued her thought. "Well, she has got to eat something, the poor dear, so I'm baking a sausage pie for her. She should like that, it has lots of cheese. And she likes sausage as long as it's cut up in small pieces, like in the pie. It has to cool for an hour before serving, so you can see why I need to get started fast."

The frying pan that Lottie had just finished washing and taken out of the sink fell from her hand and clamored to the floor with a clatter. Later, Lottie would be grateful that she had dropped the pan. Had she held it fast, she would have been tempted to whack Nellie with it.

"So that's it again, is it?" Lottie asked with a roar.

"What's it? Whatever are you talking about?"

"You're doing everything for Mrs. Woolf. Here you are helping me with the dishes, and I, fool that I am, actually thought for a damned minute that you were actually doing something for *me*. Instead you were only doing it for that skinny bitch!"

Nellie slapped the maid across her face. "Don't you dare speak about the missus that way. You know as well as I do that she puts the roof over our heads, the food in our mouths, and the wages in our pockets."

"How can I not speak of her that way? She is constantly coming between us. You are always there for her, always doing things for her. What about me? When is it my turn, goddamn it?"

Nellie grew irate. "Bloody hell, I am so sick of hearing the same thing over and over again. You know bloody well how I feel about you. I work for the lady, same as you do. And yes, I care about her. Call the constable. I'm human that way. That doesn't diminish my feelings for you, damn it. If you can't get that through your bloody thick skull, than maybe you're the one with the problem here, not me!"

Virginia was passing through the foyer outside the kitchen when she heard the commotion. She poked her head inside the doorframe, only mildly curious as to the goings-on.

"Is there a problem, ladies?" She inquired in that short, quick tone that she used to convey her disdain.

Both servants looked downward, shamefaced. "None that need concern you, ma'am," Nellie responded.

"Is that true, Lottie? Am I truly not to be concerned?"

Lottie gave Nellie a long cold stare, as if threatening to reveal the entire truth. In the end, her anger gave way to practicality.

"'Tis true, Mrs. Woolf. Just a row over work details. There is nothing at all for you to worry about. It's over now anyway." To support her statement, she flung her right arm around Nellie's shoulder and patted her back affectionately. It seemed to be the most they'd touched in weeks.

"Glad to hear it then. Good day," Virginia returned to her bedroom, the idea for a scene in her book flashing across her mind.

The women waited until they heard the lady's bedroom door close with a thud before resuming their argument, though with considerably less punch than before.

"Everything is fine, Mrs. Woolf, nothing that need concern you, Mrs. Woolf," Lottie mocked. "Why didn't you tell her the truth? We could have gotten it out into the open, once and for all. What would be the harm in that?"

"I don't know, Lottie. Why didn't *you* say something? She asked you especially, so she must have sensed something was amiss. That was your chance. Why didn't you take it?"

"Because, goddamn it, I was thinking of you! I always think of you, Nellie, you should know that by now."

"Well, I'm only thinking of you, too. I'm doing what's best for you, for both of us."

Nellie was being less than truthful, no matter how much she was to deny it. She was not doing what was best for Lottie. She was doing what was best for Virginia. It was Virginia who was her chief concern. Not that she didn't love Lottie. Lottie came first in her heart. But Lottie was self-sufficient. Lottie was a survivor. It was Virginia who was fragile, Virginia who needed Nellie, even for something as seemingly simple as getting to sleep at night. Therefore, it was Virginia that Nellie thought of, first and foremost. And Lottie saw it. Nellie knew this was going to be a problem.

Interlude

I ate dinner alone that night. Thomas had an engagement that he could not get out of, and I anyway was getting a bit weary of having company for every meal. Over the years since Lottie passed, I had begun to get used to eating by myself. The solitary life is not so bad, once you get used to it. And once you are used to it, it's hard as all heck to go back to anything else.

He had asked, however, what my plans were after dinner. I told him I was staying in; with such a magnificent room, why would I want to go out? He asked if he might ring me up after dinner if he got done with his engagement before it was too late. He wanted to talk again, but privately this time. He wanted to meet in my room, if that was okay with me. I figured it was more than safe, seeing as how I was so much older than he was and all. Besides, he knew the score. I told him to ring me up whenever he was ready. I'd be in the room waiting for him.

When he rang, I was reading *To the Lighthouse*. It was the book dedicated to Mrs. Sackville-West, Mrs. W's close companion. Now there was a strange one for you. If you saw her with her husband from a distance, you'd have been hard-pressed to tell which one was the man and which was the woman. But I got no room to judge how anyone else chooses to live their life, not after how I've lived mine. I had just gotten to the part where Lily Briscoe was sitting at Mrs. Ramsey's knee, in one sense longing for the older woman and in another sense, wanting to *be* her. I was imagining the scene in my mind. I could smell the odor of the ointment I thought Mrs. Ramsey probably had on her arthritic knee. I could see Lilly looking up at Mrs. Ramsey as though the older woman were Minerva, about to divulge all the secret wisdom of the universe. Of course, that was just when Thomas rang. He said he'd be up in a half hour. I told him that would be just fine.

I barely heard it when he knocked on the door. His knock was so soft, it was a bit effeminate. That would be the only thing effeminate about him, for sure. When I answered the door, he bent down slightly and kissed my cheek. We had become comfortable enough with each other for him to do this without either of us feeling awkward. I led him into the sitting room, anxious for him to see the surprise I had waiting for him.

"Why, Nellie, isn't this lovely?" Thomas exclaimed, a wide smile on his face. I had ordered up room service: a pot of Earl Grey tea and some Viennese pastries (I remembered him saying that they were his favorite). I had put a Mozart concerto on the phonograph, the volume turned halfway up.

"I thought if we were going to talk private, we might as well snack, as we were doing it. Sit down, Thomas, make yourself comfortable." I pointed to the sofa and love seat. "And by the way, this"—I pointed to the room service tray—"is on me."

He chose the sofa, sitting on the right side, his arm on the side. I first sat on the love seat next to him, but got tired fast of having to pivot my body to look at him while we talked so I moved over to the sofa (it was big enough for us to sit on together without being too cozy). Suddenly remembering my manners, including the fact that this was my room we were in, not a restaurant, I got up and poured two steaming cups of tea, the cup and saucer rattling slightly (I never did get used to using saucers to serve tea or coffee. I thought they were a nuisance). I took a plate off the tray and handed it to him. I would have served Thomas a pastry, but I didn't think it polite to touch food he was about to eat, and since I didn't have silverware, I let him serve himself. When he had served himself, I took one for myself. We munched wordlessly for a few minutes, Mozart filling in the silence creating a tender mood.

After he had finished his pastry and poured himself a refill of tea, Thomas got to the point of his visit.

"I wanted to ask you about homosexuality in the Bloomsbury circle. It seems to have been abundant, yet it is not really mentioned anywhere for sure. I'm a bit confused by it, to be frank. Was it there or not?"

"Well, yes, in a way. But you have to understand that it was not talked about, not ever. Mrs. Grant's husband had many affairs with men, including her brother, Adrian. While they were living together as husband and wife, he was carrying on with David 'Bunny' Garrett, who also lived with them. It was sort of a well-kept secret that everyone knew."

Thomas nodded. "The love that dare not speak its name, to quote Oscar Wilde," he interjected.

I continued with what I was saying. "Mrs. Grant wasn't thrilled, you can wager, but she lived with it. For a while there, the three of them lived together. Who knows what went on beneath that roof!"

Thomas looked aghast. "Under her own roof, all three of them! How unseemly!"

I laughed at him. "Oh come now, Thomas, really. You sound so dreadfully Victorian. We are living in the twentieth century after all. Some things have changed."

"I know, but it seems so bohemian. Duncan Grant, E. M. Forster, Harold West, my lord, there were so many. How on earth did they all find each other? Was there a club they all went to or something?"

At this, I nearly spit up the last swig of tea I had just taken; I laughed so hard. "No, there wasn't a club. Although E. M. Forster did refer to people like us as 'members.' I guess it sort of was a club, in its own way."

Thomas laughed heartily. "Yes, I see what you mean."

He might have thought he understood what I meant, but I was not so sure if he really did understand. Later that night, when I reflected on the day's conversation, the futility of Thomas's mission occurred to me. How could he possibly understand what it was like for people then, people who were born decades before he was even conceived and people who wrestled with feelings he did not have and were born into a society unwilling and able to treat these people as everyone else? Was it possible to understand intimately the flesh and blood people who stand in the shadows behind names in a history book? Something inside me screamed "No!" I was most definitely not convinced that Thomas really understood what I said, what was going on. I was not sure it was possible that he could ever understand.

The more I thought of it, I realized that I wasn't sure about much of anything at all.

Chapter Nine

Richmond
1920

The relationship between the lady and the cook grew. Even Leonard became concerned. He had married a wife, a partner, an intellectual equal. Yet for all her literary genius, he sometimes felt that he was losing her to a dimwitted cook. Whenever he turned around, they were together, whispering, conspiring, planning menus, having rows. It was as if Nellie comprised a secret part of Virginia's life, one in which he could have no part. He had heard Virginia speak sometimes, as she would later write, about women gathering together to form a Society of Outsiders. But now, standing here watching this, Leonard began to wonder, for the very first time, just who exactly was meant to be the *outsider* and who was the *insider.*

  He spoke to, of all people, Clive Bell. The irony of the situation did not escape him, Clive having proposed to Virginia before he eventually "settled" on Nessa, and Virginia having unceremoniously turned him down, but not before leading him to believe his advances would be welcome. Whether the two had ever had intercourse, Leonard was uncertain. His wife most assuredly would not have answered him about this if he asked her. In any event, he would not ask. He did not want to know.

  Clive was in the library when the maid announced Mr. Leonard Woolf had come to call. He let out a long puff from the cigar he was smoking. The smoke curled in the air as it disintegrated to nothing. He prepared the martini; Leonard always liked a dry martini. When Leonard came in, that ugly brown hat tucked away under his right arm, a book under his left, Clive lifted an eyebrow in a perfunctory greeting before the two clasped hands.

"Nessa is in town at the moment, she is picking up some new art supplies. I've hardly seen her for the past few days, she has been so holed up in her studio." He motioned for Leonard to sit and handed him the drink.

Leonard smiled in gratitude. Sipping it, he let out a groan of pleasure.

"Ah, a dry martini! Is there anything else so wonderful this side of heaven?" he asked rhetorically, as he kicked off his left shoe, extending his left leg and resting it on the nearby ottoman.

"Perhaps not," his brother-in-law conceded, but then said, "Man's reach must exceed his grasp or else what's a heaven for?"

Leonard grinned at the Browning allusion, but inside he was wincing. It always bothered him when people, especially family (and like it or not, Clive came under that category), felt the need to quote poets and novelists whenever they were in his presence. It was like some goddamned inferiority complex. Funny that they never did it with Virginia. Fey! Although she'd throw a fit at the suggestion, she did not measure up to Leonard as a writer. People must have sensed this; that was why they never felt inferior around her. Oh sure, she was very bright and her novels sold well enough, but forty or fifty years down the line, it would be *his* work they would be remembering, his work they would be studying in the universities, both in England and America. Of this he was certain.

"So, Leonard, what can I do for you? We've never been overly chummy, so I assume this is not purely a social call. Furthermore, I doubt you are here simply to sample my martinis."

"No, not quite." He took a short breath. "This is a bit difficult for me, but I was wondering." He paused for a moment and took another breath before continuing. "Does Nessa's attention ever … wander …?"

Clive's curiosity was piqued. "I'm not sure I understand exactly what you mean, brother-in-law. Wander where? To infidelity?"

"No, no, not that, I hadn't even such a notion, I assure you," Leonard answered in the most reassuring tone of voice he could muster.

"Good, because I am quite certain I would be loath to discuss the matter with you if that were the case, which, thank the good Lord, it is not. But what then could you mean?"

Leonard gulped the remainder of the martini, swishing the olive around in his mouth for a moment. He pulled out a pack of smokes and the lighter his father had given him. He had smoked in this house hundreds of times, and his host sat smoking this very instant. Yet, he still thought to ask before lighting up.

"Yes, of course, old chap, go ahead," Clive responded, eager for Leonard to get on with it, so he could put an end to this unwelcome visit.

Leonard lit the cigarette and took a long inhale. He paused for a brief moment before explaining. "I mean, does she ever develop friendships, deep friendship, with anyone else?"

Clive laughed too loudly. "Well, of course, she does, old chap, she is a woman. Women do these things after all. There is no harm in it, and certainly no stopping it. I wouldn't want it any other way, believe me. Like that fellow Grant she is always palling around with, going to museums and art galleries, fey! Enough of that! Glad I am that they don't invite me on their womanish excursions. Although I can't say I'm much surprised that Grant would want to take part in such things. Based on some of the things I've heard …" He let the sentence dangle in the air unfinished for a moment before completing it, "Well, let's just say that if Marlowe were alive today, the old boy would be in his glory." Leonard said nothing.

"But this time that she spends with him, or anyone else for that matter, doesn't it make you feel, I don't know … less important somehow. As if you are not the focus of her life, her everything, as a husband is supposed to be to his wife."

When Clive laughed this time, it was a roar that came from his belly. "But don't you see, Lennie, that's it, the price we pay."

"The price we pay for what?" asked Leonard, who hated worse than the pain of death to be called Lennie.

"For marrying the women we did. Let's face it, Leonard, we did not marry ordinary women. We cannot expect them to act as any ordinary women do. They are rather extraordinary."

Leonard reflected on that statement while he sipped his martini. "True, but they are still *women*. We cannot allow them to have minion over us. If that should happen, better Hitler should spread his wings across the continent."

At the mention of Hitler, Clive fell silent. Leonard's words loomed in the air. After a moment, Clive broke the tension with a slap of his hand on his left knee.

"You may be right, Leonard, though God take us if what you say ever should come to pass, but nonetheless, our wives are cut from different cloths than the wives of others. This we must accept. It is the only way we can live with them and ourselves."

Leonard left shortly thereafter. He thanked his host for his time. The maid gave him his top hat and coat, and he walked briskly into the crisp fall air. He was sorry he had come; he felt no better, only worse. He would handle the matter in his own way. And most of all, he would never go to his foolhardy brother-in-law again for advice. As it was, discussing such a personal matter with a man who was at best irritating and at worst irascible left a bitter taste in Leonard's throat. He felt the need to drink plenty of water.

Leonard decided not to go home just then but boarded the nearest Tube station. He wanted to go into London to Hatchard's. Visiting bookstores usually helped him clear his mind. He loved the musty smell of the shelves, the quiet unassuming clerks who manned till stations.

He decided to purchase an old biography of George III. He found it buried in a pile of books in the far left corner of the basement. The books, covered with a thin layer of dust, seemed forgotten about. The biography of "Mad King George" was at the bottom of the pile. He had almost missed it. Leonard brought the book upstairs to the till and paid the clerk and began reading it as soon as the sale was complete. He declined the offer of a bag.

Chapter Ten

Richmond House
February 1922

Kathrine Mansfield dropped in for tea unannounced, as she had a habit of doing. Nellie was in a tizzy. She was, as usual, quite fastidious in her tea preparations. She would prepare exactly enough for whoever was expected—always the Woolfs, sometimes the Bells. Unexpected guests were a constant source of irritation. More irritating still was the cavalier attitude of the mistress about such an inconvenience. It was as though the cook's time and feelings did not matter.

"See if *she* had to go about scrambling for extra tea and sugar, and slicing the pie extra thin hoping that no one will notice. She'd sing a different tune then, I'd wager."

Lottie was unsympathetic. "Pah! You're full of hot air. You could put a stop to it if you really minded."

"How exactly could I do that, may I ask? Throw the lady out on her arse?"

"By failing to make such provisions," Lottie responded. "If you were not so adept at finding the extra needed to accommodate interlopers, they would not come so frequently."

Nellie did not answer. She never answered when Lottie was right.

Nellie was bent over the oven taking a lamb pie out to cool while Lottie got the tray ready. As she blew on it, she thought of something funny. "That hat that she wears, what the devil does she keep in that thing do you think? It's twice the size of her head."

Lottie laughed. "A friggin' rat, maybe, who knows? And what difference does it make, anyway?"

A rogue image flashed through Lottie's brain. "Do you think she takes that thing off when her husband fucks her?"

"She must, or it might topple onto him and kill him." Nellie leaned over holding her side, her chuckle now a roar of laughter. At Lottie's shushing, she quickly composed herself, lest she be heard by the mister and missus and their guest, who would all be in the parlor engaging in polite small talk while their stomachs undoubtedly rumbled. She placed the pie, cups, and silverware on a large rectangular copper tray and moved into the dining room, nodding to Lottie before she left the kitchen.

Leonard poured Katherine a white wine. She sipped it, telling a slow-moving story of a trip she had recently taken to America. She spoke of staying in a New York hotel and seeing a show. Virginia listened with feigned interest. Having experienced every luxury London had to offer, she could not imagine why anyone would want to go elsewhere.

"Tea is ready, ma'am," Lottie stated abruptly, having barged into the room with no announcement of her presence and no regard for the guest whose narrative she had just interrupted. The company moved themselves to the dining room, Leonard helping his wife off the sofa and offering her his right arm, while he extended his left to Katherine. Both women accepted the proffered arm in kind. Having settled in the dining room, they began eating and talking, the emphasis on the latter. Katherine was hungry; however, imitating her hostess, she mostly picked at her plate.

Leonard was grateful for the unexpected visit, as it saved him the trip out to Katherine's place (he had an inherent mistrust of the post and used it as infrequently as possible). He had a check ready for her. It was partial payment for her latest book, *The Garden Party*. He handed her the check, along with the advance copy of the book. Katherine gave a gleeful grin at seeing the amount of the check, took it out of the envelope, folded it neatly, and tucked it hurriedly away into the small pouch inside her purse. The book was a collection of stories. Katherine turned the pages slowly, examining their contents with great discernment, as if she herself had not written them. As she did so, she could not help but mentally calculate how much money the stories might bring her in sales. She had the money spent before she earned it, hoping to spend some time in the south of France within the next few months. Murray hated to use their savings; this would be her treat to him, for both of them actually. Katherine was glad she could give them this. It would make her happy.

"So, Katherine, do you have a favorite story in this volume?" Virginia asked pointedly in between bites of the meat pie, which seemed to her particularly bland today. She was anxious to move the conversation to something she actually cared about.

"Yes, actually, I do. 'Ms. Brill' I think is the most darling of them. The heroine is quite sympathetic, you know, a spinster, living her days alone, devoid of human companionship. I hope the reader will want to reach out and kiss her."

"Pah!" Virginia exclaimed. "I remember that story well. Your reader will not, as you put it, want to kiss her. He will pity her. That is the worst thing in the world for a woman, to receive a man's pity. Speaking for myself, I should rather be dead than be pitied by anyone."

Katherine let an exasperated sigh escape her lips. "Dear, Virginia, you are forgetting one thing. You are a real person, with real-life feelings. Whereas Ms. Brill is fictional … although, as her creator, she feels quite real enough to me," Katherine added.

"Yes, but literary characters must reflect the people who read them or they have no use," Virginia pontificated in a tone sterner and a volume louder than she intended. "Don't you agree, Leonard?" She shot him a cutting glance as if daring him to side against her.

"Well, in a sense, I suppose. I have always felt that literature, especially contemporary literature, reflects the society it portrays, yet I understand Katherine's point as well. We really must not blur the line between fact and fiction."

Virginia smirked. He had evaded the question. She had a clever husband.

*****

Nellie had used up the last of her patience. She had other things to do today. She was in the workroom, tucked away behind the dining room, where she alternated between sitting in an uncomfortable chair and pacing back and forth in the small room, out of sight of the gentle folk. Lottie was lying down downstairs, having had one of her fits of exhaustion that made her too tired to attend to the dishes. Nellie had promised she would take care of it, but she still had a lot to do if dinner was going to be ready by seven, the usual time. "That bitch better not think she is staying for dinner, that's all I've got to say," she muttered to herself *sotto voce* as she wore out the linoleum with her pacing.

She entered the dining room without ceremony. "Is everything finished? Lottie is unwell, and I'd like to get everything washed and dried before I start dinner preparations." Nellie tilted her head in Katherine's direction. "I'd be pleased to invite you, ma'am, but seeing as there isn't enough, I'm afraid I can't. Maybe if next time you see fit to calling before you arrive, things will be different."

"Nellie!" Virginia's rebuke was sharp. "How could you?" Pointing to Katherine, she said, "This is a guest."

"How could I what? Speak plainly? Easily, ma'am. If you'll pardon me for saying so, someone who comes when expected is a guest. Someone who simply shows up is not a guest, but an imposition."

An outside observer would have been hard-pressed to determine who was more red-faced during this exchange, host, hostess, or guest. Katherine muttered half-coherent apologies, Virginia said something under her breath about the uncouthness of servants, and Leonard stared into space. Nellie gave an indignant grunt then set about clearing the places of anything that was finished. She put the dishes into the tray she carried, which would ultimately wind up in the sink. Once she had cleared the room, Leonard regained his composure and dared to speak.

"I am really quite sorry about that, Katherine. Nellie is not usually so impertinent. I don't pretend to know what's come over her, but I will make certain she is reprimanded."

"No, please don't trouble yourself. It is hardly worth it. She has a point, besides, she undoubtedly has enough of her own troubles already to consider. I wouldn't want to augment her burden."

"That is most gracious of you." Virginia added, "But then again, why shouldn't you be gracious, as you always are." Privately, Virginia sided with Nellie, being able to imagine the burden it must be to have to provide for someone without any notice. In public, however, she was forced to maintain a different stance.

The two women chatted endlessly about their writing: three of Katherine's published stories along with as well some of Virginia's plot sketches. Leonard had left the table at four thirty to go back to work on his press. He found literary conversation stimulating, and Katherine was a valued client, but there were limits to the amounts of time that could be dawdled away. One did have to earn a living, after all.

While she was refilling her cup with the last vestige of boiling water, Virginia made a bold confession. She was modeling this version of Mrs. Dalloway, at least in part, on Katherine. Mrs. Dalloway would be upper-class, somewhat of a snob, yet would have some loveable qualities about her. Men would be beguiled by her, at least some men. Her husband, perhaps, and an old flame, an admirer, Peter his name might be. Katherine was touched and muttered something trivial about the greatest honor a writer can give another writer is to blah blah blah …

Her words meshed together in Virginia's mind. She was no longer listening, but mentally planning out the character of Mrs. Dalloway. She was certain men would find her alluring, perhaps even beguiling. Would women? Moreover, whom would Clarissa want, if indeed she wanted anyone? Was there a single woman or man whose attentions she craved more than any other's, any other person on earth, perhaps? Virginia trembled as her inner voice spoke volumes, her mind spinning with endless possibilities. She had to work them out in her head.

"Goodness me, I had no idea of the time." Katherine's words suddenly pulled Virginia back into the present reality. The guest hurriedly wiped her mouth for any loose crumbs, patted down her dress, and stood upright. "Sorry to have kept you so long, Virginia. It is always such a delight talking to you."

Virginia stood as well, reaching for the side of Katherine's arm to pull her close. "It was wonderful to see you as well. Thanks ever so much for stopping by. You know you are always welcome here, regardless of the hour." She said the last part with added emphasis, for the benefit of Lottie, who was hovering nearby, having been overcome, it would seem, by a sudden compulsion to dust.

"Thanks so much. You're an absolute dear. We simply must have you and Leonard over to our place sometime soon. And do thank Leonard again for the check, so considerate he is, always paying me on time."

"Yes, well, that's my Leonard, always managing the accounts. It drives him to distraction to have to wait for his money, so he never keeps anyone else waiting for theirs."

Lottie wanted to dance as she closed the door behind the obnoxious woman. She thought she would never leave. She said not a word to Mrs. Woolf but began clearing off the tea dishes. Virginia thought about going into the kitchen to say something to Nellie but changed her mind. Instead, she went to her room, closed the door, sat at her desk, and wrote several pages of notes about the character of Mrs. Dalloway.

No matter what happened, Virginia knew Nellie would be there. Trusty old Nellie, the essential angel, often as despised as she was necessary, who existed to watch over the writer, her very own Mrs. W.

Chapter Eleven

Richmond House
1921

Mrs. Woolf became unwell again. It was while she was in the middle of writing the first draft of *Jacob's Room*. Leonard was stunned when it happened.

He had come into her room on a Friday afternoon, not long before tea was to be served. She was standing in front of her dresser, staring into the mirror blankly, as if in a trance or semi-catatonic state. Her notepad and blue pen lay flat on the dresser, an ink smudge in the center of the page where she had laid down the pen, careless of the fact that the ink had not dried yet (an action that, in of itself, signaled trouble; Mrs. Woolf hated ink smudges and went to great pains to avoid them). In her left hand was a glass of water, filled to the brim. In her right hand was a handful of pills. Leonard simply stared for a long, intense moment. As her right hand raised itself to her mouth, it was then that he was galvanized into action.

"Virginia, NO!" He lunged toward her, his open arms extended, shoving at her hands with his full body weight pressing against her frail frame. The glass fell to the floor and shattered, the pills scattered (strychnine, he would eventually learn when he brought them to the chemist to be analyzed). They both fell to the floor with a thud, he on top of her. On the way down, she whacked her head on the metal steam pipe. She shrieked in pain. The wooden floor beneath them shook as they hit it.

Nellie was in the kitchen waiting on an apple pie she had in the oven, a treat she was preparing especially for Mrs. W. Hearing the commotion above her, she raced up the stairs, taking them two at a time (something she never did). Seeing the spectacle, she cried out. Lottie was already in the room. She had been across the hall in Mr. Woolf's bedroom, dusting, when it had all started. She had seen nearly everything, a fact Virginia would surely come to regret.

"Mr. Woolf, ma'am, what is it?" Nellie asked, the panic rising in her voice despite her best efforts to keep it down.

Leonard lifted his head for a second and saw the servants standing there. Returning his gaze to his wife, whose body he was still half covering, although he had by now shifted most of his weight off her, he noticed the blood. The pipe had left a gash in the center of her head. Bright red blood pooled there. For the briefest of moments, he was afraid that she might have a concussion. He swiftly dismissed the concern from his mind. A concussion, if indeed she had sustained one, was the least of their current worries.

"Lottie, get me two hand towels, one damp with warm water and one dry. Nellie, help me lift up her head." Lottie scurried to get the towels, and Nellie rushed forward, crouching down to the left of Leonard.

"Don't worry, ma'am. You're safe now. We're here, we won't let anything happen to you, ma'am," she said to Virginia who was in a daze, only partially conscious. Cradling Virginia's head in her hands, Nellie shot her employer an inquisitive glance.

"A suicide attempt," he answered flatly. "It was pills." He motioned to the floor.

"She was about to take them when I came into the room. Thank goodness she hadn't had the time to swallow any, or they'd have to pump her stomach."

"Where is Lottie with those towels?" Nellie muttered. No sooner had she spoken the words did Lottie appear, towels in hand. She handed the towels to Nellie, who began applying them expertly to the wound, alternating between wet and dry. When the bleeding finally stopped, they loaded her into the car, sprawling her across the back seat, placing a pillow beneath her head and covering her with a wool blanket (Lottie had thought of the blanket, remembering how cold the mistress could get). The servants sat squished together in the front passenger seat next to Leonard (for this was not the time for convention), who drove like the devil himself was chasing him. They brought her to Dr. Savage's office, not bothering to ring ahead, given that this was an emergency. Leonard was sure the doctor would be in; he would see them straight away.

In the oven, the apple pie sat smoldering, now burned beyond all recognition.

*****

It was her family, her own family, that drove her to her emotional precipice. Leonard may not have had a clue as to what precipitated his wife's suicide attempt, but Nellie knew. It was her work on *Jacob's Room.* The hero, Jacob, the namesake of the novel, was modeled largely in part of her late brother, Thoby. As Virginia wrote the novel, the voices in her head became more pronounced, more vocal. They were not just the voices of stray characters, begging authoress for more time on the page, but the voices of the dead. Thoby spoke to her during the night, the words he said resounding in her ears when she woke up in the middle of the night, scribbling down the words she heard into the small notebook at her bedside.

The descent to madness had begun slowly. It was imperceptible to someone like Leonard. He was always running from pillar to post, barely having enough time to drink his coffee (he was forever taking it in long gulps, scalding his esophagus) and grab one of Nellie's biscuits with a slab of butter as he headed out the door running to the trolley stop. He liked to leave the car for the women, just in case they had to rush Virginia to the doctor, as was sometimes necessary. Besides, the truth was he hated driving. He preferred a trolley or the Tube, where he could read proofs or a newspaper undisturbed. No, Leonard had no time, not even to notice his wife's deterioration, right before his eyes.

Their friends hadn't seen it either. To Katherine Mansfield, E. M. Forster, and the others, she was Virginia, their fun-loving, stalwart, and often sarcastic friend. In short, she was fine. But the servants knew something was wrong, as they naturally would, before anyone else. They were around the lady more than anyone else and were trained to always be in the background, circling the periphery.

Lottie saw it first. She had gone into the study to polish the bookcase (a colossal task, considering that every volume had to be removed from every shelf, and then rearranged in the exact order; once, when Virginia had not been able to find a book she had been reading for a review she was writing, she swore terrible oaths, ranting for over three quarters of an hour; she twice threatened to sack Lottie if she dared rearrange a single volume again without her approval). Lottie knew to proceed with caution.

It was that caution that made Lottie stand a bit straighter when she crept into any room her mistress occupied. She did not knock. The Woolfs liked servants to slip in and out unobtrusively, performing their chores swiftly. The mistress was alone in the study, talking to herself, a common enough occurrence when she was writing. Lottie had overheard her once saying that talking to herself as she was writing fiction helped her get into the minds of her characters and listen to them. The talking would be low-key, monotonous. This time was different. Virginia was talking excitedly and loudly and in different voices. Lottie smelled trouble.

"Nellie, luv, we have a problem with the missus," Lottie said, after finishing as quickly as she could without disturbing the lady and tiptoeing surreptitiously back to the kitchen to warn Nellie.

"What is it now, Lottie?" The cook, standing with her shoulders hunched, rolled her eyes, leaning over her wooden cutting board. Her eyes were visible only to the onions she was mercilessly chopping on the cutting board. She was convinced that the maid invented trouble, simply to have another reason to mock Mrs. W.

"It's the voices, they're back."

Nellie instantly snapped to attention. Her entire body felt as though someone had run an electric current through it. "When?" she murmured.

"Today, just now, probably still happening. I don't know how long they've been back, but I'll wager all day."

"Oh, dear, this may be terrible. The last time … well, we don't need to go there again."

Lottie nodded in agreement. "Mr. Woolf needs to know. I doubt she'll tell him. Poor thing, she may not even realize it herself." Nellie was touched. Lottie did not like their mistress one iota, and she made no bones about the fact, yet even still, she showed genuine sympathy for Virginia's plight. Perhaps there was hope for humanity yet, Nellie thought. Suddenly she had to stifle a laugh. Imagine it, the hope for the entire human race lying on the shoulders of Lottie Hope! The thought was too ridiculous for words.

Nellie knew in her heart, in the core of her being, that Mr. Woolf needed to be told about the voices. She knew Lottie was right; it was the only sensible thing to do. But Nellie was not always sensible. In fact, as her oldest sister, the mother figure in her life, told her quite often growing up as she was growing up, Nellie often did not think at all. Nellie *felt*. Feeling was not always a good thing. Sometimes thinking was better.

Later, when she would think about the incident that had happened, combined what *would have* happened had fate not intervened and sent Mr. Woolf to the room at that precise moment, Nellie would realize how serious a blunder she had made. She never admitted her error of omission to anyone. Lottie just assumed she had passed the information along. The guilt of the unacknowledged sin weighed heavily on her conscience. It would come up and eat at her whenever she and the missus had a row.

Virginia spent three weeks at Tickingham, enduring a rest cure. She was allowed no visitors the entire time. For such a social person, the lack of contact with anyone not wearing a white coat or starched white uniform was painful. Far worse was the loss of books. All her books and writing materials were confiscated. She yearned for them as an alcoholic yearned for a scotch. The one luxury she was allowed was her cigarettes, an irony she never failed to appreciate. She would sit in her room (as far as she was concerned, it might as well have been a cell) puffing away indiscriminately. While she was there, Nellie maintained the household. She directed Lottie's cleaning and shopped for the groceries and visited the butcher all by herself. She did not need to pay anyone. Leonard had accounts with the butcher and the grocer, just as he had with the doctor. They would provide whatever was needed and send an itemized bill at the end of the month, which Leonard would scrutinize and then pay, all the while grumbling about extravagant spending, inflation, etc. At first, the merchants were reluctant to approve such an arrangement. Whoever heard of giving a Jew credit? But Virginia had gone to the merchants privately and assured them of payment. Only then did they agree. Leonard had no idea. He would have been infuriated.

The day Virginia was scheduled to come home, Nellie was up at dawn. She had scrubbed the kitchen from top to bottom, for Lottie had enough to do in the rest of the house, and had both the oven and the stove going. There was a meat pie in the oven, porridge on the stove, and ingredients for a salad. A special chocolate pudding was planned for dessert. Nellie was pulling out all the stops. Even Lottie seemed today to be putting extra effort into her polishing and dusting, trying to do her part in the welcome.

Virginia came home at two. Leonard had gone to get her. When she arrived, the servants were in the parlor, smoking, sharing the single ashtray they had brought from downstairs. When they heard the car door slam shut (for Leonard was always too forceful in closing car doors), both women extinguished their cigarettes and leaped to the front door expectantly. Lottie opened the door wide and stood all the way to the right, Nellie to the left. As Virginia walked through the doorway, her right arm being gently supported by Leonard, the women smiled broadly at her and uttered, "Welcome home, ma'am," *sotto voce* (as if no one should know of her return).

Virginia grimaced. The tension in the air was palpable. The two women approached her carefully, as if coming at her too quickly might send her away, arms flailing into the cold brisk air. As they grew closer, the stale smell of tobacco that lingered on their uniforms caused Virginia's stomach to do a back flip; at the sanitarium, she was the only smoker. She had quickly grown accustomed to the smoke-free clothing of others. The initial wave of nausea passed without incident, and she greeted her servants with a warm smile and a solicitous "How has everything been here?"

The women began talking at once, trying recapture the events of several weeks and shape them into a mold that could be neatly packaged into the space of two minutes. The missus nodded considerately, occasionally injecting a "How interesting" or "That's wonderful" into the boisterous babble. Finally, she announced that she was tired; she would go to her room now. No, there was no need for anyone to accompany her; she wished to be alone for a while.

Virginia walked up the stairs to her room, having removed her hat as soon as she entered the walkway. She gripped the banister forcefully, as if she might topple down without it. She climbed each step with determination. She could feel the eyes of the others piercing through her from behind. She was being watched again, and she hated it; she absolutely hated it.

She was almost at the door to her room when she made an about-face and called out. "Nelly," she called, in a voice that was much lower than she intended. The rest cures always weakened her voice, not being given much opportunity to use it. She cleared her throat, swallowed, and tried again. This time, she bellowed. "Nelly!"

"Yes, ma'am, what is it?" Nellie inquired.

"I believe I should like tea a bit early today. I hope that will not unduly trouble you." She gave a coy smile and a wink.

"No, ma'am, no trouble whatsoever. You go freshen up, and I'll be callin' you when it's ready." Nellie reconsidered her words. "Better yet, I'll come up to your room and get you, so you needn't listen for me. You can doze if you like."

Virginia turned back and finished her ascent. Walking into her bedroom, she inhaled deeply the scent of potpourri mixed in with the smell of nicotine that seemed to permeate through every surface of the house and was constantly yellowing the wallpaper. Stopping in the center of her room, she poured some water from the pitcher that was on her dresser (Lottie kept it fresh with ice water) into the glass next to the pitcher and downed it in one quick gulp. She put the glass down and plopped herself into the recliner by the window.

They had dinner alone that night. Katherine Mansfield had rung saying that wanted to come by, but Virginia discouraged her. She was not ready to receive company on her first night home. Even Nessa stayed away. She said she would come tomorrow, but she said she would not bring the children, despite Virginia's insistence that they were just fine to bring along. Once dinner was over, Virginia sipped coffee and nibbled on some dessert. Leonard read the evening paper and puffed on a Cuban cigar nervously. The coffee grew cold before it was more than halfway done, and she did not bother to have it warmed. She left the table without a word and returned to her bedroom, closing the door behind her, reveling in the privacy she had been missing for the past few weeks.

She sat on her bed in total silence, barely moving. She faced the open window and leaned her eye toward it, trying to take in the sounds of the night. A cricket chirped softly in the azalea bushes and the occasional car strode by, its motor hushed. The church bell tolled at nine o'clock, as it always did, for what reason, only God knew. Virginia privately wondered if it was the rector's way of calling "curfew," as if all residents nearby were children under his watchful care. Or perhaps it was a bidding of "good night." The reason for the bell was a source of hours of bewilderment for Virginia in idle hours, the more so since she would most likely never know the answer. Meanwhile, she breathed in the fresh, crisp night air and exhaled slowly, willing herself to taker her time. There was no need to rush; she had all the time in the world. She could do things at her leisure, beholding to no schedule except her own. She could sit here and indulge in the exhilarating fresh air for as long as she pleased. She could do what she liked and avoid what she disliked. At long last, she was home. She was safe.

Interlude

By the time I told him about the pills, I think Thomas was ready to take some himself. He seemed shaken by what I told him, as if my words had permanently altered some mental picture he had about Virginia Woolf. It was as if the alteration was unforgivable. When I finished the story, it was over lunch the day after he came to my room and munched on room service. He looked as though he might vomit or faint, or both.

"That was amazing. To think that the end nearly came so many years before. It is unconscionable. All the work that would have never been written. It boggles the mind."

"You can imagine, then, how I felt, how we all felt." She paused, taking a sip of the wine they had ordered with lunch. "You see, Thomas, there is a world of difference between us, if you'll pardon me for saying so. You know and love the writer, through her written words. You want information about the person behind those powerful words. *I* on the other hand, and Lottie, may she rest in peace, knew the person, intimately. I have an entirely different perspective on all of this. I loved the *woman first*, the writer second."

Thomas gaped. "Of course, that is why I wanted to meet you and talk to you, to get your perspective. If you'll recall, that is exactly what I told you the day that I first contacted you."

He was right; he had said as much that day. It seemed like a lifetime ago despite the fact that it was fairly recent.

"Then you understand, Thomas. This was an extremely difficult time in the house. We all felt that we were walking on eggshells. Nothing seemed to be the same. Fortunately, a day or two after she came home, after she settled back into the house and ate a few meals, Mrs. W felt stronger. She unpacked her writing utensils [the nursing home had placed them into a brown paper back when she was admitted, and returned the bag to Leonard when she was discharged]. The fact that they did not return her materials to *her* irritated her, but she stayed silent. The day she unpacked the bag, she began writing again."

Thomas was in dismay. "Did she ever explain why she wanted to kill herself so much? There was more than one attempt, we know, and then of course …"—his voice trailed off—"the last time." At the last word, he lowered his voice, as if ashamed to utter it.

"You know it wasn't just her, he was just as prone to suicide, except you don't hear about it so much."

"Really? Fascinating; do tell me about it."

"After Hitler gained power in Germany and aligned himself with Mussolini, both the mister and missus thought the end was near for England. But they were too proud to be taken prisoner or see their printing press destroyed or seized by the Nazis. They kept a wide array of pills, tranquilizers mostly, which they stored in his bedroom nightstand. The plan was, if England was ever invaded by the Nazis, or if Hitler, God forbid, won the war, they would together down all the pills they owned, killing themselves rather than being killed. He was right in it with her. That wasn't the only occasion, either. There were a few other times too that he was ready to end it, yet only she gets dubbed in history as having suicidal ideations. It must be because he was a man. It don't look good, I suppose, for a man to want to kill himself. Certainly not a man who thought himself as important as Mr. Woolf did, that's for sure."

I brought us back to the topic at hand.

"Meanwhile, as soon as Mrs. W was writing again, she wrote a new character into *The Hours*. She'd had visions of him during the ride home from the nursing home. Of medium height, a rough beard that he rarely shaved, and an unsteady right hand, perhaps part of the reason why he rarely shaved, a war veteran, possibly a hero."

"Septimus Smith," Thomas commented. "Clarissa's parallel."

"Exactly." I smiled with satisfaction. "She envisioned him as a shell-shocked veteran, trying desperately to cope with life in the civilian world. She knew he would have a secret obsession. I'm not sure if she knew from the beginning that the obsession would be Evans."

"Not to deviate from the point, Nellie, but it could be argued that Septimus's obsession isn't Evans at all, but rather, his own guilty feelings about the death of Evans."

I laughed, a bit louder than I intended. The couple next to us looked up from their soup and glared at me for a moment. I half-muttered an apology.

"You've never had intense feelings for another man, have you, Thomas?"

"No, I guess I haven't."

"Then you can't possibly understand what this character could be feeling. All these conflicting emotions that well up inside of you, you feel the way you do and you want to acknowledge that, embrace it even, because you know you can't change it, yet you also know that it is wrong. How could you not know? Everyone tells you so. If they don't say it straight out, they say it without saying it. All the advertisements you see are all about families—men and women, along with their children. Heaven forbid you should not fit into this picture—well, then you are out of the picture, so to speak. You simply have to conform to what they want, play by their rules. Anything else can easily be death."

Thomas let out a short gasp of air. "Death? Aren't you being just a bit melodramatic? I doubt it would be that bad?"

I shook my head. "No, not at all. As a matter of fact, that sort of thing happens all the time, actually. Anything that is different from the norm is punished."

"And what of Rezia? Speaking of punishment, don't you think she is punished terribly, being married to a man who doesn't want her, sexually?"

I glared at him, getting a bit impatient with his density. "He doesn't want her, period. His distaste for her is total, not just sexual."

"But he married her, of his own free will. He must have found her appealing, or at least tasteful, even if he did not love her."

"Again," and now I struggled to keep my voice on an even keel, remembering all the expense he was going to on my account, "all of that happened *before* he went off to war. Don't you see, the war changed him, permanently."

"Nellie, are you saying that war made him homosexual? That would be the ultimate irony, wouldn't it, considering how homosexuals are viewed by the military?"

"Yes, it would, but no, that's not what I'm saying at all. Course, being a woman, I've never been in war, and from the looks of you, with your fancy college education, I'd wager that you haven't either." His nod of the head told me my assumption was correct. "But from what I read from my one brother's letters, God rest his soul, and my other brother who came home and couldn't stop talking about it, the friendships you make in the trenches are lifelong and are enduring. They become more important than anything else. That's one of the goals of *The Hours*, excuse me, *Mrs. Dalloway*. I still think of that book by the original title, even after all these years. She wanted to get into the head of a soldier and see the world from his eyes, feel what he feels. That's why she was such a genius."

Fresh tears began to well up in my eyes, even though it's been more than a decade. I guess there really was no timeline for grief. I let out a long exhausted breath, embarrassed that I had carried on like that. Years of repressed emotion was let loose, I suppose. For the briefest moment there, I thought I saw Lottie smiling at me from above. She always said I didn't speak up enough.

Thomas did not say a word. The two of us sat there for the longest time, the silence hanging thick in the air.

"Wow. I never thought of it that way, before," Thomas commented. "I guess it would be difficult. I see where she gets her ideas for Septimus, feeling as he obviously does for Evans. But what of the war?"

"What of it?" I asked. "You know, I'm sure, everyone does, that she was a pacifist. So she had to make Septimus a returning veteran. She had to show her audience what war does to a man. He returns as only a shell of a man."

Thomas nodded, his right hand covering his mouth, massaging the side of his face.

"But what of his wife, Rezia?" What is Woolf saying about her?"

"Poor thing, I think she is somewhat deluded by her own sense of self. She believes she has more of a hold over Septimus than she actually does. Truth be told, he'd rather die than live under her watchful eye. She finds out that she never knew him after all, just like Gilbert finds out about Angela in 'The Legacy.'"

"Ah yes, 'The Legacy,' her last story, enclosed with her suicide note to Leonard. I doubt many of the people who will read my book will have read that story, or even know about it for that matter," Thomas remarked. "But I digress. We were talking about Rezia Smith." He began a character analysis.

"You know in some ways, I think she is supposed to represent Leonard. Like Leonard, Rezia thinks she knows what's best for her spouse. She decides for him, she attends to him, medically. And like Virginia, Septimus would rather die, and does die, than subject herself to the doctors' intervention. Virginia kills herself at the onset of another breakdown. Septimus lunges out of a window when he hears the doctor coming up the stairs to take him to hospital." He smiled, apparently pleased with himself.

I nodded, adding my own insight to complement his.

"And how she suffers in the book. Sitting there, forced to watch her husband wallow in his own despair and being incapable of doing anything about it. Her suffering is real. She is just as much a victim of the war as he is, yet somehow, her suffering does not matter. The scenes with the two of them are not entirely about Septimus, as one might think. She matters as well, if only as an afterthought."

Thomas nodded. "I believe I am beginning to understand some things."

Not for the first time, I wondered if that were really true. Maybe nobody could understand who wasn't there. But I did what I had always been trained to do.

I kept my mouth shut.

Chapter Twelve

Nellie was ready to quit. Mrs. W was totally unreasonable lately, Mr. Woolf was never around, and the pay, quite frankly, was a bit less than what her friends were making. It didn't help that she was already feeling irritable. Lottie was spending time at Mrs. Bell Grant's house, having been "loaned out," as it were. Lottie did not mind so much; Mr. Grant was known to slip the servants some extra cash for a job well done. Plus, it was only a couple of blocks away, well within walking distance if they wanted to visit for luncheon or just simply to have a cup of coffee and exchange some gossip. For her part, though, Nellie could not help being angry at the move. It made her feel like they were not servants but slaves. And Nellie Boxall was no slave to anyone! Her mother hadn't died after bearing and raising eleven children so that her children could become someone else's slaves, even if the "someone else" was basically, she had to admit, a decent person.

    It was with this attitude that Nellie prepared the afternoon's lunch. She was making a meat pie. The butcher never flattened the meat enough in the store. She always had to pound it more when she got it home. Today, she pounded harder, longer, and louder than she needed to, just for spite. It was a quarter after noon. The missus still had another forty-five minutes left to write. The study was directly upstairs from the kitchen. Nellie knew the missus could hear the noise from the kitchen and that it would make her crazy. Nellie gloated.

    After enduring ten minutes of the pounding, Virginia could stand it no longer. She charged down the stairs as though she were headed into battle. She lunged at Nellie as if she would strike her.

Nellie stepped back, her rump clanging against the pans hanging on the rack.

"What the devil is all that noise for? I can't think enough to write a single word!" the lady of the house bellowed.

Nellie gave her a perplexed look as though she were totally caught off guard by the question.

"Why, Mrs. Woolf, good afternoon to ya, ma'am." Nellie made a mock curtsy as she wiped hands on her white apron, hopelessly stained from other endeavors. The formality was a setup. She only called Virginia "Mrs. Woolf" under one of two circumstances: either Leonard was present or when she was ready for a row.

"Never mind your good afternoons. Answer me, damn it, or damn you to the deuce, whichever you like!"

"I'm just making meat pie, ma'am. I have to flatten the meat out, you know that, I've done it many times. I'm sorry if this time it distracts you." She picked up the cleaver as though she would strike it again on the table. Virginia came closer and, with both hands, yanked the cleaver out of the cook's hands and slammed it down on the carving board. Her hand stung from the effort.

"Damn you, you know bloody well what you are doing. You are deliberately to try to make me crazy because you're upset. Well, talk to me then. I'm here, you've won. You have my attention."

Nellie bellowed, "It isn't about you, goddamn it. Believe it or not, ma'am, not all of life is about you! But then how would you know what life was about, you who sit in your room writing your books, living your characters' lives rather than your own. The coward's way out!"

Nellie's words about her writing seemed to Virginia to be a particularly vicious personal affront. It always bothered Virginia when anyone criticized her writing, particularly her fiction writing. It is the very nature of genius, she thought and planned to write, to mind terribly the opinions of others. The heart of a genius leaped for joy upon receiving praise and wept aloud at scorn. But Nellie's opinion mattered more than most. She was more than a cook. She was a cherished friend and confidante. Virginia was entirely dependent on her.

Nellie's words had wounded her deeply. No matter, she would not show it, not here and not now.

"Better my scribblings than your rantings, to be sure. You think I am deaf to your complaints and your insults? How you bitch and moan about missing your half-witted friend, and conspirator, no doubt. Well, I am not, and neither is L—Mr. Woolf." This comment, Virginia knew, even in her anger, to be singularly untrue. But for paying their wages and entertaining (if not approving) the occasional request for an increase, Leonard was oblivious to the servants' desires and needs.

Nellie wanted to grab her scrawny neck. "Lottie is my friend. And you just took her from me like that, poof! No one asked me how I'd feel about it. For that matter, no one asked Lottie either. It was decided for us, we were not consulted. It's like small children who are one day told by their parents that they are moving. No one asks the children's opinion, it does not matter. Well, let me tell you something, Mrs. Virginia Woolf, Nellie Boxall is no child and neither is Lottie Hope. And we ain't slaves, neither. We are free to do as we please."

Virginia had enough. The anger was burning in her stomach like a furnace, coupled with her overwhelming desire to get back to the essay she had on her desk, only half-written.

"You certainly may do as you please, Nelly, in your own home. When you are mistress of your own house, you may do as you wish, come and go whenever you like. However, as long as you are in my home, you will do as I see fit, come and go according to my pleasure. That goes for Lottie as well."

"Fine." Nellie crossed her arms over her chest, resting them over her ample bosom. "In that case, consider this my two-week notice. I'll not work here a day longer!"

She picked up the cleaver and, with all the strength she could muster, slammed the piece of meat in front of her with a loud boom. The mistress did an immediate about-face, makes an obscene gesture, and retreated to her study, slamming the door behind her with such force that a book tumbled off the shelf.

Virginia slumped into her chair and got back to her essay. She wrote a sentence, crossed it out, started a new one and crossed that out as well. She shoved the essay aside, throwing her pen down. She got up and grabbed her journal off the shelf. Carefully putting the date at the top of a clean page, she began a diatribe about the insolence of servants who did not know their place and the anger she felt at "being at the mercy of one's servants." She knew herself well enough to know that only when she got all the anger out of her system could she write the essay. By that time, unfortunately, it was shortly after one, past her self-imposed deadline. Besides, she was too tired to continue anyway. The argument had taken away her strength.

In the kitchen, Nellie sat, slumped over on her stool, her hands pressed tightly against her stomach. She wanted to heave, but instead simply sat and cried. She loved Mrs. W and hated their rows. But she really didn't like the way she was being treated. She sat there for a few minutes, then wiped her face, washed her hands, and resumed her work. There was the matter of her notice; she would have to rescind it. She would do that later, after they had both cooled off. Besides, she was sure Mrs. W knew her well enough not to take her notice seriously. Still, though, there was always that chance that the lady *would* take her seriously. What would Nellie do if the missus replaced her? The thought made her queasy.

She rescinded the notice two days later, after they both had had time to cool off, and the missus had time to stew. Virginia accepted the apology of sorts, and they moved on. To celebrate the end of the strife, Virginia proposed a ride on the Tube into Hyde Park, where they would wander the grounds of the magnificent park and feast on lamb pie at the British Museum.

Shortly after the reconciliation, Lottie came home. Nellie was overjoyed. She had everything she wanted.

*****

Things improved, for a time. Lottie was happy to be home. She had relished in the extravagant attentions of Mr. Grant and found him quite amusing, especially the way he lavished his attentions so freely on Mr. Garnett, Bunny, as he insisted she call him since everyone else did, even though she was just the maid. But that house was just a house. She did not feel at home there. When she dusted the cabinets and vacuumed the floor, she felt as an imposter, an interloper. But that was only part of the reason for her discomfort. It was really about Nellie. Houses came and went. Home was wherever Nellie was; be it Buckingham Palace or a two-room flat on Oxford Street. As long as Nellie was there with her, Lottie would call it home and would cherish it, just as she cherished her.

Mrs. Bell Grant came over with the children often. Lottie was not fond of the children. They were pleasant enough, but exceedingly loud. It grated on her nerves. The children adored the pudgy maid with bad teeth and missed seeing her every day. For her part, Lottie smiled, feigned excitement well, and kept her the obscene epithets she muttered under her breath, inaudible to others. Nellie pitched in as well. She prepared and Lottie served cucumber sandwiches and boiling hot tea to the adults, franks and ices to the children. The children gobbled down their franks with nauseating speed. When the children came into the kitchen, Nellie helped them in getting whatever it was they wanted and then politely shooed them always. She never forgot her place. She told them there was a blueberry pie in the oven, and if they were really good, she would give them each a giant piece, with a scoop of ice cream on the side of it. The children were happy; the adults chattered away.

"Nellie, we need some more sandwiches. Mr. Grant is quite hungry today, it seems."

"Right away, ma'am." She went back to the cutting board and prepared more sandwiches, wondering just how much that man could possibly eat.

Lottie came into the kitchen, having been lying downstairs for the last hour or so (it was her time, and her cramps were terrible). She walked into the kitchen wrapped in an old blue blanket, a hot water bottle pressed firmly against her belly. She draped her right hand over Nellie's left shoulder; her fingers brushed against Nellie's breast, causing her nipple to visibly harden underneath her blouse.

"How's my favorite cook?" She half-whispered into Nellie's ear.

"Just fine, how are you feeling?"

"Oh, fine, a little cramped still, but I'll survive. Though if I drink any more tea, I think I'll float away." Lottie laughed loudly, causing Quentin to run in to see what was going on. He never liked to feel that he was missing out on anything, particularly anything fun.

"What is it? What's happening?" he asked, a bit breathlessly, streaks of chocolate ice smeared across his mouth.

"Nothing, dear boy, I was just telling Lottie a joke," Nellie improvised. Quentin was excited.

"Tell it to me, please. I love jokes, I tell them to my friends all the time."

Lottie's expression turned sour. "It was an adult joke. Now, you go back to your brother and never mind! You got better things to do than to be eavesdropping on the help in the kitchen."

Quentin wanted to say that he had not been eavesdropping; the women were loud. But his mother had taught him to be polite to his elders. In any case, he had seen enough of Lottie, especially when she stayed with his family, to know her mannerisms. When her voice got that certain edge to it … well there was no point in arguing. He turned back and left the women alone, more than a little miffed at his rebuttal. He thought of telling his mother, but decided better of it. He liked Lottie too much, and Nellie always made great treats. He decided to say nothing. He went back to his brother and played. Soon after, Nellie was calling them for some chocolate milk.

Vanessa was quite content. Lying slumped in an easy chair on the porch (Nessa always had terrible posture, much to her late mother's chagrin), she held a glass of port in her outstretched left hand and puffed on a cigarette.

"You know, Ginia, I can understand your problems with Lottie. She really is terribly moody and doesn't take instruction very well. She was a terrible burden in some ways. And Bunny was at his wits' end with her many times." Nessa exhaled a cloud of smoke and giggled softly. "We were well rid of her, by Christ, though she does polish extraordinarily well. Our china never shined so brightly."

"I know it. Her polishing is the only reason *we* have kept her as long as we have. That is why we tolerate her. Not a speck of dust or dirt escapes her watchful eye, ever." Even as Virginia spoke, both she and Nessa knew full well that she was lying. The reasons Virginia kept both Nellie and Lottie on (for it was entirely Virginia's doing; Leonard would have given both of them the sack years ago) had nothing to do with culinary or housekeeping ability. There was dozens on Trafalgar Square who could do just as well, if not better. The reason had to do with her relationship with the servants. She felt a bond with them as women, mutually dependent on each other and on their "father," as Woolf would later write. Dependence of any sort infuriated Virginia, who often wondered who was more dependent in an employer-servant relationship: mistress or maid? Regardless, she felt tremendous loyalty to her servants, especially to Nellie. The servants must have reciprocated the sentiment, for it surely was not the pay that kept them on. Virginia had no need to articulate all this to Nessa. Her beloved sister knew Virginia better than anyone. Nessa often thought she knew Ginia better than Ginia knew herself.

When the company finally left, Nellie and Lottie were both relieved and utterly exhausted. They cleaned up together, the dining room and the kitchen, and were downstairs in the basement within three quarters of an hour.

"Oh, those kids are so loud and obnoxious," Nellie exclaimed once they were in private. "Really, Lottie, I don't know how you were able to put up with them as you did. I think I'd lose my mind."

Lottie chuckled, the truth of the statement apparent. "Truly, you don't even know the half of it, ol' Nell." She relished calling Nellie that, a residual from the one Dickens novel she had ever read. She gave Nellie a sly grin. "But now they're gone, and I'm back. What's say we make our own noise?" She reached her hand into Nellie's nightshirt, squeezing her right breast with just the right amount of pressure. Nellie lurched her body toward her and kissed her wildly, passionately on the lips.

When it was over, and they were both spent, Lottie lay flat on her back, totally content, thinking that there must be nothing else so grand this side of heaven.

Chapter Thirteen

Vanessa was having a party. She and Duncan had just purchased a new dining room set, and she was dying to show it off, along with some paintings she had just finished. Naturally, Virginia and Leonard were invited; they accepted straightaway, as did all of Nessa's friends. The difference was that *to this* party, Nellie and Lottie were invited. They were not to be extra help, but guests. They would be sitting at the same table and drinking the same wine as their betters. This was unheard-of bliss! Nellie was determined to look her best this evening; one must put forth considerable effort.

Vanessa had said not to bring anything but Nellie had been brought up better than that. Mrs. W wanted to go into London as soon as she was finished writing. Nellie was to accompany her. Knowing she'd be busy, Nellie asked Lottie to stop by the florist in town and pick up a bunch of irises; they were Vanessa's favorites. Nellie did not want it said that she was not a gracious guest.

By the time the afternoon came, Virginia was edgy. She was ready to resurrect Clarissa Dalloway. She referred to some notes she had scribbled that day, now some time ago, that she had proposed the idea to Nellie. The title was there, in the center of the page, in her own handwriting: *The Hours: A Woman's Life in One Day.* Now she was ready to stop thinking about it and start working on it. She felt a bit distracted. She was writing an outline for the book and a detailed plan of attach. She always planned in great detail when beginning a book. Leonard often joked that the prime minister hadn't planned so thoroughly when attacking the Germans. Nellie thought the joke tasteless. The war was over, thank God, may there never be another, but mangled bodies and ruined lives were nothing to mock. It was all very well for Leonard, a Jew, who would never enlist, to mock the war, but Nellie had many nephews who had gone off to the war and came back in body bags or wheelchairs.

Nellie stood by the door of the study. "We'd best be going, Mrs. W, or we'll miss the train."

"Oh, all right," Virginia conceded. "I'm stuck anyway." She looked at Nellie askance, as if trying to invoke sympathy. "I finished the entire outline, but I don't have a first sentence. The first sentence is imperative. The entire book flows from it. All my books work that way. If I cannot come up with a first sentence … well, all the outlines in the world won't make a book." She put her pen down, stretched her arms above her head, and craned her neck left, then right. "The worst part is, I've been at it so long that my neck and shoulders are just in knots."

Nellie smiled. "Well, you know, ma'am, I don't know much about drafting outlines or first sentences, but stiff necks and shoulders I know well. I can help with that." She approached Virginia from behind, placing her hands firmly on the lady's shoulders. She began to rub, and Virginia began cooing with delight. Nellie's hands were strong, imposing, the result of years of carrying grocery bags, scouring pots, and lugging ten-pound bags of potatoes up and down steep stairs.

"Oh, oh, that feels so good," Virginia moaned as the tips of Nellie's rough fingers worked their way into Virginia's flesh through the cotton of her blouse. Nellie continued for minutes that seemed like hours until Virginia noticed her groin starting to respond to Nellie's touch. She immediately became uncomfortable.

"We'd best be off now," Virginia declared, abruptly ending the massage session. She stood up, her shoulders still tingling, and put her papers away. Nellie excused herself for a moment, promising to get their coats, train fare and meet Virginia by the door. On her way, she stepped into the guest bedroom where Lottie was waxing the floor and told her not to bother with the flowers. She would get them while she was in London.

When they exited the train, Nellie put a handkerchief to her nose to guard against the exhaust fumes of the train as it pulled away from the station. Virginia, by contrast, inhaled deeply, breathing everything her lungs could take in. Other people came to London and saw smog, crowded streets, pickpockets, and littered sidewalks. When Virginia came to London, she saw life—full, pulsating vitality. She longed to submerge herself into the pulse of this vibrant city. Her novel, aside from being a single day in the life of a woman, was to be a celebration of London. It would showcase London in all its splendor, from the magnificent parks to the British Museum, to the awe-inspiring British Library.

As they walked toward the first store on Virginia's itinerary, Nellie caught a corner flower stand out of the corner of her eye.

"Ma'am, if you please, remind me to stop there," she motioned to the flower stand with her pointer finger, "on the way back. I told Lottie I would buy the flowers myself …"

Virginia didn't hear the rest. She was too overcome with emotion.

"Nellie, I can't believe it. You've done it, you've actually done it!"

Nellie was confused. "Done what, Mrs. W? Did I do something wrong?"

"No, no, not at all, dear sweet Nellie." Virginia placed both hands on her cook's face and kissed her perfunctorily on both cheeks. The lady's cold hands stung Nellie's skin. They heard huffing behind them. When they looked, they both blushed. They were standing in the middle of the street, not realizing it. A queue was already beginning to form, of people who wanted to get past them, on their way to and fro. Virginia pulled herself and Nellie over to the side, out of everyone's way, before she ventured to explain.

"You've given me what I need most of all, a first sentence. And I could never thank you enough. Tomorrow, I can begin work on the novel."

"Well, I'm glad I could help you, ma'am, of course, but how did I do it? What did I say?'

Virginia grinned with glib satisfaction. "You said you were going to get the flowers yourself, that Lottie did not have to bother. That's it, don't you see." She paused for a few seconds. Lifting her left hand, she moved it slowly from left to right as she spoke the next words. "Mrs. Dalloway said she would buy the flowers herself." She dropped her hand to her side and remained silent for some seconds, giving Nellie time to absorb her words properly. "I've even gotten the next line. 'For Lucy had enough to do.'" Virginia suddenly got a glazed faraway look in her eye, and Nellie could tell that her mistress was writing the entire first chapter in her mind, right there where they stood. It was said that genius was unstoppable, that artists were creating even when not at their desks or easels. In fact, it was thought by some, Henry James among them, that an artist's real work was done when away from the desk or the easel. The only job when one sat at the desk was to begin putting on paper or canvas what was already finished in the artist's mind. As far as Nellie was concerned, this was absolutely true. She had been around Mrs. W long enough to know the most her creating was done when she was doing something other than writing: taking a walk, tending to her rose bushes or azalea bushes, planting her asparagus beds. And Vanessa seemed to get ideas for new paintings all the time. Nellie wasn't sure how Vanesa rated as a painter; her work sold only moderately well, and that was due more to the powers of persuasion possessed by the London dealers who agreed to exhibit her work than it was due to any unnatural genius on Vanessa's part. In the end, none of it really mattered to Nellie. Mrs. W was a literary genius, of this Nellie was certain, even if the rest of the world did not yet see it. And she, Nellie Boxall, someone whom no one would ever care to remember, in some small way, contributed to her employer's writings. The glib satisfaction in that sure and certain knowledge was beyond what money could buy.

Virginia was speaking again. Nellie had the feeling that Mrs. W had been talking the whole time and that she had missed some of what was said.

"Yes, the book will be set around a party. Clarissa is going into London to buy flowers for her party. She sees someone, who does she see?"

Nellie answered immediately. "Knowing Clarissa, it was probably the queen. Clarissa is a bit of a snob after all." She laughed loudly, her comment meant to be funny, not to be taken seriously. But Virginia took her quite seriously.

"It was the queen … or was it?" Her mind catapulted back to the present. She dug her hand into her purse to take out a few coins.

"Nellie, be a dear and go get us a couple of cups of tea. And make sure to bring back a bunch of napkins. I'll be over there." She pointed to a nearby bench, big enough for two. Nellie went off to get the tea while Virginia sat down at the bench and fished her pen out of her pocketbook. Nellie brought over the tea and some napkins; Virginia seized the napkins first and immediately began writing on one of them. She wrote intently, barely noticing the tea that Nellie placed next to her.

"Mrs. Dalloway said she would buy the flowers herself. For Lucy had enough to do." She stopped writing for a minute and gazed at the horizon. Nellie knew what she was doing. She was visualizing the scene. Mrs. W did that a lot. She would stare straight ahead, but she would not see what she was staring at. Instead, she would see, smell, hear, and probably even taste, the things that were happening in her novels. It was an extraordinary ability; one which had gotten her into a few scrapes on the Tube when she would glare at a fellow passenger for several minutes, causing an uncomfortable feeling and, more often than not, a disparaging remark. Nellie would murmur an apology to the offended party and nudge Virginia, who would quickly "come back." Nellie thought that the ability to see imaginary things so clearly was one of the benefits of Virginia's illness. Fiction and reality could, and often did, blend for her, indistinguishable.

Nellie sat next to the lady, scribbling away paragraphs on paper napkins. Nellie beamed from the inside, excited that she had once again, even in some small way, contributed to a legendary English novel. And Nellie was certain that this book would be legendary. She had no doubt. There was a certain gleam in Mrs. W's eye when she talked about this book. It would be the *one*, Nellie was sure of it. And she would help. Whatever needed to be done, she would do it. Even if meant having to entertain that dreadful Katherine Mansfield and her louse of a husband who, after a couple of glasses of wine, could not manage to keep his hands of the servants' bums.

They sat at the bench for fifteen minutes and then proceeded with their business. They went to the Hatchard's, the oldest bookstore in London. There were three floors of books, the cheapest of which were housed in the basement. Virginia always went there first because it often contained books that were discounted in price simply because their authors were not in vogue or had not as of yet been discovered by the literary masses. Once, while was down there scouring through the mold laced stacks, she had discovered a copy of *The Voyage Out*. She had immediately signed the inside jacket and placed the book neatly back where she had found it, lacking the self-confidence to identify herself to the owner as the book's author by presenting him with the signed copy.

Today, she was looking for a book on Turner, Nessa's favorite painter, whose style she tried to incorporate into her own. She meant to give it to Nessa as a gift. Knowing that Virginia would not desire help in locating the volume (on the contrary, she insisted on solitude while book-hunting), Nellie left her mistress and wandered back upstairs to the cookbook section. She loved trying out new recipes but lacked original ideas. She was forever buying cookbooks, trying recipes listed, and adding to or subtracting from their ingredients, making the recipes her own. She wanted to write a cookbook of her own but was hardly capable of such a long and arduous process. Her mind swirled at the very thought, though her heart yearned to accomplish it.

They met at the till. Nellie had her money out before they were called up by the clerk (it irked her endlessly to see people who were waiting for the till yet made no move to take out money until they were rung up, as if they had no idea they would have to pay). Virginia motioned with her hand for her cook to put her money away. Virginia paid for both of their purchases and deposited two of the pennies she had received as part of her change into a tin cup on the side of the till. It was for a Home for Foundlings. Never given the chance for children herself, she had a soft spot for them and considered unwanted or orphaned children to be the most pitiable of all of God's creations.

They left the store in bright sunlight, just as a wind gust was revving up. It hit them in the face: Nellie's scarf went flying, and she muttered half-unintelligible curses under her now-visible breath. Virginia glowed. For the first time in quite a while, she felt fully alive.

The Woolfs arrived at Nessa's party exactly on time. Virginia suggested being fashionably late, but Leonard would not hear of it, being a stickler for punctuality. Nellie and Lottie walked in standing on the left side of the Woolfs, not behind them, as would usually be the case. The change was Virginia's idea. She insisted on it, saying that if they were to be equals at the party, then they could all walk in as equals. Nellie presented Vanessa with her gift of irises.

"From Lottie and me, to thank you for inviting us," she said, flashing her widest smile.

Nessa made a fuss over the irises, too much of a fuss. Virginia realized it right away and had to make an effort not to laugh. Nellie didn't notice because she did not know Nessa so well, but she was being patronized. Virginia contemplated how angry Nellie would be if she knew the truth. The secret knowledge made laughter all the more difficult to resist.

Before dinner, Nessa took her company for a tour of the house; ridiculous when once considered that every guest there had been there hundreds of times. They began with the studio, to see some of the new pieces she had been working on. "These are the pieces that will make me, Duncan is sure of it," she intoned. They entered the studio, which from the outside looked more like a large tool shed, and the rotting wood floors creaked under Nellie's firm footing. The smell of turpentine assaulted Nellie and stayed in her nose through most of the evening. Vanessa took down the single light, hung in a corner by the door, and flipped the switch. She held it in front of her as she led the company through the various acrylics and oil paints she had displayed. Toward the back of the studio was a padded chair facing an easel. The easel was covered with a drop cloth.

"What's that?" A woman neither Nellie nor Lottie recognized motioned to the drop cloth. Nellie rolled her eyes.

"That's the piece I'm working on now. It's covered to protect the paint. When it's done, I apply the finish, and then it can be displayed. Besides," Nessa gave a sheepish grin, "I am sensitive about people seeing my work before it's finished."

Nellie and Lottie understood. When Virginia was working on a manuscript, especially in the early stages, she might talk about it a great deal, but she would be very selective in what she said and to whom. And she would never let anyone see any of its pages. She was afraid to; it was the one thing that had rubbed off on her from Leonard's Judaism. She was afraid that showing the pages would put *chana hora* (a jinx) on it.

They left the studio and walked back to the house. In the living room, they admired the new sofa. The paint on the walls was clean and fresh, and the room still smelled of the newly laid rug. After an appropriate amount of *oohs* and *aahs*, and the requisite number of compliments had been given to the gushing hostess, it was time to sit down to eat.

They took their seats. The extra maids that Vanessa hired for the day served the appetizers. Lola, the upstairs maid who had been with them for quite a while, went around the table, filling wineglasses with a French wine that Bunny had brought up from the cellar.

To Nellie's left sat two painters Nessa had shown with at a local gallery. They were talking about Nessa's last few paintings. Quietly, they snickered about them, wondering how much her dandy husband had to pay to get the gallery to let her show such rot! None of the "regular" guests heard them mocking their hostess in her own house. But Nellie had been trained all her life to live in the background, among the shadows, inconspicuous. She was used to people not noticing she was there, and she was adept at taking care of things without being noticed. What should she do? She felt torn. Nessa had invited her and Lottie out of the kindness of her heart; it seemed disloyal not to inform her of her ungracious guests who possessed such cowardice, they lacked the ability to criticize Vanessa's work to her face. Yet to say something would be against her nature.

In the end, she did what she has been taught to do all her life. She minded her own goddamned business.

Virginia was sipping the white wine that she had been nursing for almost two hours, listening to the drudgery of some half-wit discussing water colors as if he had invented them. Her head began to throb. Just as she thought him finished and she began to regain full consciousness, the blithering idiot babbled on again, flailing his arms, globs of spittle forming at the corners of his mouth. She was disgusted. As always, Nellie came to her rescue.

"How is your book coming, ma'am?" She slid herself onto the leather sofa next to where Virginia was seated, her face visibly grateful for the rather rude interruption.

Virginia smiled earnestly. "It's actually going much better today."

"Is it now? That's wonderful I say," said the half-wit, who was steadily becoming more than a little drunk.

"Yes, it surely is wonderful. To be truthful, I was getting so discouraged with the whole project that I was about ready to throw the entire manuscript into the Thames. But then a dear friend made a comment to me this afternoon. It has made the difference. The novel will have a birth, after all." She patted Nellie's right knee.

"It's wonderful when we find inspiration. I feel it myself. You're very lucky to have a husband. Husbands do provide the best inspiration. Perhaps I should get one for myself!" At that, he guffawed. "It must be so much easier for a woman artist or writer as opposed to a man." Nellie stiffened at the comment; she could practically feel the hair on the back of Virginia's neck stand straight up.

"How so, exactly?" Virginia inquired.

"Women can spend all the day working on their art while men can only do their art part-time. We are charged with earning a living. Women have no such burden."

Nellie sniffled and put her hand in Virginia's underneath the table. Virginia squeezed it so hard it made Nellie wince.

"In my household, my husband and I have a business, a printing press. We run it together." She spoke dryly, in a flat tone. "In addition, my writing, the novels, book reviews, and essays account for a significant portion of our monthly income. That pokes a hole or two into your theory, I'd wager."

The gentleman fumbled over his words. "Well, there is an exception to everything, as they say. But still, I do think lady artists have it easier than their male counterparts. Yes, I do say so."

"Yes, well, do excuse me. I find myself suddenly in need of air." She rose from her seat, putting her napkin at her place, looked to Nellie and said quietly, "Nellie, would you come with me, please?"

"Certainly," Nellie responded, repeating her employer's actions. Once they had turned away from the man and were walking, they linked arms. Nellie leaned in and whispered, "Where are we going, ma'am?"

"To the deuce, if necessary. Anywhere to get away from that buffoon. I cannot bear it a moment longer." The women laughed like schoolgirls.

They took a walk through the terrace doors and wandered out heading toward the garden. The roses were in bloom. Vanessa adored roses—red, yellow, and white alike. Duncan liked to play the suitor. Once a week, he ventured into the garden with hedge clippers and surreptitiously clipped several roses, tied them together with a thin rubber band, and presented them to Vanessa, along with a card containing a short love poem. Later, she would wish she had had the foresight to save all the poems, as Sue Gilbert had thought to save the poems of her sister-in-law, Emily Dickinson, written in her tiny hand on the back of cream-colored envelopes. But then she tended to her roses, nurturing them with almost as much attention as she gives her children. She was quite proud of her roses, and slightly ashamed of Duncan. She did not mind his proclivities, and she liked Bunny just fine, but to live with him and the daily reality of what his presence signified, that was another matter entirely.

Virginia and Nellie stopped to admire the roses. They inhaled the scent deeply, and Nellie bent down to stroke their petals. Virginia picked up a pair of clippers lying on the floor nearby, and clipped one of the yellow roses just below the petals, leaving the tiniest of stems. She straightened up and waited for Nellie to do the same. When she did, Virginia came toward her, unfastened a pin from her hair, and pinned the flower to Nellie's dress, directly above her left breast. Nellie smiled in gratitude, and the two women embraced for a moment. They glanced at each other for a long moment, then Nellie spoke.

"I suppose we'd best be heading back to the party now, shouldn't we, ma'am?"

Virginia sighed. "Yes, I suppose so, though I am sick to death of the entire affair already. Perhaps we can take our leave early, though Mr. Woolf seems to be enjoying himself immensely."

"Yes, Leonard does love these things." She laughed. "Once, when E. M. Forster had a cocktail party, he was making martinis. Well, you know how little Leonard drinks, he was drunk out of his mind within a half hour, stumbling over his words, not to mention his feet. What a rot! Leonard was frightfully embarrassed the next day. It was all I could do to stop people from teasing him the next day, especially Katherine."

Nellie laughed too at the image of her employer in a drunken stopper. He was so uptight most of the time, always in that gray suit and ugly tie. It was hard to imagine him drunk and stumbling over himself. She thought about it and could barely contain herself.

When they return to the house, the party was in full swing. Leonard was, as the women thought, having a wonderful time, his tie loosened down and lowered down to his stomach. Virginia sought out Nessa, who was chatting with the author of some second-rate novel who had already made his dinner from the appetizers before the main course was even served, then had that. Nellie looked for Lottie, who was having a lively conversation with one of Vanessa's painter friends, discussing some of the Impressionists she came to know while living with Vanessa. Lottie was enjoying herself, most especially the fact that she could put down a glass and plate like everyone else and not be expected to take it away. Someone else got to clean up after her for a change. For that alone, she was grateful.

"Excuse me, I'm sorry for interrupting." Nellie approached the group that seemed to be having a grand old time listening to Lottie tell one of her endless stories about growing up. Nellie turned to the maid. "Lottie, dear, may I speak to you for a moment, in private."

Lottie got up with a bit of a huff, clearly unwilling to partake from her audience. Her head spun a bit as she stood up, the result of too much wine taken in too short of a time frame with not enough food, though there was plenty of food offered.

"Yes, what is it?" she asked, holding on to Nellie's right arm, in an effort not to swagger.

"Mrs. W and I have had quite enough for an evening. We would like to make our way back home. I was hoping you would want to join us."

"In bed, you mean, no thanks. I could do without that privilege."

Nellie bit her lip hard. She hated it when Lottie was drunk; it made her even more sarcastic than usual. She became almost unbearable. But for now, she would keep her cool with Lottie.

"Surely you know, I meant home with us. And unless you know something I don't, Mrs. W will sleep in her own bed, and I will sleep in ours."

"What about Mr. Woolf?" Lottie asked.

"Mr. Woolf should be quite happy to sleep in his own bed, but I'm sure he appreciates your concern." Her attempt at humor was entirely lost on the drunken maid.

"Will he stay here or is he coming back with us?" The "us" made Nellie momentarily hopeful, and she answered quickly. She gazed over at her employer, who was smoking what must have been his fourth cigar of the evening, happily nursing yet another martini in his right hand, and back at Lottie.

"No, Mr. Woolf, it seems, is quite content with the company. Whereas Mrs. W and I are quite exhausted from it." She gave a pointed glance before asking again, "Will you be joining us?"

Lottie let go of Nellie's arm (she had been holding it all this time) and, with a sudden burst of confidence, declared, "I think I should like to stay longer. I will return home when Mr. Woolf does."

Nellie breathed sharply. "Well then, I guess I'll be seeing you home then," she quipped.

Leonard and Lottie came in around four in the morning; Leonard dropped his eyeglasses in the foyer and knocked over the umbrella stand. Lottie tiptoed downstairs to the basement. Not wanting to turn on a light and wake up Nellie, she fumbled her way to the bed, bumping into an ashtray, knocking it to the floor and into a million pieces. Lottie swore several oaths as she lit the gas lamp and placed it on the floor as she cleaned up the glass and threw it into the pail, lest either of them should slice a foot. She got into bed quietly, trying not to stir Nellie. Her desire not to wake Nellie was not out of consideration for Nellie as much as it was self-preservation. Nellie would only go on for minutes at a time about did Lottie know what time it was, how inconsiderate could she be, etc.? Lottie already knew what time it was; she didn't need Nellie to tell her. She certainly did not need Nellie's scorn. Besides, it would serve Nellie right for all the times she left Lottie by herself to go to the missus.

Under the covers, Nellie was already awake but pretended to be asleep. The anger inside her was smoldering; she did not want it to burst into flames.

Chapter Fourteen

Hyde Park Gate
April 1925

Vita Sackville-West came for the weekend. To make the visit more special, Virginia decided that they should spend the time at her family's home in London at Hyde Park Gate. It had been recently vacated by her brother, Adrian, who had shared it for a while with Duncan, her sister's husband. Lottie had been dispatched there three days earlier, to get the house ready. Virginia and Nellie caught the last train into London the night before, so that they would not have to rush around in the morning before Vita arrived.

Nellie and Lottie always snickered when this particular guest came over. Of medium height, with straight hair and plain unflattering clothes, a cigar (how vulgar!) or cigarette almost permanently attached to her lips, and a voice that was raspy and perpetually hoarse (likely from the cigars and cigarettes), she looked and sounded more masculine than most men did. Her husband was the effeminate one. He was shorter than she, more meticulous in his clothing, and had a higher-pitched voice. Harold, her husband, usually stayed home when Vita visited Virginia's home. Although he and Virginia had always gotten along (they respected one another as writers, they both felt strongly about Vita, and their political ideals were similar), when Vita and Virginia visited, it was private. They could not abide any interruptions from the outside world. Vita would generally come when Leonard was away on business. The servants were warned not to disturb them, upon pain of death, unless the house was on fire, someone was missing a limb, or some other dire emergency existed.

Virginia had been so excited this morning at the prospect of Vita coming for the weekend, four times she had to stop and restart the article she was writing. The spoiled stationery littered the wastebasket. At one point, she put down her pen, blew carefully on what she had written so as not to cause the ink to smudge. She put her work away for a while. She could not give it the concentration it needed. She would do some household tasks for a few minutes to work off her nervous energy, then she would sit down again and try to work. She felt quite like Clarissa, who, when she found out that Sally, the only person she has ever really been in love with, had arrived, exclaimed, "She is beneath this roof, she is beneath this roof!"

Vita was due to arrive at noon. Virginia gave up writing by eleven thirty. Everyone had impossible days. This was one of hers.

When the doorbell rang, Virginia squealed with delight; Nellie groaned with dread. Lottie was not there, having gone out to do the grocery shopping and delay running into the Sackville-West woman for as long as possible. Bad enough she would have to endure the vile creature for the entire weekend. The woman was unreasonably demanding, especially for a guest, and those damned cheap cigars she smoked were insufferable. For days after she was gone, the house reeked of them. Why it was that people with money adamantly refused to part with it, even for their own pleasure, always perplexed Nellie. It would have perplexed Lottie as well, if she ever stopped to think about it. She did not.

Virginia greeted Vita at the door with arms extended, like a child waiting for a mother's long-overdue return home. They embraced for what seemed like an eternity.

"Oh, Virginia, darling, how well you are looking," Vita cooed into Virginia's ear as her arms fastened tightly around Virginia's midsection.

Virginia pulled back slightly so she could look her guest squarely in the face.

"You're a fucking liar!" She let her words sit there for a moment. "And I love you for you." She kissed Vita on both cheeks perfunctorily and then again, full on, on the lips. The two women broke out of their embrace and walked almost skipped, to the living room, their right hands joined, Vita leading the way. Once they sat on the sofa, Virginia bellowed for Nellie.

"Yes, ma'am, what can I do for you?" Nellie asked with a slight smile.

"Oh, yes, Nellie," Virginia responded as though she had already forgotten that she had summoned the cook. "I'm sorry to trouble you, but Lottie has gone out. A sudden compulsion for grocery shopping, it would seem," she added, a noticeably sarcastic twinge to her voice. "Mrs. Sackville-West and I would like tea, please, and some of your freshly baked scones."

"Ah! Nellie, your scones truly are to die for," Vita commented. She did not look at the cook when she spoke. For her part, Nellie would have been happy to oblige the guest, with the dying part anyway, for she would gladly poison her for sixpence.

Instead, she forced a smile. "Yes, ma'am, right away."

The requested items were served fifteen minutes later. About a half hour after that, Virginia rang the bell she kept in the living room, since the bell was only used when there was company. Lottie appeared and cleared away the plates (having already returned from the market). Not three minutes later, Nellie and Lottie heard the sliding door in the living room, which was almost never used, close with a thud. It remained closed until dinner time. Every time the servants thought about the likely goings-on behind the closed door, Nellie stifled a giggle. Lottie tried to keep from vomiting.

*****

The writers spent the weekend together in happy solitude. During the day, they wrote facing each other in the study. The study at Hyde Park Gate bore a remarkable resemblance both in decor and furniture arrangement as the one in Richmond. Vita sat at Leonard's desk. She never understood why Virginia and Leonard shared a study in the first place. In her own home, she and Harold had separate studies that were sacrosanct. Neither was welcome in the other's study; it was Indian burial ground. She brought with her something special from her own study: a small photograph of Virginia in a silver frame. Nellie and Lottie floated in and out of the room wherever they were, a solicitous presence. Virginia put down her pen and called out Vita's name.

"Vita, darling, I have a marvelous surprise for you."

Vita winked at her hostess slyly; Virginia blushed.

"No, silly, not that. That wouldn't be a surprise now, would it?" In the background, Nellie was bringing in some iced tea. She nearly dropped the pitcher at the suggestion. Virginia continued.

"I have a real surprise for you. It's a new book. I have the most marvelous idea for a new novel, and it will based on us—about our relationship."

Vita was taken aback. "About us! You would write an entire novel about us—about me? How dreadfully boring!" The look on Virginia's face caused Vita to rethink her word choice. "What I mean, darling, is why would you want to write a novel about a relationship like ours? And, more importantly, who in the name of heaven would read it? I could see writing about yourself—you are such a delightfully charming little goat after all,"

Virginia delighted in hearing her childhood family nickname, confided to Vita in a moment of intimacy, and repeated by her.

"But me? There is nothing illustrious or even slightly alluring about me. And I'm not even well liked—many would see me stoned in Trafalgar Square, if the English were so barbaric as to still do such things. Better you should write about Katherine. At least Katherine is out of the public eye, reclusive actually. She would make more interesting material, dried-up old prune though she may be," Vita added with scorn.

It was no secret that Vita detested Katherine Mansfield and thought her writing to be amateurish at best. It was an area of constant disharmony between her and Virginia, especially since the Hogarth Press was Katherine's publisher. But that was beside the point right now. Now they were discussing the potential for a new novel, one based on themselves.

"Actually, I am very serious about the book, Vita dear. Katherine is quite all right, despite what you may think, and perhaps someone *should* base a novel around her, but *I* want to do a novel around *you* and around *us*. I want to tell you about it."

Vita was intrigued in spite of herself. She pushed her chair in as far as it could go and leaned her face across the desk, wanting to be as close to Virginia as possible. "So tell me about it."

Virginia beamed. "Well, I'm not exactly sure. I do know that the book revolves around two women, one older and one younger. The younger is the heroine of the book, but the older is critical to the story. It is as if the two are joined somehow."

A thought struck Vita. What was it Catherine says at the end of *Wuthering Heights*? "Whatever souls are made of ..."

"His and mine are the same," Virginia finished the quote. "Incidentally, you know it was the same with the Wordsworths, William and Dorothy I mean, not Mary Hutchinson."

Vita nodded in agreement. "I understood. Really, dear, you are speaking neither to an ignoramus nor an illiterate. I quite know the story of Dorothy and William Wordsworth."

Virginia was a bit put off by the tone of her guest. "Well, this must be one of the privileges of being a bit *older*, my dear, since I'd never heard anything about her until this past week, when I picked up a library book about her." She winked; Vita huffed.

Virginia continued, "Yes, well, this is exactly as it will be with these women. Exactly as it is," she corrected herself, "for they already live in my mind and speak in my dreams. The younger woman, Lily, is an artist, a watercolorist I think. She becomes quite taken with an older woman, married I think, probably to a brute of a husband. The woman has children, and they all struggle against the weight of this imposing male figure. Lily loves this woman, married to a man named Ramsey, I think. Mrs. Ramsey and Lily love each other intensely. The younger woman wants to possess the older woman, almost to become her. But then in the shadows, there is this other figure that I keep seeing, a young slim man with ale skin and long, slender fingers. His fingernails are slightly too long to be masculine, yet he is not overtly feminine either. I can't figure out how he figures into the plot. It intrigues me because there he is, and he will not go away."

Vita sat spellbound to her chair. She reflected for a brief time before offering a suggestion.

"Perhaps he is not in the story at all, simply a character from another book waiting for you to notice him so that he can make his way into the world."

"Yes, yes, I thought that briefly myself but was afraid. I can hardly memorialize him for a later date in my journal, I don't even know his name." Virginia took a deep sigh of surrender. "Oh, Vita, darling, there are so many books I want to write, books I feel I *need* to write, that sometimes I believe my head will just burst open, characters, plots, and half-written sentences spilling out like a river that extends from Richmond to the far east end of London. Does that ever happen to you? Have you ever experienced such a phenomenon?"

Vita nodded sympathetically. "Of course, I have. Every fiction writer has felt such a thing. You will write them, *ma cherie*, it will just take some time. Try to pace yourself, one book at a time. Do what I do. If you feel that you must work on a book that you are not ready to write, write an outline, maybe even a chapter, then move away from it, back to the book you are already invested in."

"Yes, that is what I do, as you well know. I learned from you, after all."

There were tremendous parallels between Virginia and Vita and the characters in Virginia's new book. Vita was quite a bit older than Virginia; how much older, they did not discuss. She was married—though one could hardly characterize Harold as a brute by any means.

Virginia remembered exactly as it had been when they first met. Virginia had written to her after reading one of her books. She had been so enthralled by the writing that she had wanted to correspond with the authoress. It was right after *The Voyage Out* had been released. In her initial letter, Virginia had mentioned that she too was a novelist and offered to send a copy of her first book to Vita, with her compliments. She would have included it right away, but did not want to be presumptuous or to intrude on the woman's time.

To her surprise, Vita answered her letter a week later. She thanked Virginia for her kind sentiments and assured her, yes, she would love to read her book. It had been on her list of books to purchase. (Virginia wasn't sure if she believed that last part. The book was only recently out, and Virginia was an unknown among novelists. Why would this accomplished novelist have even heard of, much less been dying to buy, Virginia's book?) Nonetheless, she was flattered. She signed one of her few author's copies and brought it herself to the post the same day she received the letter. Agatha, the day maid at that time, had marveled at the fuss made over a total stranger and the haste with which the missus went to the post.

Three weeks later, Vita sent a letter back, in her unmistakable penmanship and trademark black ink (the woman was such a fanatic, it was rumored she had once fired a maid for bringing home a blue pen from the store). The letter thanked Virginia for sending the book, wished her much success with its sales, and wrote effusive praise and some mild criticism of it. The letter was three pages long, single spaced. Virginia had been extremely touched that this well-known woman would have taken the time to write so extensively. Even the criticisms, she did not mind terribly. Virginia had written back right away, thanking the author for her comments and asking if she would like to meet at the British Museum to see a brand-new exhibit and have lunch. Vita agreed at once. The women met face-to-face, toured the museum, and lunched on mutton pie and cold ale. A lifelong friendship was born that day.

The sound of Vita laughing brought Virginia back to the present with a jolt. Virginia gave her an inquisitive look.

"I was just thinking, Virginia, how queer our conversations must sound to ordinary people. By ordinary people, I mean non-writers, people who make a living dwelling in reality, not fantasy. We talk about our characters and their desires as though they are flesh and blood people who live down the street. We worry about them more than most mothers worry about their children. It must sound ludicrous to ordinary people."

Virginia tilted her head to the left, mesmerized by Vita's words, and by her presence in general.

The chair made a loud noise as it scraped the floor. Vita turned her body around and faced Nellie, who was hovering in the background, covering for Lottie who claimed cramps, again.

"What do you think of the matter, Nellie? Surely you qualify to comment on what an ordinary person thinks." Vita offered her most condescending smile, thinking Nellie could not discern it. Vita was mistaken.

Nellie, having no interest whatsoever in what this particular guest had to say, pretended to have been daydreaming. "I'm sorry, ma'am, what were you saying?"

"I was asking what you thought about our topic of conversation. You must have an opinion."

"Ma'am, I wasn't listening as it ain't my place to eavesdrop on my employer's conversation."

Vita huffed, having dealt for too long with too many servants to take the cook at her word. "Very well then, I shall apprise you. We were saying that ordinary people must find novelists very bizarre considering that novelists talk and obsess about their characters' lives more so than the way mothers worry about children. What do you think on the matter? Do writers spend too much time worrying about characters?"

Nellie's eyes darted from one woman to the other, unsure if her opinion was actually being sought or if a trap was being set. She answered cautiously.

"Well, of course, I can't speak for all writers, not knowing them. And though a great few come through this house, most of them don't really converse with me. But I do know the missus, and from her I'd say, no, she doesn't spend too much time with characters. That's how she makes them real to her readers. She studies people, real people, and incorporates them into her characters."

Virginia beamed. "That was a fine answer, Nellie, and truly I am glad that you see it that way. Funny how you don't see yourself as the least bit strange until someone else points out that others may see you so." She glared at Vita then gave her a playful grin.

"Fortunately, my closest common reader gets it. I am not so strange after all."

"Or you are, and she is just used to it already, poor thing," Vita quipped, not to be trumped. All three women laughed, but Nellie stopped suddenly, having the unsettling feeling that *she* was the object of their derision.

"Well, if you'll excuse me, I'd best be seeing to dinner." She made two quick curtsies. "Ma'am, ma'am." And she hurried out of the room, closing the door, a bit too forcefully, behind her.

In the kitchen, Nellie reflected on the conversation and took her agitation out on the chicken cutlets she pounded to flatten for frying. She hated it when other people laughed at her. More than hated it, it made her want to kill. As a child, Nellie always read poorly and was slow with her numbers. The other kids laughed at her all the time. It lasted for eight years. She used to go home crying every day. At her best, she tried to ignore them while she was in school. She didn't want to give them the satisfaction of knowing how much it bothered her. At her worst, she would go over to her tormentors and clobber them until someone pulled her off them or got the best of her, whichever came first.

As Nellie worked now in the kitchen, she thought about Vita Sackville-West. If they were schoolgirls, Nellie would have attacked her and would probably be rolling around on the floor with her at this very moment knocking her lights out. Damned that cunt! She slammed the chicken cutlets with her mallet. Vita always seemed to take over the house whenever she visited. Even Lottie went into hiding when she came for a visit.

"I can't wait for that pompous bitch to leave," Nellie said aloud despite there being no one to hear her.

Interlude

I checked out of the hotel after three weeks. I was a simple woman, and although I liked room service and nice restaurants just fine, it got to the point where enough was enough. Besides, I got no family, and my friends pretty much died off or went to live with kin in other parts of the country. I'm the only one left alive and still in London, except for Adelaide. I wanted to check on my flat. Not that I have all that much, but I liked to keep what I had safe and sound. Adelaide offered to go into my place every couple of days to water my plants (I have a few on the windowsill in the kitchen and a couple in the living room on a rack). But I didn't want to impose on her more than that. Besides, I missed the taste of my own food and the well-worn feeling of my own bed. It was time to go home.

But, I'm not ungrateful, and anyway, Thomas was persistent. Over breakfast on the day I checked out, I invited him to come to my place for tea in three days. (I wanted some time to get settled first. I figured I'd need time to sort through the post.) He accepted graciously and walked me back to my room after we finished eating, and he paid the check for the last time. The chambermaid was passing my door as I fumbled for my key. She wished me a good trip home and asked if I wanted her to ring for the bellboy to help me with my luggage. I had to admit, I liked having people fuss over me, having done it for others my whole life, but I said "no, thank you" anyway. I didn't have much, I always traveled light, and I had nobody to get souvenirs for, except Adelaide, and I figured she'd rather have cash. I'd throw her a little something as soon as I got home. She would insist on not taking it, but I'd make her. Meanwhile, all this talk about other people's lives, other people's houses, made me have the irresistible urge to go home, reclaim my flat, because it is *my* flat. There really is no place like home.

Walking through my front door, the shabbiness of my lodgings came up and hit me in the face, as if I had never noticed them before. There's a saying I heard somewhere that poor people don't know they're poor until they see how rich people live. Standing in my flat at that moment, I understood why that statement was true. Never in the entire time I'd lived there did the place look so unappealing. I noticed every flaw. The windows were sealed like a crypt, causing a musty smell in the air. Water was on the floor underneath my icebox. My plants thrived, never looking better. Adelaide had done a splendid job with them, even if the rest of the place did look like it was being severely neglected. But then, I hadn't asked her to do anything besides water the plants, had I? I opened all the windows and got on my knees to clean up the spilled water. While I was already down there, I looked under the oven to wipe away any cobwebs that may have been forming while I was away. Yes, no doubt about it, I was home.

Thomas came three days later, as scheduled. He showed up at two, the time we would usually have tea. I lived a short walk from the Tube station at Charing Cross, so Thomas said he would probably visit the library for a while before he came to me. Everyone said the British Library was the most wonderful library still around anywhere in the world. Of course, never having left England, I wouldn't know that myself, but I tended to believe it since everyone said it (at least everyone I'd ever heard from). It sounded pretty reasonable though, since England had always been at the center of Europe, and London was at the center of England. Why shouldn't our library reign supreme? I heard that they had some great libraries in New York too, but I'd never been to America. Mrs. W always said that New York was very similar to London, but dirtier. (She went there several times to promote her books and to negotiate deals with her American publisher.) I never had the desire to go there, even if I'd had the money to go, which I never did. Why would I want to see the imitation when I lived in the original?

Anyhow, the day Thomas came, I was up early in the morning baking raspberry scones. While they were in the oven, I went out to the store to get fresh apricot jam. Thomas always had scones with jam when we would have tea in the hotel. He had been so nice to me, I wanted to make them for him special. My timing was perfect. Just as the tea kettle began whistling Dixie, my doorbell rang. I traipsed down the stairs to let him in myself, so that I could guide him up the stairs. A couple of the steps were shaky, and if he wasn't careful … well, I didn't want him to break his neck on my watch, that's for sure.

I opened the door, and he kissed me perfunctorily on my left cheek. "How nice to see you again, Thomas. I hope you don't mind the atmosphere. It's a bit different from the places we have met before."

"I'm delighted to see you again and happy you could accommodate me. Meeting here is just fine." There was a certain amount of condescending in his voice, but I was pretty sure he didn't mean it, so I took no offense.

"Great. Tea is all ready. Let's go up." Thomas smiled at me. Once again, it seemed like he was looking down on me, but once again, I ignored it.

"After you." He made a gesture with his right arm, and I led him up the stairs.

"Hold on tight to the banister now. Watch the third step, it shakes. And the sixth step is rotted on the left side, step to the right." I heard him grunt behind me, whether from strain or horror, I could not be sure of. But I was fairly certain he wasn't used to counting as he walked up stairs or sidestepping cracks. Oh well, now he could see firsthand—what was it the Americans say?—"how the other half lived."

When we got to the top of the stairs, Thomas was just slightly out of breath. A fine young man like himself, for shame! He should be at the top of his game and climbing those steps as easily as Hercules cleared the stables. When we stepped into the flat, I stopped him before he started, not wanting to be talked down to for a third time in the same day.

"Well, here we are. You needn't bother to say it's a nice place I have here. I know bloody well it isn't. What it *is* is cheap, and on my budget. Cheap beats out nice any day of the week and twice on Sunday." Thomas guffawed. The previous tension was broken. I told him to have a seat, pointing to a kitchen chair, and got busy serving the tea. Only after I joined him at the table, ready to sip my own tea, did I notice he was still wearing his jacket.

"Here, let me take that from you, like I shoulda done before," I said as I went over to his chair and waited with an extended hand as he removed his coat. It was kind of stuffy in the flat, so I opened the window over the sink while his jacket was neatly tucked under my left arm. I deposited the jacket in the bedroom, came back to the table, and sat down with a bit of a plop. Thomas began the conversation.

"Vita Sackville-West, what a character she seems to have been. Was she really as outrageous as she seems from the books about her and from her own writing?"

"Oh yes, she is something. You know, she probably should have been born a man. Lottie and I always said so. The woman doesn't act like anyone I've ever met. She is more masculine than her husband could ever be, and she wears ridiculous clothes. I've even seen her wear trousers on more than a few occasions! The woman's shame knows no bounds. Of course, she may have mellowed out with age. I haven't seen her in years except for one brief sighting at the British Museum. And even then, it was only for a minute and from across the room. I turned round so she wouldn't see me and want to start up a conversation, not that she was ever likely to start a real talk with the likes of me, but just in case."

Thomas must have noticed that I was rambling, not at all like me, actually. He made an effort to steer the course. "What was her relationship to Virginia? How would you describe them?"

He was hinting again. I was getting so tired of it. I much preferred it when a body just said what he meant, point-blank. I said as much.

"You mean were they lovers?" He blushed. "Yes, they were for a while, a rather short while, actually, though they were quite close for a very long time." Thomas must have been brazened from my comment.

"Some say the relationship was mother-daughterish, that Vita was the substitute for her long-lost mother, Julia."

"Fey!" I made a sour face. History always gets things fucked up. They were no more mother and daughter than Lottie and I were sisters. It's only that Vita was older and more established, snobbish bitch that she is, still to this day. Though I must say, she cried a whole bunch of tears at the missus's funeral, and they weren't crocodile tears either. Nothing I hate more than crocodile tears—or fake piety. Be who you are, that's what I say. Lottie, she was the same way. The woman never put on airs."

I could imagine what Thomas was thinking, that how could a maid put on airs even if she wanted to, but he had the tact and all-around good sense not to speak badly of Lottie in her own house, cause she was as much in this house now as while she was on earth.

"Vita, she was married to Harold Nicolson. Did you ever get the impression that he resented the relationship between the women?"

"No, I don't think he cared much." I chuckled. "You know, come to think of it, in all the time the women spent together and all the time Vita was at the house, I think I saw Harold only a handful of times, less than five probably. But then, those two had even less of a conventional marriage than Mr. and Mrs. Woolf did."

"You mean because they both had same-sex affairs," Thomas suggested.

"Yeah, but not just about that. They seemed disinterested in each other, even when they had parties at Sissinghurst Castle. Mrs. W always said they were rarely in the same room at the parties, and they almost never touched, not even to hold hands, like almost every married couple does."

"And yet their son and biographer, Harold, insists that they valued each other among all else, even over Virginia," Thomas commented.

"Well, I suppose I don't really know about that. He was there, so he'd probably know better. Then again, he *is* their son. Maybe he saw only what he wanted to see, as opposed to what was really there. I was a servant. I saw everything, as only servants do. Almost nobody puts on airs in front of the servants. It is only in front of people like themselves that folks tend to try to act like something they are not. No one cares what the likes of me thinks. That's how it always was and always will be." I rethought my words after a few seconds and spoke again to clarify.

"No, that's not totally true. Mrs. W—she cared about what Lottie and I thought and felt. We actually mattered to her. And she spoke to us, me especially, frequently and was interested in what we had to say."

It seemed like Thomas was at my flat forever. By the time he left, the tea kettle had been nearly drained for the third time that afternoon, and the plate the scones had been sitting on now held nothing but crumbs. By the time he stood up and asked for his hat and coat, I wanted to throw him out the door. Not that I disliked him, you understand, I liked him a whole lot, but this was *my* flat and enough was enough. I never had developed a high tolerance for company.

Chapter Fifteen

The day started off normally. Nellie was up earlier than usual, trying out a new recipe she had found for hollandaise sauce. Virginia had recently remarked a few times about how much she enjoyed having eggs benedict in a hotel when she traveled. She liked to have room service; it was the one extravagance she allowed herself when she traveled. As a complimentary treat, room service would usually send up a miniature-sized bottle of vodka and a glass of tomato juice. She would add some hot sauce that she carried in little packets in her purse and make her own bloody Mary. The hotels liked to call it an "eye opener"; Virginia suspected it was designed to chase away the previous night's hangover. Fortunately, a hangover was one malady with which she was never once affected.

So, as usual, Nellie tried to please her mistress, scouring cookbooks for hollandaise sauce recipes until she found one she thought she would do well to try. It simmered in the sauce pan for what seemed liked hours, the eggs sizzling in the pan. The English muffins were in the toaster, and the ham was frying. Coffee was brewing in the pot on the stove. The kitchen was awash in the sweet smells of breakfast.

Breakfast went over well. Virginia actually ate. She didn't just pick at her food. Leonard had his coffee and a bit of eggs but was more interested in his newspaper than the food laid in front of him. He read one article with particular interest, scarcely even paying attention to the thickly buttered toast, always Leonard's favorite part of breakfast. Just like a man, Nellie thought to herself, to have the gall to have toast *and* English muffins. No woman would do such a thing in a million years. But then, men did not have to watch their figures the way women did, damn them to hell. And yet Leonard somehow managed to keep himself in shape, with a taut body that belied his age and sedentary occupation.

It was the conversation afterward that threw everything into a fury. Nellie went into the parlor where Virginia was resting for a few minutes, her notebook and pen in her study. Virginia was sitting in an arm hair, her eyes closed tightly. To the casual observer, she appeared to be asleep. Nellie knew that the eyes closed that tightly meant that her employer was doing a different type of writing. She was writing in her mind; scenes would play through her mind, scenes that she would later sit at her desk and try to recreate on the page. That was why she was so intense and why her dreams were so vivid. They were chapters in her books yet to be written.

Nellie had walked into the room, not bothering to knock, and cleared her throat. Virginia opened her eyes, for the briefest moment stunned. Seeing the confusion on her face, Nellie explained.

"Sorry, ma'am, I was just wondering as to whether you'd like fresh or canned apple sauce on your pork chops tonight? Oh, and what type of dressing you'd like me to get for the salad, seeing as I'm off to the market in a few minutes."

"Pork chops?" Mrs. W repeated the words as if she had never heard them before. "Who said we were having pork chops for dinner?"

"Mr. Woolf, ma'am, this morning, after you got to your writing. I was finishing up some chores in the kitchen when he came in and told me to fix up some pork chops for this evening's dinner. For once, I don't think anyone is coming." She chuckled.

The rage seethed inside Virginia like a small newly set fire waiting to burst into flames. She spoke in an even keel, keeping her voice flat, expressionless.

"Am I not to be consulted then about dinner in my own home? Have the doctors declared my mind too feeble for such decision-making?"

Nellie, who knew the tone of voice quite well, was dumbstruck by its present use. "No, ma'am, nothing like that I'm sure. It's just that Mr. Woolf instructed me, that's all. Seeing as how one of you told me something, I didn't see no need to check with the other. Besides, you know how you hate to be bothered when you're writing."

"*Working*," Virginia responded with slightly more emphasis than she intended. "Writing makes it sound like I am an amateur, a dilettante with nothing else to do. Writing is how I earn money, it is my work, just as yours is the kitchen and Lottie's is the dustpan. Therefore, I was *working*. Please do not make me remind you again."

Nellie was getting annoyed. "Yes, ma'am, you're *working*," she corrected herself, her emphasis slightly sarcastic. "I saw no need to interrupt your work for something so trivial."

"Trivial! Trivial is it." Her voice was getting louder. "Excuse me, Ms. Nellie Boxall, for thinking that the food I am forced to consume is something that matters. I had no idea that what goes into my body is trivial. I must have been mistaken."

So she wanted a fight, Nellie mused silently. *Bloody hell, then, I'll give her one if that's what she wants. But I have to let it fall all on her, so I don't get the sack.*

"I don't see what the fuss is about, ma'am, truly I don't. Mr. Woolf asked me to make something for dinner, and I'm fixing on making it. End of story."

Virginia leaped from her chair. "It is *not* the end of the story because you and Leonard conspired together. Otherwise, why wouldn't he have made the request at the breakfast table, in my hearing? That would have been the normal, decent thing to do. But no! That would have been too easy, wouldn't it? Far better to stand in corners and start whispering the second my fucking back was turned."

Nellie snapped. Her fury poured out of her as a diatribe. "That's right, we were talking about you behind your back. Neither one of us has anything else to do but to talk about you. And why should we have anything else to do when after all, the sun rises and sets with your arse. Everyone in the world kowtows to Virginia Woolf, everything is about her! It couldn't be simply that *Mr.* Woolf wanted something for dinner, and I was simply obliging his request. Noooo! It could never be that because that wouldn't fit your fantasies, you narcissistic, self-righteous bitch!"

Virginia slapped her cook, hard. She could have sworn the sound echoed; the pain stung her fingers. "How dare you talk to me like that! How dare you accuse me of being such a vile thing?"

"And why the fuck not. You stand there and accuse me of conspiring with Mr. Woolf for what reason only God in heaven knows. You know damn well I'd never do anything behind your back. But then again, maybe that's just it. Maybe you'd go behind my back in a minute, and that's why you think I'm capable of such a thing, because you would do it yourself."

The author twisted her nose. "I do not have to dignify that ridiculous statement with a response. Go away."

Nellie's anger emboldened her. "Oh, I'll go away all right, I'll go anywhere you want, to Hades even, but you'll come with me, I guarantee you that, so help me, God."

Virginia pounded her fists on the small table to the right of her chair. The table shook violently to the point of almost tipping over. Virginia began to scream.

"Out, out! Get out you mindless, lazy, good-for-nothing trollop. I want you OUT!"

The dishes in the china cabinet quivered. Lottie came running from upstairs, hearing the commotion over the din of the vacuum, which she was running across Leonard's bedroom rug. Even Leonard peeked his head in for a minute as he went into the kitchen from the press, housed outside, to get more coffee. He thought about saying something but didn't.

"Mrs. Woolf, Nellie, calm down. What's the matter?"

Virginia went ballistic. "Don't you tell me to calm down, not in my own house. This is *my* house that *I* pay for, I'll not be told what to do by some half-witted maid!" She instantly regretted her words. Her tone softened, her eyes started to swell.

"Oh, dear, Lottie, I *am* so sorry," she said as if trying to convince the latter of her sincerity. "I am just so terribly angry, I didn't mean to take it out at you."

"Quite all right, ma'am, I understand," Lottie responded.

You're nothing but a snobbish bitch with too much time on her hands. That's *what I understand*, the maid wanted to say.

The three women stood there for a moment, half-trying to collect themselves and half-waiting for the awkward moment to pass. Nellie spoke quickly. "Mrs. Woolf, luv, I really was only trying to—"

Virginia cut her off. She looked directly into her cook's eyes and spoke flatly. "I don't believe I shall have anything else to say to you for the rest of the day." She collected her notebook and walked out of the room and up the stairs into her bedroom. They heard the door close with a thud.

"Don't feel bad, Nellie, my love, you know how she gets with those moods of hers. She can't help herself," Lottie said, putting her arm affectionately around Nellie's shoulder. As she talked, they sat on the love seat together.

"I know what you're saying, and you're right, of course, and I love you for saying it, but it's just that—" Nellie stopped herself midsentence. "I need some air." She shot up from the love seat and marched into the kitchen and out the kitchen door, used mostly for deliveries. The screen door whacked behind her. Lottie remained seated and sulked.

*****

Things were tense for several days. Nellie stayed in the kitchen whenever possible. Rather than serve the meals herself, as was her wont, she let Lottie serve them. If Nellie had to venture into other areas of the house, she did so with singular purpose, making no unnecessary small talk. In fact, she conversed with the missus only when unavoidable. The house was so quiet, the sound was deafening.

Virginia tried not to let it show, but she was stewing. The fact that a servant in her own house would treat her with such contempt ... it was unthinkable. Damn the cook—she was planning to leave. Virginia was certain of it. From that moment, Virginia began making plans for the cook's replacement.

For the millionth time, Virginia cursed the system of privilege that she had been born into. Having been raised with money, surrounded by servants, Virginia thought that her "privilege" was oppressive. A charwoman, Virginia reasoned, had more freedom than she. For the charwoman was free to seek employment anywhere she chose; she could negotiate both the salary and terms of her employment. She survived on the sweat of her own brow. This was unlike Virginia, who could not use the tea kettle or find the mop. Virginia was dependent on the service of others. But there it was.

Nellie smelled a rat. It was time to take action, time to have a plan. She spoke to Lottie about it.

"Lottie, luv, I think I'm about to be canned. I've gone too far this time. She will never let me stay."

"Not to worry, Nellie, she will never let you go, not even if the mister said so, and he has no reason to unless you piss him off. And he's not around enough to be pissed about anything."

Nellie nodded in agreement. "I guess it's true, but I still am worried. I really did go too far this time. I really showed her how I felt—it wasn't pretty."

"Aw, don't worry too much, honey, it will be just fine. Mrs. Woolf is bound to know you didn't mean it, you only spoke out of anger." Lottie was secretly thrilled at Nellie's predicament; not that she might lose her job but that it was *she* who had told the bitch off, she who had finally said what needed to be said and had stopped kowtowing to an overgrown, spoiled-brat nutcase! The mister was much easier to deal with, though the men usually were since they were home much less often. And Mr. Woolf was wonderful, only getting involved if it concerned the pound (he was stingy with his pounds, she'd say that for him) or his food or anything else that he considered important.

But Nellie was not consoled by her housemate's words. Something inside her gnawed at her stomach.

Nellie sought reconciliation. Lottie thought she was simply trying to keep her position, but Nellie was genuinely remorseful. She hated fighting with the missus. Besides, when she thought about it, Nellie figured she should have been used to her temper by this point. Nellie was resolved. She was ready to apologize. She would do so at tea. If someone were there, like that awful Mansfield woman, she would ask to speak to the missus privately for a moment. A guest would no doubt attribute the request to some matter of household accounts. Then, once out of the earshot of others, Nellie would make her apology. But words were cheap. She would show her remorse. The idea came to her immediately. She would get some flowers, geraniums, Virginia's favorite. She could get them easily, straight from the flower shop in town.

Nellie prepared tea early and asked Lottie if she would mind covering for her by serving the tea at the appointed time so she could go out. Of course, Lottie didn't mind, and Nellie went about her business. She bought flowers at the shop along with a small box of assorted chocolates that was on a shelf on the left side of the till. Walking home, Nellie had an extra spring in her step, confident in the effect her gift would bring.

"There would be the standard three meals a day, plus tea, of course. We are not late night eaters, so you would never have to deal with 2 AM wanderings into the kitchen. However, I must tell you that we entertain a lot. I hope that will not be a problem for you."

"No, not at all, Mrs. Woolf. I'm used to cooking for large groups. One question though, ma'am. What is the salar—?"

The sound of the chocolates clattering against the linoleum made the women jump and turn their heads. The stranger, a stout woman with hair that was mostly gray, a polka-dot dress, and thick-rimmed glasses, arched her eyebrows. Virginia's mouth fell open, and Nellie remained in stunned inertia for what seemed like hours. Then, with as much force as she could muster, she threw the bouquet on the floor and jumped in the air, landing on the petals and twisted her body from right to left. Nellie stormed out of the house, tears first beginning to trickle down her cheeks.

"Nellie, come back," Virginia called after the cook, jumping up from her seat and hastily excusing herself from the woman she was interviewing. She ran out the side door after Nellie, the screen door banging behind her. The woman being interviewed remained where she was; she took her knitting out of her bag and began work on a scarf for her gentleman friend.

"Nellie, wait, hold on!" Virginia yelled after the cook, her breath coming in short gasps. "It isn't what it looks like."

Nellie huffed. "How can it not be what it looks like? You're interviewing a cook. There is only one cook needed in this house. That can only mean one thing. You are giving me the sack!"

"No, no, it's not—"

"The worst part is, I don't really blame you for that, given how I've been acting and all. That's why I bought the flowers and chocolate, to apologize to you and hope we could go back to the way we were. I just wish you could have told me to my face rather than going behind my back like this and—"

"For the love of Christ, Nellie would you please SHUT UP and LISTEN?" It could not be said who the abrupt words shocked more, the listener or the speaker. She had Nellie's attention.

"I am not giving you the sack. I was only interviewing that woman because I thought *you* were leaving. As you bloody well know, I am helpless in the kitchen. I cannot be without a cook. I was only interviewing her in case I needed her. She could never replace you, Nellie. And if I were going to give you the sack, you should know me well enough to know I'd tell you upfront. I'd never let you find out this way."

Nellie's face was soaked in tears. Virginia reached for her, kissed her perfunctorily on both cheeks, and pulled her into a tight embrace, Nellie's ample bosom crushing against Virginia's smaller, less pronounced framing.

They stayed like that for seconds that seemed like minutes. Finally, Virginia regained her composure.

"Well, Ms. Boxall, I do believe you have a dinner to prepare." Nellie gave a weak smile and did a mock curtsy to her employer. "And I've got an interviewee to get rid of," Virginia added with a wide grin.

As Lottie told it later, Mrs. Woolf had marched back to the woman she had kept waiting and explained to her that there had been a misunderstanding, the cook was not leaving so there was no need … If anything should change, they had … blah, blah, blah. For her part, Nellie couldn't care less. All that mattered was that she wasn't going anywhere. She was safe. She breathed a sigh of relief that came from the depths of her soul. It was the closest she'd ever come to losing everything she loved.

Interlude

    I was to go to the hotel again a week later. Thomas said it was the least he could do after the hours he spent exhausting my supply of tea and sandwiches. Truth be told, I suspected that the real reason was he was tired of climbing all those steps to reach my flat. I was tired of the same thing, but then I had quite a few years on him.

    Check-in this time was worlds away from the experience I had the last time. Don't misunderstand me, everyone treated me just fine the last time, I didn't mean to say they didn't, but then I was so nervous! This time I felt like I belonged. The clerk who waited on me even remembered me; I didn't have to show my identification. Imagine that! After fall the years of practiced invisibility, someone actually took notice of Nellie Boxall. That was when I realized I had arrived.

    I got the same room again. I thought it was a coincidence, but Thomas told me that he had especially requested it. "You are used to it, and you really liked it, so why change it?" I wondered how much pull he had in this place that he could actually request a special room for someone, but that question would have to wait for another time. This time, I didn't expect him to wait in the lobby while I got settled seeing as we already knew each other. But I was wrong. Just as I was about to walk up to my room, expecting to be escorted, Thomas pulled a newspaper out of his briefcase.

    "I'll be over there," he pointed to an armchair in the corner of the lobby. "Come down when you're ready."

    "I don't suspect you'll have to wait long," I offered. "There isn't all that much I have to unpack, and anyway, at this age, you make sure you're always ready for anything.

    The room looked perfect, as if no one had stayed there in my absence. But of course, someone *had* been there, probably multiple guests. As I put my under things into the dresser drawer, I found myself wondering who had been there when I wasn't. Who used those drawers, slept in that bed, made love in that bed, while I was back in my flat? Because if there's one thing my years of service taught me, it was that you can learn a whole lot about people from looking at their things, how they keep them, and how they live in general.

After a half hour, I was almost ready to go downstairs. I used the loo, tidied up myself in the mirror, and patted my dress down. I closed my door gently and walked over to the lift. A well-dressed woman holding a purse that looked like it cost more than my entire outfit had her left arm being held by an equally dapper man wearing a tuxedo. I checked my watch; it was barely one in the afternoon. Where could they possibly be going that would require him to wear a tuxedo early in the afternoon? I shrugged. Lottie must have been right. Rich people really do live in a world of their own.

Thomas was staring intently at some item in the newspaper. I couldn't tell if it intrigued him or if he simply couldn't see it and was too ashamed to take out a magnifier glass.

"That was fast," he remarked when he saw me standing there. "Let's go have a drink at the bar. Maybe they serve something to snack on before tea." It took an effort for me not to grimace.

The entire time I had been here before, I avoided the bar area. It obviously had been designed by a man, with only men in mind. The room was constructed of old wood. Walking into it that day, escorted by a man, I noticed sprinkles of sawdust on the floor, like you might see in a butcher's shop. The odor of stale beer seemed imbedded in the wood.

Choosing a seat uncomfortably in the middle of the room, Thomas pulled out a bench for me, and I sat down, put my elbows on the edge of the table, and immediately cried out slightly. There was a splinter in my arm. I cursed under my breath and took it out. Thomas nodded sympathetically and murmured what I thought was a faint apology—whether it was for the bar or the splinter or both, I couldn't tell. When the waitress came, she took out orders. Even that was an issue. She didn't understand what I wanted when I asked for a mimosa. When I explained, I was promptly told, with an edge to her voice, that they didn't serve champagne there. I would have to order something else. Not even, would I like to order anything else? Just, I had to order something else. Indignantly, I ordered a white wine and an order of fish and chips. Thomas ordered a straight scotch and some nachos.

We made small talk about the weather, the latest programs on the radio, and such until our drinks arrived. The waitress must have been new, seeing as how she brought the drinks and the food together. We clinked glasses and got busy eating. After a few minutes of concentrated chewing, the talking resumed. This time, I steered the conversation.

"So, Thomas, we've talked about the lives of a lot of people, but one person seems to have been left out of the conversation."

"Leonard," Thomas offered. "I wanted to speak about him today. There is a lot more ground to cover where he is concerned."

"No, not Leonard," I replied with a sly grin, "I wanted to talk about someone else entirely."

"Who then?" he asked, looking confused.

"You!" He jerked his head back as if jolted by a current of electricity. Even still, he let me finish my thought. "I want to know all about you. Most specifically, I want to know why you want to write this book. What does it mean to you? 'Cause I'm enough of a judge of character and observer of people to know that this is not just some contract you're fulfilling for a publisher. This is personal for you, I'm sure of it. And I want to know why."

The look on his face just then must have been the same look the caveman had when he discovered fire.

"Me! Why on earth would you want to hear about me? This story, the whole book is about the personal lives of the members of the Woolf house. No one cares about the life of the biographer."

"Now, listen here, Thomas. We have been in each other's company for days and weeks at a time. I've told you more about myself and that chapter in my life than I've ever thought I would tell anyone. And yes, you have paid for that, and it's been appreciated, but I want to hear about you now. I want to know what it is that is behind this project. What's driving you, Thomas?"

I didn't know where I found my nerve or why he didn't tell me what to do with myself, but he didn't. Instead, he dropped his napkin into his lap, and his fork clattered against the dish. He held his head with both hands, completely covering his face. He remained in that position for several minutes. I began to fidget uncomfortably, afraid of what can of worms I had opened. After five minutes, he uncovered his face and folded his hands into his lap.

"I wasn't always a Virginia Woolf scholar. As a matter of fact, in college, I never read one Virginia Woolf novel or even cared to. My friends who had read her thought she was incomprehensible. As for me, I hardly ever read fiction anyway, so incomprehensible fiction was totally out. I had no interest whatsoever."

"So then what changed your mind, Thomas?"

"I got married," he answered swiftly, simply and plainly, as if that should be enough to explain the transformation in his reading habits. Further explanation came more slowly, painstakingly. "My wife and I met during my senior year of college. She had graduated a year before me and was in law school. She adored Virginia Woolf and had read every one of her novels, reviews, and essays. She would read the same novel over and over again, until she could recite paragraphs by memory. After we were married, in bed at night, she would read *To the Lighthouse, Jacob's Room,* and *Mrs. Dalloway.* Sometimes she would find a paragraph that particularly struck her, and she would read it to me out loud. Lisa, my wife, had these dark moods, depressions, really. I didn't make the connection at first, ever actually, until it was too late. She kept diaries which I never saw. Why would I, right? They were her diaries. Like Angela, from Woolf's last short story, Lisa left the diaries for me to find. Like Gilbert, Angela's husband, I had received my legacy. I had learned the truth. And like Gilbert, I learned the truth only after it was too late for it to be of any real use to me."

I was almost too stunned to speak. I could not imagine how I could or should respond to such a personal revelation. All of a sudden, it made me uncomfortable that he had told me, even though I had pressured him to. What was it Mr. Woolf used to say? "The truth is a terrible burden." I was starting to understand what he meant by that.

I knew I had to say something, or he'd think I was a toad. "You mean— She— Your wife—" I didn't feel comfortable saying her name, worried that might imply a familiarity inappropriate under the circumstances.

"She killed herself that afternoon. She threw herself in front of an oncoming train at the Charing Cross station. The police came to inform me. I'll never forget it. I was at my desk at work busy staring at some papers. I was so deep in concentration, I didn't even notice the two bobbies towering over my desk. One of them coughed, you know, that way people do when they want to get your attention but don't want to say anything. Well, that's what he did, and I looked up, embarrassed by my oblivion.

"'I'm sorry, officers', I said as I stood up from my chair and shook each of their hands to greet them, 'I didn't see you there. What can I do for you?'

"'Mr. Lore, we'd like you to come with us, please, sir. There's something we need to take care of right away.' I looked at them in disbelief. 'I'm kind of busy here, officers.' I pointed to the mount of papers I had been ruffling through a moment ago. 'Can it wait?'

"'No, sir, I'm afraid it cannot.' The other officer said. It was the first time he had spoken. I was becoming increasingly uncomfortable. 'I'm not under arrest, am I?' Both officers shook their heads in unison. 'No, no sir, it's nothing like that. It's just that we've got something to tell you and something that's got to be taken care of, and it'd be better done in private, that's all.'

"'Well, I'm sorry, but it will have to wait then, you see I have this deadline that—'

"One of the officers reluctantly interrupted him and delivered the news that would reshape my world forever.

"'I'm sorry to tell you like this, sir, but your wife was killed by a train. She appears to have jumped in front of it.' There was nothing in the world that could have prepared me for those words, Nellie, I'll tell you that. I remember crying for a minute at my desk. No one noticed. Then as I got up, I got strangely calm, numb actually. I was walking to the lift, and I said to my coworker, 'Lisa is dead, I have to go with these men to see her.' My coworker had been holding a cup of coffee—he dropped it, and it splashed all over his suit. I don't know what shocked him more, my words or my expressionless way of delivering them. I stayed like that, real calm like, until we got to the morgue. Once I saw her mangled body, I fell apart. I was devastated. For the rest of my life, I'll never forget what that looked like or what it felt like.

"Afterward, everything got worse. I didn't think it *could* get worse, but it did. It was time, that was the killer. All of a sudden, I had all this free time on my hands. I had no idea how to fill it. Free time is a mourner's enemy. I came home to an empty house. I had no one to help with the dishes, no one to ever notice if the dishes were done or not, no one to do anything with. And the nights, well, they were the worst. I couldn't sleep in my own bed for months. I lay on the couch until I fell asleep from crying or sheer exhaustion, whichever came first. Finally, I realized that I had to do something, so I read. I read earnestly and diligently. I read Virginia Woolf as a tribute to Lisa, and also to try to discover what Lisa saw in the woman. I began to study everything about her and wanted to know her, intimately, the way that I thought I knew my wife, but apparently didn't. That's when I thought of you. That's when I thought of this book. And you're right, this is not to satisfy a book contract. I don't have a contract for this book. I hope I will eventually, but even if I don't get one, the book is for Lisa." Tears began to stroll down his cheeks, and my own, in sympathy. He cleared his throat and wiped his face with the napkin before speaking again. "And now, if you don't mind, I never want to talk about this again."

The two of us stared at each other for a long time, not saying a word. There were times when words were unnecessary, like when you're in the company of someone you've known and loved for years and were quite comfortable with, and there were times when words paled at articulating whatever emotions you were experiencing. This was an example of the latter. We hugged each other for a long time, one of those bear hugs that people only gave each other at a funeral or when they were about to never see each other again. Finally, we let go and just sat there for another few seconds.

"I think you'd like to hear about the time Lottie got sick and Agatha came back. Talk about conflict, Lord!" I broke the silence with a smile, and Thomas responded in kind. Wiping his eyes quickly, he flashed a grin.

"I'd love to."

And so I began to tell him that part of the story.

Chapter Sixteen

Lottie was sick. She had a terrible infection in her stomach and had to go to hospital to get intravenous antibiotics. Nellie was in a state alternating between concern and panic. She wanted to be at the hospital as much as possible to support Lottie. Besides, Nellie had an innate mistrust of hospitals and the people who staffed them. When she was growing up, her sister always told stories of all the people who went into hospitals and never came out—including their own mother. That coupled with her own dreadful experience getting her appendix out at the age of twelve had helped to formulate Nellie's disparaging view on hospitals, a view that could only in part be considered paranoid. Hospitals had always been known to be disease carriers. They were often dirty places where infection spread like locusts. Florence Nightingale had drawn her last breath fighting for hospitals to maintain at least the same cleanliness expected of a coffee shop. Yet despite Nightingale's efforts, there were still places that looked as if they hadn't been cleaned ever. One doctor who came into Lottie's room while Nellie was there blew his nose, helped a nurse tie up a garbage bag, and examined Lottie, in that order. He hadn't once washed his hands. Nellie felt compelled by an urgent need to be at Lottie's side as such as possible, fearing that her absence might cause some unthinkable tragedy that could otherwise be averted. Virginia was sympathetic, but Leonard was unmoved. He insisted that his meals be cooked as usual. He could not abide any disruption to their established routines, nor would he bear the expense of eating out, not even once or twice a week. Besides, for all his complaining about too well done, burned porridge, or over-glazed ham, he was used to Nellie's cooking. Her style was unique, including her blunders. The only accommodation Leonard was willing to make was temporarily rehiring Agatha, the day maid the Woolfs had employed before Lottie came to work for them as a live-in, to take on Lottie's duties while she was convalescing. It had been pure chance that Agatha had recently moved back to the area and was looking for work again. Leonard had not been terribly pleased with her services previously, but given the situation and considering the fact that *he* had no intention of picking up a dustpan, nor could he afford for his wife to distract herself from her work to do so either, it seemed the best possible solution.

The addition of Agatha to the household was an imposition even to Nellie, who, by the nature of her position and status, was accustomed to being imposed upon. The first issue was the placement of the beds in the basement. They had long since been put together. Now they would need to be separated. Another issue was that Agatha felt entitled to run the show there. She thought of her previous employment as giving her senior status in the household despite the fact that she had been already gone for some time. Feeling entitled, Agatha refused to work around Nellie's schedule, marching instead to her own schedule. She did everything as she had done before, with zero consideration for the fact that things were no longer the same in the household as when Agatha last worked there. The only thing that had apparently stayed the same was the salary. Leonard was paying Agatha the exact amount he paid her before. Agatha complained to no end about the issue, but claimed that she needed the money so had no other choice. Nellie really couldn't have cared less. She just wanted Lottie home with her.

The blowup came a few days after Agatha arrived. She was putting some clothes into the dresser to the left, in the basement. Up until this point, most of her clothes were in her suitcase, and what remained was in a brown paper bag. She took out some of the clothes in the dresser and put them on top. Agatha then put her own clothes in with far more care than she took Lottie's clothes out. Nellie walked into the room for a break just as Agatha was halfway done. Looking at the interloper, with her back to Nellie, Nellie was aghast at what she saw.

"What the fuck do you think you're doing?" she bellowed, causing Agatha to drop the clothes in her hand and her whole body to jerk back. Agatha spun around to face her accoster, her face flushed with shame at getting caught.

"I-I, uh, needed to put my clothes somewhere. They were getting wrinkled in a suitcase and a bag, and I was tired of bending for them all the time. I thought that since this wasn't being used now, I'd use it. I didn't see no harm in it."

"Bullshit! If you didn't see harm in it, you'd be doing it out in the open, not sneaking around like a thief in the night. Lottie's not dead, goddamn it, she's coming back. She's coming back, and you're gonna be out on your arse—again."

It was a mixture of her embarrassment at being caught doing something that she really shouldn't have done without checking with Nellie first and her anger at the way Nellie was speaking to her and the way she treated her in general since her return that caused Agatha to respond the way she did.

"Don't be so sure she is coming back after all. Hospitals are known for making mistakes, especially when it comes to poor women from the wrong side of the tracks. If they killed her, it's not like anyone who matters would care. And besides, if she does get better, Mr. Woolf will give her the sack for sure. He won't be wantin' some weakling around his house fainting every time she lifts a tray. And don't be surprised if you're next, you pompous bitch."

Agatha regretted her diatribe as soon as she voiced it and so made no move to defend herself when Nellie, who had by now moved closer, slapped her hard across the face. Agatha lowered her head, the sting of Nellie's slap still fresh on her face.

"Don't you ever talk that way about Lottie again, or about anyone else I care about for that matter," Nellie hissed, the venom pouring out from her voice. "How dare you say such a dreadful thing? Who the hell do you think you are? Why don't you just pack up and get the fuck out of here right now!"

Agatha knew when she was beaten. She decided to raise the white flag.

"Listen, Nellie, I'm sorry about what I said just now. It was wrong, and I didn't really mean it. I was just angry, is all."

Nellie was not so quickly moved to forgiveness, especially when it came to a virtual stranger. Agatha tried again.

"Look. I said I'm sorry. If you don't want to accept that—fine, you don't have to. But like it or not, we're stuck together for the time being. We are going to have to find a way to make it work—for both of us."

Nellie found the words empty, but she could see the reason behind them. She spoke tentatively.

"Yes, well, I do see your point. I don't want any more friction either. God knows, with Lottie being in the hospital and all, I have enough on my plate, thank you very much. I guess I can get along for as long as it takes."

Agatha offered her right hand. Nellie grasped it and then let go in short order. She didn't trust this woman as far as she could throw her, but she had little choice at the moment. It was in both of their best interests to be civil and make it work. She doubted Agatha would cause any further trouble.

The women passed the rest of the day in peace. Leonard and Virginia never even realized there had been a problem. When Nellie got to the hospital that afternoon, she told Lottie none of this. She wanted Lottie to concentrate on nothing other than getting well, as quickly as she could. Nellie bought her chocolate-covered strawberries at the gift shop downstairs. They cost a fortune, the gift shop being extremely overpriced, but Nellie had no time to get to the grocery store before the hospital, so the gift shop would have to do. It was okay. The look of delight on Lottie's face when she saw the treat and the smile as she ate each strawberry carefully made the high cost entirely worthwhile.

"Good news, luv, the doctor thinks I may be coming home in the next few days. The infection seems to be getting better."

"Oh, Lottie, that's great. The house isn't the same without you, luv."

"Well, I'll be back in no time, you wait and see. He says my white blood cells are going down, meaning that the infection is starting to go away. Who knew that blood cells are white or red? It's fascinating."

"It sure is, but I don't even pretend to understand it." She held Lottie's two hands in both of her, tightly. As they rubbed their hands, together the calloused fingers created extra friction, and Nellie wondered for the millionth time what it must be like to have hands as smooth as Virginia's, hands that had never so much as scoured a pot, soaked in freezing cold water, gutted a fish, waxed candlesticks, or scrubbed floors. "But listen, honey, there is something I have to tell you—something you should know now before you get ready to come home."

As Nellie told Lottie about Agatha's re-emergence in the household, she tried to minimize her woman's function and downplay her own concern about the returning staff member. Lottie listened to Nellie's story with interest, but without the level of suspicion that she would have normally felt, suspicion of her employers only, never Nellie. Ever since that one incident when Nellie first started at the house, there had been not a moment of mistrust between the servants. Anger had been between them plenty of times. Lottie could not begin to count the number of rows they had had over the years, the worst ones usually being over something inconsequential. But trust was never an issue. They trusted each other to the grave.

Chapter Seventeen

Lottie came home from the hospital after two weeks. The doctor had forbidden her from doing any heavy lifting or most other forms of strenuous work. There was no room for Lottie, Nellie, and Agatha in the basement. And even if there were room, Leonard had no intention of paying an extra salary. Lottie was unpaid during her hospital stay, and of course, Agatha was paid. Now that Lottie was back, Agatha was promptly dismissed. Between seeing Agatha get the sack and having Lottie back in the house where she belonged, Nellie could not have been happier. She no longer had to make the long trip to the hospital and taste the insipid food in the cafeteria, watching nurses come and go with food trays laden down, talking loudly as they enjoyed the respite from the floors. Nellie had gotten to the point where she could easily find any room or office in the entire building. Other visitors came to her with questions. She started to think the hospital should cut her a check. On the day that Lottie was released, Nellie was overjoyed. The joy was short-lived.

With Lottie on restricted duties, it fell to Nellie to do most of the drudgery that would normally fall to Lottie. Plus, she had her own work to do. No one gave her a reprieve or even the slightest consideration. She was still expected to prepare the meals the same way, according to the same timetable, and do everything else exactly the same in spite of her doing two jobs. Resentment built up quickly. After all, Nellie had aches and pains too. She had problems too. True, she was not just home from hospital, but no one ever asked if she felt well or if she was overwhelmed. She was just expected to be fine. She was beginning to get annoyed.

It was the dishes that set Nellie over the edge.

A week after Lottie came home from the hospital, Nellie was resting in the basement after having prepared an elaborate luncheon. She was wiped out. There had been more people than she had expected, especially for lunch. Not only did Nessa come with Duncan and Bunny *and* the children, but Katherine came with her husband, milquetoast of a man he as he was. As usual, the guests left everything where it was, not giving a thought to the fact that someone had to clean up their messes. The damned children weren't even instructed to pick their toys off the floor. It was like it didn't matter. Nellie had to clean up the mess in the dining room. At least Mrs. Woolf, God bless her, had thoughtfully stooped to collect the children's toys, giving Nellie more time to attend to the kitchen.

In the kitchen, the dishes were piled high in the sink. Nellie had no chance to wash them since she was so busy running back and forth serving (something that was ordinarily part of Lottie's job description). Lottie was in the kitchen. At least, Nellie comforted herself, Lottie would get the dishes done. That would be one less thing Nellie would have to attend to, since she was already running behind schedule with dinner.

She was wrong. The dishes were piled up as high as ever. The drain board contained not a single cup, saucer, or piece of silverware. Lottie sat at the kitchen table, idly sipping a cup of coffee.

"You couldn't even do the friggin' dishes!" Nellie's outburst was so unexpected that Lottie jumped, spilling coffee onto the tablecloth. The stain spread. Lottie leaped up, dabbed a dish towel under some running water, and began to vigorously rub the tablecloth to obliterate the stain.

"Nellie, I'm sorry I didn't think about it. I'm so tired from the medicine."

"Bullshit! You are so tired and worn out that you can't lift a finger to help me"—she pointed to the coffee cup and to the cookie Lottie was eating—"but miraculously, you can do for yourself just fine." She slammed her hand on the table. It hurt. "I've been doing fuckin everything around here, and I haven't complained because I understand. I understand you can't carry things and you get tired out quickly. Really, I do, and I am happy you're home, for sure. But goddamn it, you can't wash a fucking dish. Are you really that helpless?"

"No, I'm not so helpless, but it's hard for me, Nellie. It really is, I can't explain it. I could have died in that hospital, I thought I was going to for a while. You wanted me home, and now I am. I don't understand what you want from me!" Lottie started sobbing, her head folded in her hands.

Nellie felt a little guilty, but she was too angry to let her guilt get the better of her. She sat down next to Lottie and put her arm around her for a few seconds then withdrew it. When she spoke, her voice was calm, much calmer than she felt.

"I need you to start doing some things around here. I sure don't want to endanger your health, and I don't want you to go back, God forbid, to the hospital, but I need help just the same. I'm running myself ragged doing my job and yours while you beat me to Mr. Woolf's desk on pay day. And you've never given me so much as two pence."

Lottie was incensed. "So that's what this is about? You're upset because I haven't given you any of my pay?" Her cheeks reddened and her voice raised. "Well, here then, goddamn it." She dug into her brassiere and pulled out some notes that were stuck together. "Take it." She flung the notes at Nellie.

"It's not about the damned money," Nellie responded as she scooped up the cash and tucked it into the side pocket of her apron. "It's about respect. When you treat me like this, I feel like you don't respect me, like I don't matter. And I've been told most of my life that I don't matter, but I know I do. Nobody's going to tell me that anymore, most especially not you."

Lottie was shocked at Nellie's reaction. She didn't know if she wanted to hug or hit her. She wondered and wanted to ask why Nellie put the cash in her pocket if that wasn't what she was upset over, but she didn't want to make things worse. Instead, she decided to pour on the charm.

"Honey, you know that I don't mean to hurt you. I wouldn't do that for all the money in the world, you know that about your Lottie." Nellie nodded in agreement. "It really has been hard for me since I came back. But I can try a bit harder." She leaned over and gave Nellie a quick peck on the cheek. Lottie stood up. "Now, you go back downstairs. Give me ten minutes, and I'll have these dishes done. When you come back, I'll start putting them away. You know Mrs. Woolf only likes dishes air-dried."

Nellie was appeased for the moment, and Lottie heaved a sigh of relief. Another catastrophe narrowly averted.

When dinner was an hour late, Leonard had a fit, carrying on like a raped ape. He mumbled things like how he would be better off taking his dinner in a tavern, how his sensitive stomach could not bear food late at night, and how he wanted to hire a staff that knew how to get things done. He loudly confronted Nellie for a brief moment. The irate glare he saw in her eyes gave him pause. He retreated.

Virginia barely noticed the delay in the meal. She was much too absorbed in the final revisions of her new novel, which was due to go into production in two months. It was always like this. Whenever she was doing her last revisions, "pulling the book together," as she called it, the woman had to be reminded to eat. Sometimes, she would go deeply into a trance and call the people around her, even those closest to her, by the names of her characters. The world of her creation and the world of reality would blend in mind, mixing to the point where she was often uncertain where one began and the other ended. Sometimes at this point in a book, the voices would return. Thankfully, they usually didn't stay long, just until the work was finished and the book was in production. Thankfully, there were no voices at all. Much as she loved her employer, Nellie didn't think she could deal with Lottie's infirmities, both real and imagined, and "the voices," as the household had dubbed Virginia's auditory hallucinations.

During this time, eating was out of the question but for the occasional nibble here and there. Virginia would lose five kilograms; then, her labor over, she would gain ten as she gorged on anything she could find. In anyone else, one might assume that the gorging was a self-appointed award for the hard labor of putting the finishes touches on an intense novel. But in Virginia's case, Nellie knew better.

Since Virginia hated food, Nellie often wondered then if the gorging was some type of self-induced punishment for what she perceived as another literary failure. The gorging might have been a reward for a job well done.

Nellie would never understand Virginia's attitude about her work. No matter how much praise she received from critics, how much she was clamored at bookstores by anxious shopkeepers looking for autographs, she still never thought of herself as being good enough. Years later, Nellie would wonder if this doubt was one of the things that dragged Virginia off her emotional precipice and into the Danube River with rocks in her pocket. To never think yourself good enough at what you do, to labor your whole life at an art that you perfected and yet still come up short by some ridiculous standard—it was an unthinkable burden to have to bear.

After the suicide, Nellie would wonder if Virginia identified with Shakespeare's sister, the imaginary one she'd talked about so often and written about in *A Room of One's Own*. Shakespeare's sister, who had a genius for fiction and longed to write about men and women and their ways but could get no training in her craft and killed herself in London rather than face a dismal future. No, Nellie would realize several days after the burial, there was no means of preventing this tragedy. No one could have fixed what was wrong with that part of her psyche; it was beyond anyone's reach.

But those were the thoughts Nellie would have in the future. In the present, she had but one concern that weighed on her mind and heart, keeping the household and the two women within it whom she loved more than life healthy and functioning without losing herself entirely in the process.

*****

Lottie began to recover, and the lives of all three women gradually returned to normal.

Leonard's life had hardly changed at all during all this time. He was busy, as usual, with his *work*, running to and fro. Virginia worked as well, of course; writing all those books was certainly not fun and games, but it did not seem to register with Leonard. *He* was the one who could not be disturbed, *he* was the one who *worked*, despite the fact that it was *she* who provided most of their income. It was the old double standard, played out even in the most cultured and sophisticated households.

But for Nellie, none of this mattered in the slightest. All that mattered was that Lottie was feeling better, was back to work, and Nellie was no longer responsible for doing absolutely everything. Lottie was simply happy to be feeling better and stronger every day. She felt stronger even than she had before she had taken ill. She wondered now if all those nights that she went to bed so early, exhausted by teatime, wasn't her illness, festering, unrecognized until it finally made itself known in its dreadful fashion. Virginia was simply happy to have domestic tranquility returned once again. For she who was thought to be aloof to all human emotion save her own was actually quite sensitive and perceptive when it came to the emotions of those in her own household. Her often perceived aloofness melted away. She would walk past the servants in the kitchen, see them working side by side, and smile. Everything was back the way it had been; the women were content.

Chapter Eighteen

The night terrors returned, suddenly and unexpectedly. Nellie was summoned into the study one morning right after breakfast. Leonard and Virginia were waiting for her, standing by their desks, facing the door. A chair was pulled up next to them. Nellie knocked on the door. Once given permission to enter, Nellie faced her employers and sat on the chair they indicated. Their expressions were dour, and Nellie quickly scanned her memory for recent events, thinking she was about to be reprimanded for some transgression or given the sack. But no, it was not as she expected.

"Thank you, Nellie, we won't keep you," Virginia began. Leonard followed suit in very short order.

"Simply put, Nellie, Mrs. Woolf's troubles at night have returned, rather suddenly, it would seem, and we find ourselves, well, that is to say that once again …"

"My husband is saying that once again, I require a babysitter."

"Virginia!" Leonard scolded.

"Well, why bloody not? For Christ's sake, it's what it is, is it not? You want Nellie to babysit me so I shall sleep through the night and not disturb you." Leonard blushed bright red. She spoke the truth.

"I'd be glad to stay with the missus, sir," Nellie said as if Virginia were not there. "It will be just fine. We've done it before. I am happy to be of service."

Virginia smiled weakly. "Thank you, Nellie. It is quite good of you really." Virginia was quiet for a moment while a thought occurred to her. "What of your housemate?"

"Ma'am?"

"Surely she will be unhappy with the situation? She will not wish to lose …" Virginia considered her words. "Your company in the basement for an undetermined period of time. I do not wish to create a rift between you."

"Think nothing of it, ma'am. After everything that's happened recently, Lottie won't mind a little change. I'm sure of it." Nellie meant what she said. She figured that Lottie owed her one, after the hospital business and all the extra work Nellie did while Lottie was recovering. Besides, after all the trouble the Woolfs went through to keep Lottie's job open while she was ill, surely Lottie would feel that she was in their debt. Nellie thought for certain that such a minor request for accommodation would be honored without any fuss.

Nellie thought wrong. Lottie went ballistic.

"Again! I thought we were finished with that bullshit. She's playing the victim again, by Christ! Writing all the books she does and all the articles, and she still has you believing she can't sleep without help."

"What do you want me to do? She *needs* me. You know what that is, up until very recently, you needed me too."

Lottie was outraged. "You still don't get it do you. Yes, I needed you! So what? I'm *with* you. I'm supposed to need you. She is not. She has a husband, whether or not either of them knows it. You're all I have, and I'm all *you* have, whether or not you realize it."

"Of course, I know it," Nellie snapped. "No one loves me except you! How could I forget with you reminding me every goddamn day! So help me, Lottie, one day you're going to drive me to drink, or worse. Then you'll be sorry when I'm gone. And when I'm gone, I won't be coming back. Ever."

Lottie wasn't sure what Nellie was getting at, but both possibilities that came to mind unsettled her. She tried to make peace.

"Nellie, luv, forgive me. You know I have a jealous streak. I know you have a job to do, I know that we have good positions here. And I know that the missus depends on you, I really do get it. It's just that … I hate the thought of that woman driving us apart."

Nellie rolled her eyes. "How many times do I have to tell you before you finally *get* it?" She began to speak methodically, as though she were a recorded voice being played back. "She is not driving us apart, I do not care about her more than you, I am not going to choose her over you." She wanted to add "This is a recording" to her droned-on list. Lottie was irritated at the tone but comforted by the words. She believed Nellie's words but needed to hear it from time to time.

For Nellie's part, she had repeated the same reassurances over and over again, so many times in fact that she was beginning to doubt her own sincerity. Did she really care more for Lottie than Mrs. W? If given an ultimatum, would she throw over Mrs. W to save Lottie? Pah! The thoughts were ridiculous, and she had no time to sit around considering them any more than she had time to wring her hands wondering when the world might end like the idiots she sometimes saw on street corners. She knew her own mind, and she knew her heart. It was Lottie who was insecure; and it was her insecurity that was making Nellie crazy.

Interlude

If I didn't know better, I'd think that Thomas was beginning to have designs on me. It wasn't anything he said; he was too much of a gentleman for that. No, it was the way he looked at me. Not all the time, mind you, but every once in a while, when I was telling a story about the past. He'd get this look in his eye like he was absorbing not only the story, but me, like he wanted to possess me somehow. Of course, it was a ridiculous thought. I was eons older than him, and besides, he knew the situation. So I knew I was being absurd, yet still I could not help but get the feeling sometimes.

We visited Hatchard's bookstore, the same store that Mrs. W and I used to go to so often. I had not been there since the day of her funeral. After the service was over, I went to every bookstore I could walk to. Seeing as she was a writer, it seemed fitting to spend time in bookstores on the day of her funeral. I bought copies of at least one of her books in every store I went to, even though I already had them all. I could not think of a better way to honor her.

I suppose honoring Mrs. W was really the reason I ever agreed to meet Thomas in the first place. Walking through the bookstore with him, however, was more than I could handle. I started shaking. At first, it was barely noticeable, but then it became so pronounced I couldn't hide it. I gripped the banister going to the basement with all my might (the lift was out of order), and still I almost toppled down the stairs. I could see her clear as day at the bottom of the steps, bent down, hunched over a pile of books, her oversize hat half-sliding off her head. I even heard her voice, asking the sales clerk for some obscure title that should be on the shelf but isn't, and watching the clerk's body language as he tried to mask his exasperation with this trying customer.

"Are you all right, Nellie?" Thomas's concerned hand on my elbow snapped me out of my trance and brought me back to the present. I looked around. I was still on the staircase, just standing there on the second-to-the-last step, causing an annoyance for the other customers who had to walk around me. One woman about my age swore a mild oath as she wiggled her away around both of us and muttered something under her breath about inconsiderate Londoners. I guessed she was from the country, in town just for the day.

"Yes, thank you. I'm all right, just a little lightheaded at the moment." I held out my hand, and Thomas clasped it gently. We walked down the last two steps and off to the side. Thomas led me to the upholstered armchair on the left side of the staircase. I plopped myself down.

"Was everything okay over there? You seemed upset, out of it, sort of."

I cleared my throat. "I had sort of a spell there for a minute. I don't know how to describe it exactly. It was like I stepped back in time. Everything seemed so real to me. She was there, looking through the books. I saw her! I even heard her voice."

Thomas paled, as though he might faint. "By *she*, I assume you're talking about Virginia. Mrs. W, as you refer to her."

"Yes," I answered. "You know, I do think I understand now, for the very first time, what Mrs. W felt when she was getting an idea for a novel. She always said the scene played out in front of her, as if in life. That was exactly what happened to me just now. I saw everything, a day in the life—not current life, but life as it had been."

Thomas was concerned. "Perhaps we ought to get some sugar inside you, quick. Dizzy spells are often a result of low blood sugar, hypoglycemia they call it." He pronounced the term slowly, emphasizing the syllables. He sounded rather official, almost like a doctor. It struck me funny coming from him, since it was so out of character. I wanted to laugh, the same way I'd want to laugh if I saw a six-year-old boy pretending to read the *Times* with an unlit pipe hanging from his mouth. But then Thomas was no little boy.

"It feels strange, whatever it is. I thought I'd faint there for a minute. I'm glad you're here." I grabbed his right forearm and held it for a couple of minutes. All of a sudden, it felt inappropriate. He must have felt it too, because he moved his arm away at the same time that I took off my hand. I cleared my throat, and Thomas tapped the back of his head, a silly childhood habit he had told me when I noticed it on our third meeting. He always tapped the back of his head when he was nervous or uncomfortable. I always cleared my throat.

"Maybe you wouldn't mind getting a scone across the street at the café? I'm suddenly famished!"

"No, not at all. In fact, I think that is an excellent idea," he replied. He quickly put down the three hardcover books he was holding, an apparent change of heart, and ascended the stairs two at a time as he made his way out of the store, past the curious tourists. I followed him as quickly as I could. It was several minutes before I met him outside.

Thomas flashed a bright (if somewhat forced) smile at me. "Shall we get that scone now, or would you prefer something more substantial?" He glanced at his watch. "It will be teatime before we know it."

"The scone and a nice cup of tea would do me wonders right now, thank you."

"Very well then, although for my part, I think I shall have coffee. Tea is a bit too weak for me at the present."

Not only did Thomas order a coffee, it was espresso, and he ordered a shot in it. He brought up Agatha again; I wished he hadn't. She was so dreadfully dull. Why on earth would I want to continue to speak about her when there were so many better topics? Who knows, maybe he thought she was a safe topic—someone who would shield us from … what it was, we did not know.

He droned on about her. What was she like? Did I think she was jealous of my relationship with either Lottie or the missus or both? Did I ever see her again after Lottie came home from hospital? On and on until finally I took a big gulp of my tea and said, "Agatha was a miserable, self-righteous slug. I never saw her again after that time and never wanted to. In fact, if I saw her right now in this café, I'd either ignore her completely or spit in her face."

Thomas may have been taken aback by the angry words, but they suited a purpose. Whatever awkwardness had been building between us for the past half hour or so was resolved. We were comfortable with each other again. The work could continue—which I reckoned was a good thing. We had come so far as it were, I didn't want to stop now.

As for me, I've been by myself all this time since Lottie passed and didn't plan on sharing a home with anyone else, certainly not at this point in my life. But still, that day in the bookstore, just for that one moment, I could have considered. The brain is a strange animal; that's for sure. Oh well, I'd better get to bed after all this.

Chapter Nineteen

Nellie's shoulders were hunched as she leaned over the sink. Her hands were awash in the stream of cold water pouring into the metal pot, filled with potatoes needing to be peeled.

Virginia rushed into the kitchen, her arms failing in the air. "Nelly, Nelly, I have the most *wonderful* idea. I know exactly what my next book will be about, and it is the best ever." She paused for a moment, expecting a response. Nothing.

"Did you hear what I said?" Virginia inquired.

"Sure I did. You have an idea for a new book. That's nice, ma'am."

Virginia was aghast. "That's nice? I'm telling you about the best thing that's happened to me in a long time, and all you can come up with is a simple that's nice." When Nellie did not respond, Virginia grew incensed.

"For God's sake, Nelly, put down the damned potatoes and say something to me. Say something more substantial than a simple 'that's nice.'"

Nellie made a sour face and dropped the potato she was peeling and the knife she was using to peel it into the sink. She wiped her wet hands on her apron and looked at her employer squarely in the eyes. "You want me to say something more, fine. I have to get these potatoes done now, or Mr. Woolf will not be happy when the pot roast has a side of nothing. So whatever it is you want to tell me, I'd appreciate your making it snappy, if you don't mind."

Virginia was so indignant at Nellie's attitude, she almost didn't tell her. But Leonard was out for the day, and Lottie wouldn't have cared in the least. She had no one else to tell at the moment.

"I am going to write a book for Vita, in her honor. I know exactly what it will be about, I even know the protagonist's name."

Nellie knew she was supposed to ask. "What is it, ma'am?"

"Orlando. The protagonist's name is going to be Orlando. He will be a man living in the Elizabethan time—but over time, he will become a modern-day woman. No one has done this. *It* is unheard of. It will be a smashing success, and it will all be for Vita."

"How does she fit into this? What does she have to do with it?

Virginia rolled her eyes, exasperated. "Don't you get it? Look at Vita! She is so masculine in some things, yet she is a woman. She smokes that pipe like a man does, and acts more like a man than Harold does. Yet she is a mother, something no man can do … nor I for that matter." As she spoke the latter part of the sentence, the sting of it struck her fresh. Their lack of children was Leonard's decision. It had been he who had not wanted them, he who felt that the strain would be too much on *her*. She had been given no say in the matter. Sometimes she thought she would not want them, but often times she did. Today was one of the day she did.

Nellie was afraid of the last comment and wanted to redirect the conversation. "Right, I see what you're talking about. It's like she is both man and woman, so your character is going to be both also, just not at the same time."

Virginia threw up her hands, rushed to the sink, and kissed Nellie on both cheeks. Such effusive behavior put Nellie off, but she understood her employer's excitement and was glad for her happiness, however fleeting.

"Congratulations, ma'am, I just know it will be a success. I am sure of it." Virginia smiled gleefully at her cook's words. Nellie smiled back. "Now, if you'll excuse me, ma'am," she pointed to the sink, "the potatoes aren't going to finish peeling themselves." She grasped the peeler firmly in one hand and the half-peeled potato in the other. She turned the cold water on and returned to work. Virginia shook her head and walked away wordlessly, bewildered as to how anyone could care about such a thing as peeling potatoes at such a momentous time as this. A new novel was conceived, possibly the best of her career, and the woman was worried about potatoes. Ah, the minds of the lower class! Virginia would never understand them at all.

Lottie had been upstairs dusting when Virginia came down ranting. When Lottie came into the kitchen an hour later, Nellie told her what had transpired, her voice brimming with righteous indignation.

"The nerve of her coming in and interrupting me like that. I told her Mr. Woolf was expecting the potatoes. What did she think, they were going to take care of themselves?"

"Aw, Nellie, I've told you, she doesn't get it. She's not like us. No one's ever expected her to have dinner ready by seven. She doesn't live in the same world as we do. She doesn't understand."

Nellie heaved her chest. "Damned if I don't know it. But still, a little consideration goes quite a long way."

Lottie smirked. "No such thing. Nellie dear, when are you ever going to learn? The only people who have consideration for us are us."

Nellie could have responded about how, whenever she was behind in her work and needed help, Lottie would have work to do in another part of the house. Today was a perfect example. True, the dusting did need to get done, but would the world have ended if Lottie lent Nellie a hand before she tackled dust bunnies? Nellie thought such things but wisely chose not to say them. A row between them now would serve no purpose other than to create aggravation—and Nellie already had enough aggravation.

"You may well be right, Lottie. I guess there is still a lot I need to learn, about more than one thing, too." Lottie noticed the undercurrent in Nellie's tone but ignored it.

"It's not that you need to learn so many things, Nellie. You just need to understand her. You have to see her for who she is, and I think you are starting to, finally. You're getting smart when it comes to her."

Nellie was not sure that Virginia was the one she needed to get smart about, but she once again decided to say nothing, for the sake of peace.

"You see, Nellie dear, give a body enough time, and their true colors always come out. She can't hide who she is, a selfish uptight bitch."

Virginia was standing behind the kitchen door for most of the servants' conversation. She fumed, especially at Nellie for letting Lottie's accusations go unchallenged, but remained silent. She was holding a juice glass. She deliberately let it fall from her hand, shattering on the floor. Hearing the glass break, both servants jumped up, exchanged a worried glance, and rushed out the door. They saw Virginia hunched over, attempting to clean up her mess.

"No, ma'am, you shouldn't be doing that. Let us take care of it, you might hurt yourself."

"Thank you." Virginia shook slightly. "I don't know what came over me. I was bringing the glass inside for some orange juice when my hand just let loose. Before I knew it, it was out of my hand." Virginia impressed herself, both with the skillfulness of the lie and the deftness with which she told her. Usually she was a terrible liar.

"Think nothing of it, ma'am, we're glad to do it." She glared at Lottie who went immediately to get the broom and dustpan. Nellie swept while Lottie stooped. Virginia watched, silently satisfied.

"Was there something you wanted, ma'am?" Lottie inquired as she swept up the broken pieces.

"I'm sorry?"

"You were coming into the kitchen, not a usual occurrence, if don't you mind my saying so. So I figured you must be wantin' something."

Virginia blushed. "I suppose I did want something, but after the commotion I created, I have clean forgotten what it was, totally." It was her second lie in a matter of minutes. She impressed herself.

Lottie grunted, then cleared her throat to cover her impudence. "Yes, of course, ma'am. Well, when you remember, we will certainly be here, anxious to hear whatever it was you had to tell us."

"Yes, when I remember," Virginia mumbled feebly, already having lost interest in the exchange.

Virginia never came back; no one expected that she would.

*****

Three weeks later

Leonard was fit to be tied. Bad enough that dinner had been late for the past four nights! Now when he brought E. M. Forster over (albeit unexpectedly) for lunch and some cocktails, he was mortified to find the dining room in disarray. It seemed that after months of Virginia's complaining, probing, and pleading on behalf of the china cabinet, Lottie had acquiesced. It was Leonard's ill fortune that the precise day and hour the maid chose to clean the china cabinet, where dust had been accumulating since the time of creation, it was when Leonard was bringing his company. Leonard was mortified. He had brought E. M. Forster home to woo him, in a sense. Leonard wanted him to leave his current publisher and sign on with the Hogarth Press. Forster's books were selling like wildfire, and he had another one in the works that was sure to be a hit. Leonard wanted to publish the next book. When they had gotten to the house, Leonard had given him a tour of the printing press, housed in the converted garaged that was adjacent to the house. Forster seemed impressed, with the quality of the product, if not with the outlay of the machinery or the space that housed it. Leonard was certain that he had him. He and Virginia had known EM (for everyone called him EM, so much so that one would be hard-pressed to identify his first name) casually for years. He was part of the same circle of friends. History would dub them the Bloomsbury Circle. At the time, however, he was just another writer that Leonard wanted for his business.

Once his guest was seated on the terrace, with a martini in his hand, Leonard sought out Nellie and had her whip up a fresh chicken salad with some mayonnaise. There were some croissants Leonard had brought that morning from town. He had her stick them in the toaster to serve on the side. They could use them as bread to make sandwiches. Nellie got busy straight away, and Leonard returned to the dining room to find Lottie. As he anticipated, she was leaning her entire body into the china cabinet, spraying the glass shelves and wiping them clean. Normally grateful for her rare diligence, today, Leonard was put off by it.

"Lottie, I'd like you to put up a pot of coffee and bring it along with cups and saucers to the terrace. Three cups and saucers will suffice."

"Yes, Mr. Woolf, I will do it as soon as I finish this, for sure."

"Lottie, you misunderstand me. I want this done right now."

Lottie stuck her head out of the cabinet. "I intend to get this done right now, sir, then I'll be getting to your coffee. Otherwise, I'm pretty sure Nellie is in the kitchen."

Leonard could not hide his annoyance. "Nellie already has an assignment. In any event, as master of this house, when I issue a directive, I expect it to be followed at once. You are to stop what you are doing at once, prepare the coffee, and serve it on the terrace." He pointed to the starched white apron that was part of her uniform. There were several stains on it, cleaning supplies mixed with dust and dirt.

"You should change your apron," he stated matter-of-factly and watched her as she left the room. He swore an oath under his breath and returned to his guest. Lottie did as she was bidden.

They were just finishing their chicken salad when Virginia walked out onto the terrace. She walked slowly and steadily, as if on automatic, her small notebook clutched tightly in her right hand, along with her customary blue pen. She plopped herself into the chair next to Leonard.

"EM, you certainly are looking well. How is your writing going?"

"Nicely, thank you, Virginia. I am working on a somewhat secret manuscript at the moment. I don't know if I'll publish it, but I want to write it nonetheless."

"I'm intrigued. What is it about?"

"It is the story of an English young man from a privileged background who goes to an English boarding school. While he is there, he finds himself quite taken in by one of the older boys. He develops feelings for him, feelings that others deem quite unnatural."

"How interesting! Does he get him, physically, I mean? That may be a problem for the censors. They don't generally like to read graphic descriptions of buggery."

"I'm not sure yet. I've only done the outline and a few preliminary chapters. As for the censors, it is irrelevant. As I've already told you both, I'm not planning on publishing it, or even trying to."

"Nonsense," Leonard chimed in, "why on earth would you or any other sane person go through the time and energy it takes to write a book if it is going to sit in a desk drawer collecting dust. Books are meant to be published, for millions to read [and hopefully buy], discuss, and review. That is why writers write."

Virginia made a face. "Leonard, God bless him, thinks that *The Wise Virgins* makes him an expert on what it is to be a novelist, what we go through to preserve our craft."

"Not just *The Wise Virgins*, Ginia, but as you recall, I *publish* novelists. I see what it is to bring a book from an idea to a finished product, all the work and rework that goes into it. I know the creative process—how difficult it is. And I also know that no one does it for nothing, for themselves. Even Emily Dickinson, in all her obscurity, wrote her poems for someone else, Sue Gilbert. Even if they were never meant to be published formally, and God knows the Americans can go on with that debate ad infinitum, she still was not writing merely for herself. The poems were meant for her sister-in-law to read. Granted, they were meant to be read in private, but still, the situation remains the same."

Virginia coughed. She always coughed nervously when she was uncomfortable, and nothing made her more uncomfortable than being bested in a discussion. She changed the topic without warning.

"Do you think Hitler can be stopped without England going to war?"

EM's face turned stone cold. A pregnant pause that seemed interminable filled the air as he considered his response carefully, almost as if fate were to be determined by his answer. Beads of sweat formed on his brow and trickled down his face.

"In truth, I am not so sure. But in the name of all that is good on earth and in heaven, I do hope so. The last war …" All three of them shuddered at the mental images conjured up by the mere mention of such an atrocity. "Well," he said, alternating what he was going to say, "may it never be repeated."

The thought of the war disturbed Virginia greatly. She began to mentally detach from the conversation. She thought of another time, about a month before, when the subject of war was broached to her, quite unusually and unexpectedly.

It was a Tuesday. She had received a letter in the post. That was not unusual; she could in a given day receive twenty or thirty letters (her record was fifty). They were often solicitations from organizations, letters from friends, acquaintances, and business associates, and, invariably, a letter from a fan. Fan letters were the ones she answered first. Her fans, mostly women, were the ones who supported her by buying her books. She owed them. Besides, she enjoyed the exchange with these strangers who were moved enough by her words to want to contact her yet kept a respectful distance by sending a letter.

This letter was different from the usual ones. When she looked at the return address, Virginia instantly recognized the name. It was a man, a diplomat who was rumored to carry some influence with the prime minster. She had met him once, she remembered. He seemed pleasant enough, but he was fat, and he sweated profusely. She had been put off by all the sweat. No matter. She now held his letter backwards in her hand and opened it carefully with her letter opener. After the customary salutation, she was puzzled at the opening sentence which read, "How are we to prevent war?"

"Nellie, come look at this letter I received in the post today. See how absurd it is!" Virginia called out as she strutted into the kitchen, amused, sitting herself down at the table where she had her breakfast. Nellie sat herself opposite where Virginia was sitting and reached for the letter in Virginia's hand. She read the first sentence and then put the paper down on the table.

"Bunk!" Nellie exclaimed. "Why on earth would he write such a first line? Why ask you that?"

"Exactly my thought, Nellie dear," Virginia responded. "Why ask a woman about preventing war. Women don't create war in the first place. Men create war. How can woman prevent what man creates?"

"Maybe he thinks you can do the impossible. Maybe he figures that with your writer's imagination, you can create a world without any war, a world without conflict."

"Oh, how dreadfully boring that would be," Virginia remarked then, seeing Nellie's expression, quickly explained.

"I don't mean the part about a world without war, of course, dear. I mean the part about a world without conflict. Conflict is the essential ingredients in fiction. It is what keeps us going in life. Without problems to solve and obstacles to overcome, what would the human brain do all day long? Even us, Nellie." She gave her cook a lighthearted, playful slap across the face. "Where would we be without our occasional rows?"

Nellie laughed at the dig, intended for laughter. Virginia continued her response, more thoughtfully. "Dear Mr.———," she began composing aloud, "how can I, as a woman possibly be found fit to answer such a question as to how are we to prevent war?' Women do not make wars. Women are the bystanders of the wars of men. Women are most assuredly, in many cases, the victims of men's wars, either used like pawns. How silly then to come to a woman for the answer."

Nellie agreed. "Maybe the king will commission a special appointment for you, ma'am." She moved her right hand as though scrolling it over a page. "Virginia Woolf, renowned novelist *and* keeper of the peace of the United Kingdom."

Virginia instantly imagined herself wearing some absurd cap and a long gown, like the kind they gave university graduates. She bellowed with laughter at the image, doubling over with her hands pressed tightly against her abdomen.

"Yes, can you imagine such a thing? As if I don't have enough on my plate as it is, writing all the things I want to write." The conversation ended shortly thereafter, and the women went on with their respective day.

At bedtime, just before she turned out the lights on the day, Virginia scribbled on a piece of scrap paper four words, "can we prevent war?" She left the note on her nightstand. The next morning, she asked Nellie for some eggs and sausage. She liked to fill up on protein anytime she was about to do something out of her comfort zone. She was quiet over breakfast, barely saying a word to anyone, a half-muttered thank you to Nellie when the food was put in front of her sufficed. She vaguely recalled asking for more coffee at some point, but wasn't sure if she had verbalized it or if she had only thought it and Nellie had brought it anyway, anticipating the request. She stared at the food she was eating, as if she expected it to jump off the plate and dance before her very eyes.

After she finished eating, she took the paper that Leonard was reading before he abruptly left the table to go to another one of his interminable "business meetings." She started at the front page, her attention focused on a headline in the lower right-hand column of the first page. It had two words, *war looms*. Two simple words, yet Virginia found herself transfixed by them. War seemed to be surrounding her wherever she looked. The letter she had received seemed like a portent. Providence was speaking to her; she needed to answer. But the question remained, how could she as a woman possibly prevent war? It seemed a conundrum that stopped any intelligent response she might make.

After breakfast, she went for a walk into town and sat at her usual bench on the side of road. She was alone; something that was rarer and rarer these days. It seemed that there was always someone she had to see, a book she had to promote, a guest to entertain. But on this walk, she was entirely alone. The leaves rustled near her feet; a bird chirped above her. Virginia closed her eyes for a few minutes, willing herself to bask in the relaxation of the moment.

She remained perfectly still for minutes that seemed like eternities until a harsh, crude image jolted her like an electric shock and caused her to become rigid. She squeezed her already-closed eyes even tighter, trying to repel the image. But the apparition would not leave her. It was a mortally wounded soldier, his breath barely sustained, with two bullet holes in the center of his chest from which blood gushed out like rivers.

Barely audibly, the soldier cried out to her, "Don't let this happen."

"How shall I stop it?" she answered, terrified.

He made no response but collapsed on the ground in front of her, dead.

When she opened her eyes, she was momentarily startled beyond knowing where she was or what she was doing there. Her face and neck were in a cold sweat, and her hands trembled at her sides. Her throat was parched. She wanted to get water from the fountain up ahead but did not at this moment trust herself to stand. She feared her legs might betray her. Her voice cracked as she spoke. "But *how*," she pleaded to the dead soldier who was not really there but who seemed frightfully real to her. "How am I to prevent war?"

She left the park, still shaky but grounded enough to trust herself to get home without being trampled by a horse or run over by an automobile. She spoke not a word more but let herself into the house and went straight to her study.

By the time she got to her desk, Virginia knew that she must write this now. She must answer the letter she received. She must resolve for herself how one could prevent war. Furthermore, she must answer for herself, how she as a woman (married to a Jew no less) could possibly know anything about the subject, and how any opinion she had could possibly be given any merit.

She took out a few blank sheets of paper, picked up her trusted blue pen, and began to write.

> Dear Mr. ———, it seems incredulous to me that you, a man, should ask me, a woman, how we can prevent war? *We* do not make wars—men make wars. Therefore, we (women) cannot possibly prevent what we have no part in creating.
>
> That being said, I do think that there is way to achieve what you are hoping for. Funny that you should write to a woman, because I do believe that the solution lies in women. Parliament declares war. If women were allowed

in Parliament, there would be a drastic reduction in the number of wars declared. The reason, contrary to what you might think, has nothing to do with bloody sentimentalism. One need hardly look beyond Mary Tudor or Catherine de' Medici to know that a woman's heart can run as cold as a man's given the right provocation. No, the difference is motherhood. No woman could possibly sign a bill that would send her sons, or the sons of any woman she knows, to their deaths in a war. She simply could not bear that on her conscience. Therefore, I have at least a viable solution. Put women into Parliament. If you make women an integral part of the government, there may indeed be a chance for war to be eliminated once and for all. As it is now, however, women have no place in the government, we do not participate in politics, and we are unwelcome in the government. How can we possibly prevent war, poverty, or any other effects of the ministrations of government?

The second suggestion I can offer, entwined with the first, is to allow women admittance to university. As a woman possessed of some modest talent for putting words onto paper, and as someone fortunate enough to have been born to a literary biographer in a house where books were prolific, how much more in depth and knowledgeable would my writings be if I had the benefit of a university education? The only reason I have the limited knowledge I have of literature is because of my access to books in my father's library. But what if I had not been born to the class I was? How would I then know anything about the literary greats? What of the daughter of the collier who has a brilliant mind but no place to exercise it? Is her mind doomed to atrophy *ad infinitum* simply because she had the misfortune of not being born to a literary critic and biographer? Is she never to be able to rise above the unfortunate circumstances she was born into? An education would be able to expand her mind. This would give her power. Women can never hope to prevent war or participate in any other serious business if we are deprived of getting the same education available to just about any Englishman who can read. If that can happen, if women can be admitted to university, then I think we may be onto something. There may then be a way for women to help to prevent war—by giving them the power to stop it.

Virginia blew softly on the ink and put her pen down gently. She stood up and stretched her arms to their full length; the slight cracking sounds signaled to her that she needed to take a break and get some exercise. She opened the door and was about to go through the terrace doors to take a walk in the garden when Lottie passed her in the foyer, on her way to change the bed sheets. Virginia stopped her in her tracks.

"Lottie, I am going for a walk in the garden to stretch my mind, to say nothing of my legs."

"Yes, ma'am, I'll let Mr. Woolf know if he is looking for you," Lottie responded, anxious to get on her with work.

"No, you misunderstand my intent, Lottie. I would like you to come with me."

Lottie nearly fainted on the spot. "Are you feeling all right, ma'am? You're sure you don't mean Nellie and are a bit confused?"

The lady bit her lower lip. "I am certainly not confused. I ought to know my own servants. Now, if you please …"

"Begging your pardon, Mrs. Woolf, but I was just about to change the bed sheets—"

Virginia waved her right hand in front of her face. "Fey! The linens are not going anywhere. And I doubt Scotland Yard will be dispatching anyone to inspect our bedrooms. I would greatly appreciate your company on this walk." Mrs. Woolf fell silent; Lottie understood that she did not have a choice.

"Of course, ma'am, I'd be glad to come with you. I just didn't realize how important it was to you, is all."

"Fine, then. Shall we go?" Virginia led the way with Lottie quick at her heels.

They walked around the gardens, admiring the azalea bushes and asparagus beds then stood by the coy pond in the center of a bed of red and white roses. After some minutes of a somewhat uncomfortable silence, Virginia asked a question.

"How is it to be a servant, Lottie?"

"Beg your pardon, ma'am? What do you mean?" Lottie was a bit put out by the question, thinking it a tad insulting.

"Sorry, what I mean to say is that I want to know how it feels to be a servant, to always be attending to the houses of others rather than your own, to live in the house of others, rather than your own."

Lottie's resentment dissipated. "Well, sure, sometimes I think it would be nice to have my own place. And yes, I get jealous sometimes when I see people who have no more brains than me be catered to just because they were born into the right family, one with money, and I wasn't." She thought better of her words. "I don't mean you, Mrs. Woolf, any fool can see your genius." The compliment was sincere.

Virginia blushed slightly and patted Lottie's hand. "But always watching other people, always being there but somehow not, do you ever feel out of place?"

"No, because that is my place. Servants are supposed to be on the outside of things. We are outsiders, that's why we only associate with each other, why we form such close bonds with each other"— here, she was obviously speaking of Nellie in particular—"it's almost like we have our own society."

"Yes, I see your point, Lottie. It's the same with writers, I think, we seek each other out because we understand each other. Like speaks to like, as they say. I could never imagine explaining the difficulty of my work to someone who has never written professionally, nor could I presume to understand what it is to scrub floors, polish silver, or launder bed linens."

Lottie smiled, feeling finally recognized for something. She wasn't sure, but it felt like the lady and she were at last beginning to understand each other.

"The hard part I guess is feeling less than. I don't mind feeling less than my betters, they are my betters after all. I *do* mind feeling less than human."

Virginia blanched. "I certainly hope I never do anything that makes you feel less than human. I would never want to do such a thing."

Lottie explained. "It's nothing that you or Mr. Woolf do, it's not even about the two of you specifically. It's the structure of the whole thing. If I gave my notice tomorrow and went to work for someone else, it would be exactly the same. Truth be told, much as I hate to admit it, you and the mister are probably among the easiest employers to work for, really. But being outsiders all the time, always there for the action but never being part of the action itself … well, after a while, it gets to you."

Virginia was intrigued. "I wonder if Nellie feels this way, and if Nessa's servants do as well."

"They do, ma'am. As I told you, it is not about you and Mr. Woolf, it is every household. All servants feel as I do. it is our biggest topic of conversation when we get together."

"I see. I think I am slowly beginning to understand."

In bed that night, Virginia could not sleep. Her conversation with Lottie kept replaying in her mind. She kept hearing the word *outsider*, like a phonograph record that is stuck. Then she heard the word *society*. She recalled what Lottie said, "it's almost like we have our own society."

"A society of outsiders," Virginia murmured to herself. Only not just for servants, but for all women. All women were outsiders. But there were advantages to this. It should not be given up so easily. That was what Lottie didn't understand.

Virginia picked up the spiral notebook that she kept on her night table and scribbled the following:

> Society of Outsiders
> All Women
> Positive thing—don't give up outsider status
> Letter about the war—work it in

> How can women remain outsiders and yet gain access to the "inside?" How do women get what men already have without sacrificing that which makes us women? How do we gain rights without giving up who we are? If there only were an answer ... If I could come up with such an answer ... maybe then we could also know how to prevent war.

Virginia closed her notebook and forcefully shut her eyes, though her mind reeled After much concentration at relaxing and mentally turning herself off, she went to sleep. But even in sleep, she could find no respite from her creativity for it exhibited itself in her dreams. She dreamed she was looking at a group of women standing on the corner of Piccadilly. She could see them clearly but was invisible to them; it was as though she were standing on the hidden side of a two-way mirror. The women she observed were standing outside a cinema house, complaining that the manager would not let them inside even though it was pouring raining. They were all in their forties or fifties, and they wore the same oversize straw hat, tan with a pink ribbon that wrapped around the middle. One woman, who seemed to be leading the group, pounded on the wood frame of the door. The glass rattled.

"We are the Society of Outsiders. Open the door for us. We are the Society of Outsiders. Let us in at once!"

Even in her dream, Virginia caught the ironic humor of the woman's statements. The spokesperson had just proclaimed herself an outsider; bloody hell, let her stay outside then! Virginia guffawed, not just in her dream, but in her sleep as well. She kept hearing the voices echoing, *Society of Outsiders, Society of Outsiders, Society of Outsiders* ...

Nellie heard her employer's louder-than-normal rumblings as she passed her room and decided to go in to check on her. She deliberately passed Mrs. W's room every night. It was the last thing before she retired to the basement for the evening. If she heard nothing, she kept walking. If there was even the slightest hint of trouble, she would investigate. Slipping into the room soundlessly, Nellie noticed the white afghan quilt that was a permanent fixture on the bed (it had been knitted by Vita and was a birthday present) in disarray at the edge of the bed, crumpled up like a discarded sheet of paper. Nellie smoothed its edges and covered her employer with it. Virginia was tussling about, still in the throes of her dream. Nellie put her hand firmly but gently on Virginia's side. Almost instantly, the authoress stopped fussing. Assured that the missus was now fast asleep, Nellie went down to the basement and got into her own bed. It had been a long day. She was dead to the world within minutes.

Chapter Twenty

Hogarth House

When Lottie recounted her impromptu chat with Virginia about the nature of servitude, it was all Nellie could do to keep from laughing in the maid's face. Despite the fact that Lottie had recounted the event in great detail, the whole notion was too absurd for words. Yet it was the very absurdity of the notion that made it doubtless in Nellie's mind that her housemate spoke the truth. She knew without question that the event had happened, exactly as Lottie had said it (although Lottie was often known to exaggerate details, especially if they were in her favor).

"My darling, Lottie, you must surely understand how preposterous it all sounds to me! A famous writer like she is, interested in the likes of us. What could it possibly matter to her what it feels like to be a servant? Why would she care?" The laughter escaped her now and erupted like a tidal wave.

Lottie's face reddened, and the bile churned in her stomach. She slapped Nellie across the face, hard. Nellie stopped laughing.

"What the fuck was that for?"

"What was that for? Are you serious? You're fucking jealous. That's what that is for. All the times I complained when you shared her bed, wiped her arse, or did anything else, you told me there was nothing to be concerned about, I was being foolish, do you remember that, Nellie, foolish? Well, now that the tables have turned for five minutes, you're the one who is jealous. You're so friggin' full of yourself that you can't even consider the idea that she might be interested in someone else's opinion other than yours. She wanted to talk to someone else for once, and it's making you crazy."

Nellie's shoulders stiffened and her back arched. Part of what Lottie said was true; she was a little jealous, not that she would ever admit it.

"That's absurd, Lottie. Of course, I don't care whom she speaks to, and I'm glad that for once the two of you may have bonded—"

"Hold on, I didn't say anything about bonding with Mrs. Woolf. We simply talked, is all."

"Still, all the same I *am* glad the two of you got to talk a bit. It's just that I can't possibly understand why she would ask you such a ridiculous question, or how you could possibly answer it. How could anyone answer such a question? We are what we are born into. If we know of nothing else, how can we explain what it is to be who we are."

Lottie hated it when Nellie waxed philosophical, especially since she couldn't keep up. Lottie had always believed that if Nellie had been born a man, she would have been sent for further studies, maybe even sent to university on scholarship.

"I don't know anything about that, but I still can't believe you are upset over one conversation with that jerk," Lottie answered.

"I'm not upset;" Nellie retaliated. "I don't care that the two of you spoke without my being there. I just don't get the point of the conversation."

Lottie grinned devilishly. "Now I've put my finger on it, for sure. You don't care that she asked my views, that's all well and good. It's the fact that she asked for my viewpoint *instead* yours. *That's* what's sticking in your craw. She wanted to know what I think and not you, and it's eating your guts out. Why don't you just admit it?"

Nellie's sullen silence only served to further fuel Lottie's anger. "You think you're the only one who is something around here. You think I'm fucking trash, I know you do, like I could never compete with you. Well, maybe I can't." Unbidden tears began to well in Lottie's eyes and threatened to erupt like Vesuvius down her cheeks. "But let me tell you something, Ms. Nellie Boxall, I am Lottie Hope, and I AM SOMEBODY. I grew up being told I was nothing, common trash, so much so that I got to believin' it myself. But no more. I am someone, I matter, and I ain't kowtowin' to anybody, especially not the likes of you, being of a station no better than mine."

Nellie dropped the issue quickly, partially out of guilt, but also out of fear. Nellie had never seen her housemate so enraged. Who could tell what the result might be? In spite of herself, Nellie still could not understand the point of that ridiculous garden chat. What could Mrs. W possibly have been thinking?

When she would later reflect privately on the chat with Lottie, Virginia would likewise fail to see the point of the questions she posed. They seemed as futile as the supposedly learned Talmud scholars who spent countless hours debating whether or not a goat has a soul.

No matter how frivolous her questions may have been on that day, Virginia would be forever grateful that she had asked them. She felt certain that the information she had gathered would be used at some point. She had no idea where or how she would use it, but she would; of that she was certain.

Chapter Twenty-One

Leonard was on edge. Hitler was advancing; all of Europe feared his prowess. The Woolfs were taking precaution. The bottle of lethal poison sat in the garage, ready to be consumed the moment the Nazis should, G-d forbid, occupy London.

It was the last week of the month, and as usual, Leonard was preparing the checks that were due at the beginning of the month. The monthly was singularly painful for Leonard. At dinner parties, Virginia liked to recount the time that Leonard had been to the dentist and had four infected teeth pulled out. She joked that before seeing the dentist and throughout the entire lengthy procedure, Leonard never said ouch. Only when the receptionist handed him the bill for the procedure did he begin to feel any pain. She would roar when she told that story, insisting that once again, his heritage was to blame. They all pinched pennies, she would joke endlessly. Leonard found her jokes wearisome, though he rarely said so.

So there was Leonard, going over the household expenses, like he usually did, with a fine-tooth comb. When he came across the grocery bill, he let out a yelp. "Nellie!" he bellowed. "Nellie!"

Nellie ran in from the kitchen, slightly out of breath and still holding a knife in her left hand (she had been dicing onions for soup when the master started yelling). She had no idea what she was in for, half-expecting him to be bent over in agony, blood gushing from his chest.

"What is it, Mr. Woolf? What's the matter?"

"This!" he exclaimed, holding up the grocery bill and shaking it in the air. "How can this be? Look at the amount here." He stood up angrily and thrust the bill in her face. She wanted to take the knife in her hand and plunge it into his heart. He had frightened the wits out of her. Instead, she exhaled slowly, dropped the knife on the desk, and took the bill from his hand. She glanced at the "total amount due," skipping the itemized charges, and nodded in the affirmative. "Yes, it is all in order, what is the trouble?"

Leonard was ready to hit the ceiling. "All in order? You can look at this balance and stand there with a straight face and tell me it's all in order? How is that possible?" Nellie remained silent. "Don't just stand there staring at me, damn you, tell me. Explain yourself." The obstinate silence remained, bringing Leonard's temper to a boil.

"Look at this bill" He began to shake the paper violently in front of her. She gently tapped his hand to get it out of her face. "The bloody royal family doesn't consume this much in groceries in one month."

"Really now? I had no idea you were so well-acquainted with not only their majesties but their grocery list as well."

Impudence only infuriated Leonard further. How dare she be so flippant with him! The whole world was holding its breath, and this simpleton was spending money like it was flowing up the Thames.

"How can you justify such outrageous expense? Did you do the grocery shopping at Harrods for Christ's sake?"

"No, at the usual stores," she calmly responded to the smart aleck remark that made her want to smack him upside the head. While she refused to take the bait, she would stand up for herself.

"As far as justifying the bill, I think I've worked here too long for me to have to *justify* anything. I bought what we needed or what the missus or you told me to buy. I can't help it if Hitler's threats are causing a panic and driving all the store owners to triple their prices. But I'll not be accused by you. No, sir, I've never been dishonest a day in my life, and you damn well better know it."

Leonard's anger was now tempered with a twinge of shame. "I know you are honest, Nellie. You'd have gotten the sack after the first week if I had any doubts. That's not the issue. I'm sorry if that's how it sounded. The issue is that this bill is outrageous. We need to be conservative these days for precisely the reasons you mentioned."

"Yes, Mr. Woolf, I do understand for sure. But as I said, I bought nothing out of the ordinary." She pointed to the upper portion of the bill that itemized the expenditures. "If you'll take a look here, you'll see that there's nothing I don't always buy. Everything is exactly as it is every month, it's just that everything has gone up, is all, like I said before."

Leonard, of course, had no idea what was usually purchased. He normally scanned the bill, making sure there were no charges for anything outrageous, then simply checked the balance and wrote out the check. So examining the bill too closely would have been moot. Nellie knew this well and used it to her advantage.

"Well, let's do try and cut back, wherever we can. We just can't go on spending like there is nothing wrong in the world and everything is the same as it always was. We must be judicious, always judicious."

By this point, Nellie was vexed and in the mood to challenge. "I see. And exactly how judicious are *you* being when you purchase those endless bottles of wine and brandy for your company and smoke those dreadful cigars that stink so badly, the missus gets positively ill and Lottie has to air out all the rooms and shampoo the carpets?"

"Well, sure I … I mean …" Nellie was satisfied. Leonard's sputtering was a sure sign that he did not know what to say.

"Never mind, Mr. Woolf. It is surely your money you are spending, if you care to spend it on things to appease your friends, however boorish they may be, it is your privilege, I can't deny. I'll try to be more cautious in the future." The issue was resolved. Leonard was satisfied with her deference, and Nellie was smug with her victory. Both of them were pleased with themselves, and they went on with their respective days.

During a walk after dinner to take in some fresh Richmond air and get in a little exercise (for she was getting a bit stout, if her dresses were any indication), she reflected on the confrontation with Mr. Woolf. Despite the brevity of the conversation, and the fact that everything had been settled between them, the thought of it even now enraged her. *The bastard doesn't trust me!* she said to herself and bit her lower lip so hard it almost bled. *He says he does, but he doesn't.*

If he did, he never would have confronted me that way. He would have done it differently, as a question, not an accusation. For sure, he wouldn't come at Mrs. W the way he did me. She'd have stuck him in the eye with her pen. He's lucky I didn't go after him myself. The nerve of him! She pounded her foot on the ground. A stray cat yelped and then gave a short hiss. She had unwittingly pounced on its tail.

What angered her most of all was not his lack of trust, she didn't care about him enough for that to really matter. It was the desperateness of the situation; that's what bothered her most. He was the employer; he held all the cards. All she could do was grin and bear whatever he decided to dish out. She thought, not for the first time, about the situation of the Negroes in America, long freed from slavery but barred from enjoying most of the privileges the white people took for granted. She thought her situation was parallel. Like him, she was free, but subject to the whims of someone else. Like the Negro, she was expected not to want to eat at the table, but to be grateful for its scraps. The whole experience of it sickened her to the pit of her stomach.

She truly believed she was important; she believed she was worthwhile. She had her purpose in life and it was an important one. Yet moments like what had happened earlier, despite a hundred apologies that might come after, were just reminders of how terribly unimportant she really was and of how little she really mattered. The shame of her station burned through her body the way brandy did when she would take it to clear up her indigestion.

Two nights later, Leonard came home with a treat, a transparent but appreciated nonetheless attempt to smooth things over with Nellie. Gertrude Stein, the renowned French novelist who lived openly with another woman, was coming to give a talk at the British Library in a few weeks. The event was by invitation only; all of London Society was going to be there. It was said the Prince of Wales himself was planning to attend. Leonard secured not one but four invitations. It was because he was her publisher, but he was certain everyone would think it because he was a fellow Jew. When he presented the tickets as a surprise to the household, the reactions were mixed.

"Leonard, how absolutely charming! To hear Gertrude Stein speak is a once-in-a-lifetime chance. I've wanted to meet her ever since you got her as a client. Oh, we'll have a grand old time, won't we, Nellie!"

"Why sure, ma'am, it isn't every day that one meets someone as notorious as that lady. She is known all over the world, I'd wager." Nellie gave it some thought. "Maybe I can fix a special dinner for her, assuming Mr. Woolf can persuade her to eat with us. It might be very nice."

Virginia chuckled. "Oh, no, Nellie dear, this occasion is much too splendid for a home-cooked meal. No, this is a situation to be celebrated grandly. Not that your cooking isn't grand, my dear, but this occasion warrants going to a restaurant." Virginia went into one of her famed trances, talking half to her audience but mostly to herself.

"Yes, a lovely little restaurant right by Green Park. A place with character, with paintings on the wall and a real Georgian feel to it. Gertrude Stein is used to the finer things in life—to class. We must go out of our way to give her first class treatment."

Leonard nodded in agreement. "Absolutely. The sky's the limit, especially when it comes to someone like Gertrude Stein. The money we make off her books alone keeps the Hogarth Press afloat for half a year, by Christ."

Virginia patted the left side of Leonard's face, as though he were a dog she was petting. "That's my Leonard. Always keeping the pounds in perspective, no matter what else may come. The king himself could stand on our doorstep asking for tea, and the entire time, Leonard would be calculating the cost."

"Well, someone has to think of money, my dear, if they," he pointed to Nellie and Lottie, "are not to be in the street with us lying next to them." The resentment in his voice was palpable.

"Of course, darling, I know that. I wasn't implying anything. You mustn't read into anything I said."

"After all, not all of us have an annuity coming in every month," Leonard grumbled, just loudly enough for Virginia to hear him. He walked away from the women, and Virginia chose not to follow him, despite her annoyance at the callous remark. She had learned long ago that a row with Leonard was pointless. They were both too pig-headed to admit defeat. Nothing was ever resolved.

Virginia meanwhile turned her attention to the servants. "Won't this be the most divine evening ever? I can hardly wait. We must look our best for this, all three of us. We'll have to get new dresses, no matter the heart attack Leonard will have at the suggestion."

"None for me, ma'am, but thank you anyway." Lottie's interruption surprised Virginia and Nellie. "I appreciate the offer, I really do, but if it's all the same to you, I'd rather pass. Hearing writers talk never did do much for me." There was a brief pregnant pause. "Not meaning you, of course, ma'am," Lottie added, only half-hiding the smirk on her face.

"Of course not," Virginia responded coldly. "Well, Lottie, if you choose not to avail yourself of the opportunity, I certainly am not going to force it on you. You are excused from attending."

Lottie resented being excused, for it implied that she needed to be excused. She was not a child requesting release from the dinner table but a grown woman making her own decision.

"I shall ask Vita to come. I know she will be delighted."

"What a grand idea, ma'am. I'm sure she will be thrilled." Nellie smiled sweetly. She could have killed Lottie right there and then.

*****

The grand event came. Gertrude Stein spoke in the main reception area of the British Library. A makeshift stage had been prepared for her, at the center of which stood a shaky podium and a microphone that made more static than anything else. On the side of the stage, Alice Tokalas, Gertrude's longtime lover, twitched nervously, not bothering to sit in the chair provided for her. The slightest crackle in Gertrude's voice sent Alice rushing over to pour water into the writer's glass. If Gertrude reached for her papers, Alice was there again, arranging them for her.

The event was standing room only. The twelve rows of chairs that had been set up were filled before noon; Gertrude was not scheduled to speak until two. The first two rows were reserved. In the first seat of the first row sat the Prince of Wales, the prime minister sat to his right. To the right of the PM was the Speaker of the House of Lords. Leonard sat at the end of the first row, his face gleaming. Four guards stood by the first row, two on each side, lest some well-read lunatic attempted to ambush the dignitaries. Virginia and Vita were in the second row, behind the PM and the Speaker, respectively. Nellie sat in the third row, behind Virginia, squashed between a man who reeked of garlic and an overweight woman who sweated profusely and appeared to be morally opposed to bathing.

The reading lasted an hour; the question-and-answer period another half hour. As soon as it was over, Leonard approached the podium to introduce himself to the writer and to offer himself as an escort. Alice intercepted his gesture of chivalry by pushing aside his hand and letting her lover grab her own hand instead. Gertrude smiled at Leonard and grasped Alice's hand firmly.

"Ms. Stein, I cannot tell you what an honor it is to meet you in person," Leonard gushed.

"Thank you, Mr. Woolf. I am very pleased to meet you as well. Your checks are always exactly on time. In all my years of dealing with publishers, I cannot tell you how rare it is to find one who pays his bills promptly. Some of them are so slow that by the time the check comes, you could starve to death."

"Thank you for the compliment. It means ever so much coming from you." Leonard quickly got to his intended point. "Ms. Stein, my wife, Virginia," he pivoted and signaled for his wife to approach, which she did posthaste, "would like to invite you out to dinner tonight, on us, of course." He smiled and then, looking into Alice's eyes, hurriedly added, "That invitation is open to both of you, of course."

"Thank you very much. Alice and I would be pleased to come."

Leonard beamed. "It is settled then. We shall pick you up at your hotel. I understand you are staying at the Savoy, is that correct?"

Gertrude nodded in the affirmative. "Yes, that is quite right. The Savoy is the *only* place to stay in London."

"The Ritz is quite nice as well, I think," Alice offered. The look on her companion's face told Alice that she had spoken out of turn. Virginia noticed the look and felt immediate sympathy for the speaker.

"Oh, yes, I quite agree that the Ritz is lovely, I've stayed there myself. But I'm afraid Leonard also prefers the Savoy."

Gertrude scoffed. "Well, *we* are at the Savoy. Shall we say seven?"

"Splendid," Leonard exclaimed. "We will pick you up around six. I'll ring your room from the lobby when we arrive."

The foursome arrived at the restaurant promptly at seven. Vita was invited but declined. She had the strange feeling that she would not be welcome, her invitation notwithstanding. Virginia had the foresight to ring ahead to make a reservation, so their table was ready when they arrived. Gertrude lit up her cigar as soon as they were seated. Alice shifted uncomfortably in her seat and discreetly covered her mouth with the cloth napkin. She coughed into it once.

"Oh, Alice, please. Grow up," Gertrude rebuked.

"Shall we decide on what we all want?" Virginia led by example by opening her menu and scrutinizing it, suddenly regretting having had the idea for this get-together and wanting to get it over with as quickly as possible.

Leonard had the poached salmon, Virginia the filet of sole, Alice the Caesar salad, and Gertrude had prime rib. They talked mostly about books. Gertrude and Virginia had opposite tastes in novels. Virginia adored George Eliot and found James Joyce intolerable. Gertrude thought Eliot ridiculous, borrowing Virginia's phrase about "silly women novelists." Joyce was everything there was to know about in literature, according to Gertrude. They argued briefly, without animus. Leonard and Alice chatted briefly about politics, both of them being having political leanings more to the left. Mostly, their talk was meant to diffuse the tension created by the writers.

When dinner was concluded, they went to the Woolfs' home for coffee and dessert. Lottie had met them at the door and ushered them in. She gave not the slightest inclination of awareness of who was in her midst. As far as Lottie was concerned, the women were just two more pesky guests she would be expected to serve and clean up after. Nellie's approach to the visitors was a different matter. She extended her right hand in greeting, telling Gertrude how much she enjoyed her talk and how wonderful her books were to her. She rather ignored Alice, deeming her at once to be nothing more than a shadow of the lamp of greatness.

The novelist did not respond well to Nellie's salutations. Rather than offering her hand in kind, Gertrude recoiled, as though Nellie were some deadly contagion. Nellie looked over at Virginia, who gave her a sympathetic nod. She herself was quite tired of this overbearing woman. She would much have preferred to visit solely with Alice; but Alice was not the legend. It was not Alice who sold books. Alice did not make large sums of money for the Hogarth Press. And yet one felt entirely comfortable with Alice, and entirely uncomfortable with Gertrude.

Once the hosts and guests were seated, Nellie went to make the coffee and take the dessert out of the icebox. She had made her best dessert: a cake made of chocolate pudding in between layers of graham crackers. She kept the cake in the icebox, since it was best served cold, with generous helpings of cool whip. It was in the icebox for several hours now, in prime condition to be served. She brought out the cake first, so they could admire it, while Lottie set the table. Nellie returned to the kitchen and put on the kettle because Alice requested tea. Nellie took out a lemon, just purchased that morning, and sliced it thinly, putting two slices on the side of Alice's cup. Coffee and tea were served, and Lottie dug into the cake, serving each person according to the size of a slice requested.

Within forty-five minutes, dessert was over, the coffeepot was drained, and Alice had finished her tea. Lottie was about to ask if more tea was desired when Gertrude gave Alice a certain look, and Alice jumped up from her seat saying that they needed to get back to the hotel, it was late, they had had a long day, etc., etc. Virginia saw them out the door, and Leonard drove them back to the Savoy. As soon as they were in the car, safely out of earshot, Nellie let out a loud sigh of relief.

"Whew! Thank heavens they're gone! I don't mind telling you, ma'am, that lady is cold, real cold. I mean, did you see the way she reacted when I went to shake her hand?"

Virginia nodded. "Yes, like you would poison her with your very touch. Disgraceful. It certainly does not speak well for the manners of the French." She began to talk to herself again. "But still, to have had Gertrude Stein in one's own home, to have drank coffee with her and found her distasteful, or divine, or devilish, it doesn't matter, you see. All that matters is that one has met her. It is a sign."

"A sign, ma'am? A sign of what?" Nellie asked, though instinct told her she shouldn't.

"It is a sign," Virginia paused before continuing, "that made one's mark. It is a rite of passage."

The servants did not answer, but cleared off the table, putting the dishes into the sink. Lottie washed them while Nellie wiped down the table. Virginia went off to her study, despite the hour, to record the meeting in her journal.

Back in the privacy of her hotel room, Gertrude Stein made no mention of the day in her journal. In fact, she would never mention the experience, either in writing or verbally, again.

If Gertrude failed to be impressed, Alice succeeded. She thought her brief hostess quite remarkable, though she kept her opinion to herself. And she had to admit, Virginia had more of an affable, outgoing personality than Gertrude, who was much sterner. Many accused Gertrude of not having a sense of humor and of being incapable of laughing. Privately, Alice thought she agreed with Gertrude's detractors in this regard, though she would never admit as much to her lover. Alice was so enchanted with Virginia after their brief meeting that she began buying all her books. She kept them locked in an old trunk her grandmother had given her; Gertrude never touched that trunk. At night, after Gertrude had gone off to bed, or during the day while she was at the library, Alice would read Virginia's books voraciously, taking notes in the margins in blue ink for articles she herself wanted to write but knew she never would. One writer in a household was more than enough. Yet still she yearned for something more.

Chapter Twenty-Two

London
February 1928

Dusk fell over London. The bone-chilling wind heralded snow. Nellie was hurrying down Regent Street trying to catch the next Tube at the Oxford Station. The scarf that she had taken with her when she started her trip (with her susceptibility to colds, she really could not be too careful) was now wrapped tightly around her face, partially obscuring her vision. In her left hand was Leonard's briefcase, a worn-out brown leather briefcase with a combination lock that had broken long ago. The briefcase was heavy. It contained the corrected galley proofs of a thick manuscript that was due to go to press within the next few months, a few checks, signed contracts, as well as other miscellaneous items. She was tired. Her mission involved having to trek on the Tube from the house to the solicitor's office to pick up the signed contracts, then walk to the author's house to get the corrected galleys, then walk back to the Tube and get home from there. Ordinarily, Leonard would have handled this business, but he had spent most of the afternoon reading and furiously editing a new manuscript submitted to the Press. He became so involved with the work that he had simply lost track of time. He asked Nellie to go in his place, as a favor. He hated using couriers; they were so expensive and were often unreliable. When Nellie agreed to go, Leonard showed his appreciation by offering to take Virginia out for dinner that evening.

Nellie quickened her step, trying to get to the train before the snow started. As she was crossing the street, a young man with sandy blond hair and a wide smile driving a black car—whose make Nellie would later wish she had noticed—pulled up into the crosswalk, blocking her path. He rolled down his window, and she noticed something bizarre. He was wearing dark sunglasses. Here they were, outside after dusk, and he still wore sunglasses. Later, she would wish she had attributed more significance to this oddity, but at the time, she thought it simply a quirk of young man's nature.

"Excuse me, miss, can you give me directions to Piccadilly," the young man called out.

Nellie spoke, still several inches away. "Make a right at the next corner and then …" A car horn blazed in the background followed by a store alarm. Nellie's next words were inaudible.

"I'm sorry, I didn't hear that. Could you come a little closer?" the man screamed. She complied, wanting to be helpful but also anxious to get on her way; the wind was whipping up.

The gun aimed at her was small and black. The barrel was pointed directly at Nellie's chest. The blood drained from her face in an instant.

"Get in," the young man ordered. Nellie froze for a moment, unable to think. "I said get it now!" Nellie's eyes scanned the immediate area around her. "Don't even think about it. Get in!" She put her hand on his door and tried to open it. It felt like lead. "No, the back door," the man hissed. She opened the door with considerable effort and slid across the seat.

The young man turned off the engine and stepped out of the car, stretching to his full height. The gun was hidden in a pocket on the right side of his jacket. He opened the back door nonchalantly, as though he were reaching in to take out groceries, unzipped his trousers, and pulled back his underwear. His member stuck out, fully erect, like a second weapon pointed directly at her. Nausea swept over her like a tidal wave. She thought she would vomit the moment he got close to her.

The man slithered his way into the back seat, holding the gun firmly with his left hand, and reaching for her face with his right. He rubbed her face roughly; his calloused hand felt like sandpaper on her skin. He moved in to kiss her. When she reflexively recoiled, he smacked her with all his strength across the face. She was stunned for a moment and thought she had lost a tooth. He took advantage of the moment to force her head toward his lap with the hand that held the gun while simultaneously reaching up her skirt with his free hand. Nellie struggled underneath him but was no match for his brutish strength. He pushed his cock closer to her mouth. It touched her lips just as his hand was reaching behind her to her buttocks. At that very moment, she could not hold it down any longer. She retched, all over the car, his lap, his cock.

He jumped back, dropping the gun. Nellie saw her chance. She grabbed the gun and kicked him in the face, as hard as she could, knocking him off balance. She reached for the door; when he tried to overtake her, she fired the gun, shooting out the car window. The glass fell on him, and she ran out the door. She ran to the hospital down the road with all her strength. When she got to the emergency room door, she realized she was still holding the gun. She emptied the magazine, sticking the bullets into her pocket, and she tossed the gun into the large trash barrel directly behind the hospital. Shaking violently, she ran into the emergency room, past the guard at the door and the white-haired volunteer who smiled at you while she asked for your name and insurance information and gave you some forms to fill out. She ran toward the triage desk and attempted to go straight into the treatment room when a burly guard with a salt-and-pepper beard and oversize belly from too much beer and donuts and not enough exercise stopped her dead in her tracks.

"Sorry, ma'am, you can't go in there," the guard said as he leaped to his feet. He put his hands on either of her shoulders, gently, to get her to focus on what he was saying. Nellie jumped back and started shouting, "No, no, get off me, get off me!"

The triage nurse was a slender woman in her forties wearing a starched white uniform and a hat that sat lopsided on her head on her head half-unpinned. She was experienced and knew a woman in trouble when she saw one. The nurse got between the guard and the patient. "Let her go, Joe, I'll handle it," the nurse said.

"But I was only …" The nurse gave him an understanding glance, and he did not finish the sentence. He didn't want her to think him boorish. She turned and assessed the woman in front of her. She was shaking violently and wore a vomit-stained dress torn in the crotch area. The nurse spoke calmly in a low soothing voice, almost as if she wanted to lull the woman to sleep.

"What's the matter, dear?"

Nellie's shaking increased as she spoke. "I was attacked, at gunpoint. He could've killed me." She began sobbing uncontrollably. The nurse stood up straight as a board and flew into action. "Joe, call the constable at once." Turning her attention to Nellie she said, "Now, now, it's all right dear, you're safe." Gradually, Nellie stopped shaking. "My name is Abigail. What's your name?

"Nellie, Nellie Boxall."

"Well, Nellie, why don't you come with me so we can talk and get you cleaned up some. May I take your arm?" Nellie nodded in the affirmative, and the nurse led her gently to a cot in the far corner of the exam room. The nurse helped her to get onto the cot, whispering reassuring words to her at regular intervals. From the nurse's calm and assured demeanor, Nellie guessed that she was not the first woman with this problem that the nurse had encountered. She felt bad about the guard; he didn't do anything wrong, but she could not think about that now. She would apologize later.

The nurse pulled the curtain around them, ensuring privacy. She gave Nellie a gown and helped her change. She was calm when the doctor came to examine her. The constable was waiting outside when the nurse drew back the curtain. He asked so many specific questions, Nellie got the impression he might not believe her. It particularly vexed her when he asked if there was anything she wanted to add to her story.

"My story?" she asked. "My story? Do you think I'm making this up?" She pointed to her dress. "Do you think I ripped my own dress and bruised my own arm? My face is bruised. Did I smack myself too?"

The constable coughed apologetically. "I didn't mean anything by that, ma'am, just an expression. Poor word choice, I guess."

Nellie was mollified. "You have to understand, I work for a novelist, Virginia Woolf. She writes stories, when I hear stories, I think only of fiction."

Abigail intervened. "Of course, dear, but as the constable just explained, he didn't mean anything by it." She tried to lessen the tension. "Did you say Virginia Woolf? How lovely! I just adored *Night and Day*, though I am still trying to muddle my way through, for the second time, *Mrs. Dalloway*. Why don't we ring her up? Someone is going to need to come get you. We certainly can't have you taking the Tube."

"Mrs. Woolf doesn't like to go out so late. Mr. Woolf will probably come in the—oh no!" she shouted. "The briefcase. I lost it."

"What briefcase? What are you talking about, dear?"

"It was the reason I was out in the first place. Mr. Woolf asked me to pick up papers and the galley proofs of a book he is going to publish." She covered her mouth. "Oh no, everything's gone. Everything was in the briefcase. I think I'm going to be sick."

Abigail shooed the constable out of the area and got a pail for Nellie. The cook vomited her guts up for the second time in less than a few hours. Abigail placed her right hand firmly on the cook's back while she was bent over the pail. When it was over, Abigail took the pail away and came back with a washcloth, dampened with warm water, and a paper cup filled with ice water. She handed the washcloth to Nellie to clean off her face and then gave her water to drink. The nurse held her while she trembled and paid no attention as she rambled on about the briefcase. Abigail had been a nurse for more years than she cared to recall. It was common for victims, particularly crime victims, to focus their energies on some inconsequential matter, in this case, the briefcase. Abigail thought it was the brain's way of protecting the victim from fully processing what had happened, at least temporarily. When all seemed better, Abigail rang the Woolf house. Leonard answered the phone and promised to come right over. Lottie would come with him, bringing a fresh change of clothes.

When the officer returned, the conversation shifted from a narrative of what happened to a description of her attacker. Nellie could not give the officer much to go on. The only thing she remembered about the car was the color, black, and the fact that the car had four doors. She could only describe the man who attacked her in the most general of terms. Given what she said, half the men in London under thirty could be rounded up as suspects. The odds of her attacker being brought to justice were slim, the officer said. His tone seemed accusatory, as if it were her fault that she was not more observant while she was fighting for her life. But then, given her emotional state at the moment, she could not tell if she was reading into his words something that was not actually there.

Leonard drove to the hospital at breakneck speed, despite the snow that was already beginning to cover the roads. Lottie was sitting in the front seat along with him, totally forgetting protocol. Leonard did not notice the breach either. All he cared about was getting there quickly and safely. He pulled into the empty spot in the emergency room parking lot. Rushing inside, their hoods propped up, they quickly found their way to the white-haired woman, now reading a magazine, and gave her Nellie's name. The woman directed them to the appropriate spot. Abigail had come out and given Nellie's name at the desk, remembering that Nellie had never actually registered, so it would be impossible for anyone coming to get her to locate her. Leonard and Lottie rushed to the right area and found Nellie, sitting upright on the cot. Abigail was standing next to her like a guard.

The women embraced for what seemed like hours while Leonard stood by uncomfortably. When they broke apart, Nellie spoke to Leonard.

"Mr. Woolf, I'm so sorry. I lost the briefcase somehow in the struggle. I didn't even realize I didn't have it until just before the nurse rang you up. Whatever it costs you, I'll pay you back. I don't know how I lost it."

Leonard waved his hand in the air. "No, don't give it another thought, Nellie. The only important thing is you. You survived, that is what is important. You are part of our household, our family. Nothing else is more important than that. We would be devastated if something, God forbid, should have happened to you. Mrs. Woolf is home right now biting her fingernails to the bits waiting for us to bring you home safe and sound."

Lottie helped Nellie get dressed while Leonard headed for the billing office to discuss payment arrangements. To his delight, because Nellie was a victim of a crime, there was no bill for him to pay. In the event that the perpetrator was apprehended, he would be responsible for the charges. If not, the City of London would take care of it.

Snow was falling heavily when Nellie stood just outside the emergency room door, supported by Lottie holding her arm and the nurse with her hand on her back. There was a long wait for a wheelchair and an even longer wait for an orderly to escort the patient downstairs. Nellie just wanted to get out of there so they had improvised, by having her walk, closely attended. When she reached the cold snow-filled air, Nellie remained still, breathing sharply. The cold air hitting her and the snow falling on her face affirmed that she was alive. She had survived. Staring at the snow, Nellie noted the irony of the pure white snow, which looked so clean, in direct contrast to how dirty and impure she felt. Soon enough, Leonard was sticking his head out of the car window, encouraging the women to hurry. Nellie snapped back to reality and allowed Lottie to lead her into the car, where she was driven home.

The reunion at the Woolf house was full of tears, comforting words, and embraces. Virginia had spent the past hour wearing out the linoleum in the foyer, pacing back and forth, unable to remain still. She could not concentrate on anything except Nellie's return home. She would have been devastated if Nellie hadn't returned, if the bastard had killed her.

Nellie spent several weeks on bed rest, ordered by Mrs. W and encouraged by the doctor. A temporary cook was brought in, and would remain until Nellie felt up to resuming her duties. Leonard, grateful for Nellie's safety and overcome by a spirit of generosity and benevolence, paid Nellie during the entire time of her convalescence. He did not complain once, not even to himself, despite the significant hardship wrought by the lost briefcase. The contracts had to be re-drawn and re-examined by the solicitors. Leonard had to pay the extra fees, since the contracts were in his possession when they were lost. But the galley proofs were the worst of the lot. Thank God he had an extra copy of the MS that he could work on, re-doing all he had already done. He had to ring up the author in order to try to explain why the proofs would be delayed another few days. Authors were temperamental by nature. He did not want to panic the poor soul. Authors were more possessive of their books than most parents were of their children, but Leonard felt the man was owed a truthful explanation. The author understood what happened and said it was all right, but his tone conveyed annoyance. Oh, well, it could not be avoided. Uncharacteristically, Leonard did not even care about the man's moods, nor did he worry about him possibly withdrawing his MS and submitting it to another house, though he would have hated to see that happen. For once, finances did not factor into Leonard's thinking. At the end of the day, all that mattered to him was that Nellie was safely home.

Nellie's assailant was discovered three weeks later by a bobby on foot patrol in a back road on the outskirts of London. The man had been shot dead in his car. Death was recent. The medical examiner determined time of death to be probably no more than two or three hours before the officer had found him and radioed his superior. Based on Nellie's description of the car and the man, the Scotland Yard detective who had been assigned to her case rung up to request that she come to the morgue to make a positive identification. If it *was* him, the detective told her, she would also need to go to Scotland Yard to fill out some paperwork, so she should set aside about two hours—three to be safe. She might want to bring someone with her, a man perhaps. Women were known to become hysterical in those situations. Nellie declined the offer, preferring to go alone.

The coldness of the morgue frightened Nellie. Not only was the temperature very low, there was also a chilly feeling when you stepped into that room of white washed walls, tiled floors, and steel drawers, almost like filing cabinets. No artwork hung on the walls, no plants by the window. The room was devoid of emotion.

Nellie stood on the opposite side of a door with a large pane of glass that separated the section where the medical examiner would be with the corpse from where Nellie stood with the detective. The corpse was covered with a heavy green blanket.

"Now, Ms. Boxall, in a minute I am going to signal to the ME to remove the blanket. When that happens, I am going to ask you if you recognize this man. I must warn you, whether you recognize him or not, seeing the man's dead body will likely be a bit of a shock for you. I'll be standing right behind you when the cover comes off, to catch you in case you faint." Then he added, "You wouldn't be the first woman to faint in this room."

You don't know this *woman*, Nellie thought to herself.

"Thank you, I'm ready now," Nellie assured the detective. The detective nodded to the medical examiner who was standing patiently to the right of the corpse. Upon seeing the detective's signal, the medical examiner gripped the edges of the blanket with his gloved hands and pulled it down to around the man's chest.

"Ms. Boxall, do you recognize this man?"

Nellie stared at that face through the glass for several seconds before speaking. "Yes, I do recognize him," she eventually responded.

"And from where do you recognize him?"

"He's the man who assaulted me several weeks ago. He tried to rape me."

The identification over, the ME was about to cover the body and put it away when Nellie spoke up.

"No, wait, can I go in there and see him, up close?"

"Well, it's not usually done but …" He opened the door that separated them and spoke quickly. "Roger, hold it for a moment. The lady would like to see the perp up close."

The ME uncovered the body and waited. Nellie went into the room and stood up close to the body. She stared at him, reaching her hand out for a moment, almost touching him but holding back. Suddenly, she hocked up her throat and spat, right on his face. The detective blanched, and the ME was just dumbfounded. Nellie walked out of the room without saying a word. The detective brought her to the adjacent office to sign the necessary paperwork. Neither of them said a word about what she had done.

The amount of forms seemed endless. Apparently, even death had its red tape. Who would have thought? Nellie signed her name multiple times on multiple forms. The detective signed underneath Nellie's signature on each form, as a witness. The forms were necessary, he said, to close the case. Hopefully, this would give her closure. She would be able to put the whole awful experience behind her and move on with her life.

Of course I'm going to move on with my life, Nellie thought to herself. *What other choice is there? But how do I put this behind me when it is all I think about all day long?* The images of the attack played in her mind, like a picture film that kept playing, rewinding and playing again; a machine that would not turn off no matter how many times you pressed the button. She had supposed a trial, telling the world what had happened to her and looking her attacker square in the face when she told it, would stop the film from playing in her mind. She wanted to see in her mind the person she was before she was attacked. She wanted to be that person again. She wanted the satisfaction of seeing him rot in prison. She was owed that—that much was coming to her. No more.

When she left the office, Nellie was crying, not over the man's death, but over the fact that she would never get to see him go to trial, never get to see him locked up.

She was crying because she had been cheated. She would never get the justice she was due.

Chapter Twenty-Three

Richmond
April 1928

Recovery was slow and painful. Nellie still shook involuntarily at random times, and she jumped out of her skin at the slightest noise. While looking through peppers in the bins outside the local fruit-and-vegetable store, a car backfired. Nellie fell to the ground in an instant, the basket she was holding flying across the curb. She remained there, quaking, for several minutes, tears running down her face, until she realized what had happened. She felt ridiculous. She pulled herself up, still shaking in her shoes, and felt the perplexed stares of her fellow shoppers. Part of her wanted to say something, to explain, but she did not. To do so would only have made her into even more of a freak show than she already was at the moment. She stood at her full length, dusted herself off, and picked up the basket and its contents now lying on the ground.

    She went back to the peppers for a few minutes. Suddenly, she flung the basket down, covered her face with her hands, and cried hysterically. The people who had been staring at her moved away in fright, now convinced beyond a doubt that she was mad. When she composed herself, she ran off at breakneck speed, back to the house, where she fumbled with her key until it turned in the lock. Virginia was by the door when she got in and saw the frightened look on Nellie's face as well as the eye makeup streaked down her face.

    "Nellie dear, my heaven, what is the matter?" Virginia immediately went over to the cook and put an arm around her shoulder.

"Oh, ma'am, it was terrible. I was shopping for peppers, and a car backfired. It was nothing, but I am so edgy these days that I jumped out of my skin. I was so frightened I dropped the basket and threw myself down like a ninny. Everybody was watching. Then all I could do was cry. I was such a sight! Oh, I can never go to that store again."

"Fine. In that case, we can have Lottie do the vegetable shopping from now on. Will that help the situation?" Virginia winked, and Nellie began to relax. Both women chuckled. The tension of the moment was broken.

For the next few weeks, Nellie was the center of attention, for the first time in her life. Lottie and Virginia were attentive to her every need, making sure she was comfortable in every situation. Leonard stayed home more. After the vegetable store debacle, whenever Nellie needed to go shopping, he would suddenly and miraculously need to go somewhere in the same direction. He would go with her, either driving her or simply accompanying her on the Tube or for a walk. His rouse was obvious, but it was heartfelt, and it touched Nellie deeply. The entire household was united in one task: helping Nellie to get back to normal, as quickly as possible.

Friends and acquaintances did their part. E. M. Forster sent a bouquet of flowers with a card that read "one day at a time." Katherine Mansfield sent a note of support, in her cryptic handwriting. Friends of Nellie's who served in neighboring households came by all the time, gathering in the basement, offering to help fix dinner, or whatever else they could do. Nellie had never felt so supported and so loved. Even women who didn't care for her, those who were jealous of her position or the fact that she had someone, or whatever, sent cards or small token gifts. One cook in a nearby house, someone Nellie ordinarily detested, felt so terrible about what had happened that she cooked two nights of meals and sent them over to the Woolf household, with a note to Nellie saying, "I've been where you are. It gets better." The generosity of people overwhelmed her.

Over the next few weeks, that horrible film that in the first few days after the attack played in her brain nonstop paused and began to play only a few times a day. After a couple of months, it was down to once or twice a week, and before six months were passed, it turned off for good—except for snippets that would pop up unbidden and unexpected, but she could handle that. What got her through was the incredible support she received from everyone around her. Yes, the young man had taken something from her, so that she would always be angry. But through the experience, she had also gained something that was invaluable. The people that surround her showed her how much she meant to them. More than that, they taught her that "love conquers all" was more than just a catchphrase, and that family was not some abstract concept nor was it limited only to people who share blood. Nellie's family was here, in the house where she lived, the people she cooked for. She had never felt so close to them.

Interlude

"Wow! That must have been a dreadful experience for you."

Thomas gasped after I recounted the assault and its aftermath. He began to stare at me, like he was seeing me for the first time, even though we had met many times, and I certainly had not changed from the day he first met me at the Ritz. I shifted in my seat, slightly uncomfortable with his eyes piercing through me, as if to my soul.

"Yes, it was terrible, but it made me a stronger person. I looked evil in the face, and I did not balk. It was monumental. Besides, everyone was so supportive, even the nurse in the hospital. I never experienced anything like that before or after."

"It's only a pity that it took such a tragedy to make people come around."

I started to think maybe he had the wrong idea of what I was trying to say. "It wasn't like people were against me or anything like that before. It's just that I wasn't important, or didn't think I was anyway."

Thomas scratched his head. "And being attacked told you that you were important?"

I laughed. "Ironically, yes, it did." I felt I should explain. "In the sense that it made me realize that people cared about my welfare. You have to understand how it is with my kind of people, servants, I mean. We're supposed to fade into the background, blend in like the furniture. And I'd always done just that. I was quite good at it too. But then after the attack, things changed. All of a sudden it was all about me. People were talking about me, worrying about me, and not in terms of what was I going to make for dinner, or when would I go to the market. They were worried about my health, my happiness. As I said, I wasn't used to all that fuss, and it felt real nice."

Thomas got that look on his face again. I knew it well. It was that look that told me he was thinking about something that was bothering him. He stared at me for a few seconds; it looked like he was staring *through* me. I waited. He spoke soon enough.

"When my wife died, everyone was really nice to me too. People would stop over to see if I needed anything, women cooked for me, I think my icebox was full for weeks, though about half of it went into the trash because a lot of the time, I couldn't bring myself to eat. Yes, everyone was concerned about me. It should have been touching, I suppose. 'The milk of human kindness,' isn't that what they call it?" It didn't seem like he wanted a response, so I didn't give him one.

"But no, instead of being grateful, I was angry." This surprised me. "At first, I was gracious. Nothing offends charity givers more than ungratefulness on the part of the recipient of their charity. But inside I was boiling. How dare those people be there now, when Lisa was dead, when they should have been there while she was here. Maybe if anyone had paid attention, if someone had seen the warning signs …"

I felt the need to reassure him. "Thomas, I am sure there was nothing they could have done. I mean, from what you told me it sounds like if—"

"If *I*, her own husband, couldn't do anything, what could I expect anyone else to have done, right? Yes, I know, and the guilt of that weighed me down for a long time, threatened to destroy me, believe me. But even still, knowing that did not make me less angry at these people, no matter how angry I already was at myself. I was especially furious at Debbie, her fucking sister. They were so close, though God knows why—the woman is a parasite, always was and always will be. Debbie was up Lisa's arse for everything. Whenever she needed or wanted anything, there she was, asking. The one time my wife needed her, she couldn't be there, couldn't see the handwriting on the wall? Maybe if Debbie had seen past her own selfish needs just *once*, Lisa would still be among the living."

My heart ached for him, but I knew from experience there was nothing I could say that would make the hurt any less, no matter how long it had been. If he was still looking for answers, he was seriously wasting his time. There were no answers; an educated man like him should now that, should have figured it out a long time ago. I remembered when Lottie died. At first I looked for answers, but that didn't last more than a few days. I gave it up real quick, not because of all the people saying "it was God's will" or it was "all part of God's plan" or some equally meaningless dribble. No amount of church or sentiment made me feel any better. Certainly, nothing helped ease the pain of the long lonely nights. I learned real fast that there are some things you just have to go through.

"Thomas, it's terrible I know. When Lottie died, I didn't know what to do with myself most of the time. And to make it worse, like you, I also felt guilty."

I could see his interest was piqued. "You never told me. How did she ... pass?"

"It was a heart attack. She was simply having a cup of coffee when she, all of a sudden, clutched her chest and said she couldn't breathe. There was nothing anyone could do."

Thomas shook his head sadly. "I am so sorry, I had no idea how it happened." There was a look on his face before he spoke again. "Forgive me if I'm prying, but there is something I don't understand. Why do you feel guilty? She had a heart attack, it was a natural cause. What is there for you to feel gui—"

"I called the ambulance."

"I beg your pardon."

"I called the ambulance. I was right next to Lottie when she doubled over. I screamed and ran to the telly to ring up the ambulance. The ambulance came and took her to hospital. I rode with them. She died within a few hours."

Thomas's face softened. "You did everything you could. You were reassuring right up until the end. I'm sorry, but I still don't see why you should feel guilty."

Now I was getting real frustrated. It was hard enough as it was to relive all this. A college man like Thomas should have been able to put it all together without me having to spell it out for him.

"Don't you see, I told her everything was going to be okay when deep down I knew it wasn't. I lied to her, in her last hours of life." Now the tears were streaming down like rivers. "And I let her down. She died in a hospital bed, surrounded by strangers, instead of dying in our bed, with only me to watch. That's the way she wanted to, and that's how I should have let her go. She should have been able to expect that from me. It was only right."

Thomas looked as though he didn't know whether to hug me or slap me. I thought for a split second that he might opt to do the latter, except I knew he was too much of a gentleman for that. It might be that he thought I had no right to feeling the way I did, considering how much more of a tragedy he went through, but every person's tragedy was their own. Everyone had their own cross to bear. I didn't think he had a right to be comparing tragedies, if that's what he was doing at all. But then, I read into things too much, my big sister always said so.

"I understand your heartbreak, I really do. But you are punishing yourself for a crime you didn't commit. You called an ambulance, she died in the hospital. What else could you have done? It's unfortunate that she had to die there instead of at home, but at the time, you had no way of knowing if she could be saved. Every day, people have heart attacks and live. You were doing what you had to do, no more and no less. I'm the one who has to live with what I didn't do, the help I didn't call for, the cries that went unanswered simply because I couldn't hear them."

All of a sudden, I started thinking about Mr. Woolf. "I wonder if Mr. Woolf felt like we do after the suicide. I wonder if he spent time thinking about what he could have done, the signs he maybe should have seen, or whatnot."

"Maybe. It would be natural if he did go through that, but from what you told me about him, I doubt it."

I was starting to get annoyed that he didn't understand, again. Maybe you had to be there in order to really understand anything. Maybe the whole thing was so weird that no one else really knew what was going on. But either way, I was getting annoyed.

"It wasn't like he didn't care about her, you know. He absolutely did. It was just different than most husbands care about their wives. But then again, Mrs. W was not most wives. He was jealous of her, not that he would ever admit it, but he still wanted the best for her. He was very shaken up when she was in hospital. And then … I went to the funeral and passed by the house a few times afterwards. He was devastated, wore the same brown suit for days on end. Mrs. W would have yelled at him, for sure. I don't think he even realized it."

Thomas grew somber. He had this tendency to pout, not fully, like a five-year-old, but enough that it was noticeable. I gave him a look, and he snapped out of it.

"I see. Well, for someone who cared about her, he seemed to have a funny way of showing it, monitoring her medicine, treating her like she was her patient."

"I know what you mean, but you have to understand how it was. He had no clue what to do, he was terrified that she would kill herself at any moment. It wasn't like he was a control freak or anything, he just wanted to save her life."

"And protect his meal ticket, no doubt," Thomas said. After he said it, it looked like he regretted it, like he was afraid he'd upset me. He had, but not that much. He wasn't there; he didn't get it.

"I'm sorry about that, Nellie, I didn't mean to—"

"Forget it, it was nothing. But you have to understand. It's not that he was a saint or that everything was so perfect, but those two really did love each other, in their own way. Whatever he did, I'm sure he thought he was doing the right thing. I can't believe that he would deliberately try to hurt her, no matter how women's history has painted him."

"That could be very true, or it could be that you were too close to the situation to see it objectively. Or … the other possibility is that your memory is clouded with nostalgia."

That made sense to me, I guess. It didn't seem like I was remembering things any different than it was, but I couldn't see it. I guess we were going to have to just agree to disagree.

The more I thought about everything, the more nostalgic I became.

Chapter Twenty-Four

Richmond
1935

Virginia was finishing proofs for *A Room of One's Own*. She was sitting in St. James Park, a few blocks west of the Ritz (a fact that meant nothing to Nellie at the time). As usual, Nellie was with her. Normally, they would sit on a bench, but today was different. Today, Virginia wanted to get as close to nature as possible. They sat directly on the grass, without so much as an old sheet to protect their dresses. Spring was in full bloom, and the park was filled with the many colors of life. Unfortunately, the trees were also in full bloom, putting Nellie's hay fever into high gear. The missus always complained she had hay fever as well, but seeing as they had been sitting there for over an hour without so much as a sneeze from the missus, Nellie thought the condition was imagined.

As always, Nellie had been the first to read the manuscript, even before Leonard, though he would have pitched a fit if he knew. Virginia was so excited about the book that she talked about it endlessly.

"Karl Marx had his Communist Manifesto. This is my Feminist Manifesto. This book will be about women alone, and in many ways, it is for women alone. I doubt many men would want to read it anyway, ha ha."

Nellie laughed along with her mistress. "Not after the way you talk about men in the book, especially Professor X."

Virginia smiled and gazed into the horizon for a moment. She could see it, clear as day, a lecture hall, such as the ones in Cambridge or Oxford. Hordes of young men cramped into their seats were scribbling notes. In the front of the room was a podium made of old wood. Resting on it was an open manila folder containing pages of handwritten notes, typed and mimeographed handouts, and an exam. Leaning against the podium, speaking animatedly was a woman. Yes, a woman was giving the lecture—a woman was teaching the class. What a divine sight! Virginia could *krell* at the thought (a Yiddish expression she had learned a long time ago from her mother-in-law).

She turned to Nellie and stated, *sotto voce*, "Perhaps one day Professor X will be a woman."

"Sure, ma'am, anything is possible," Nellie replied although in her heart she thought it impossible to fathom.

Nellie had named the book in a moment of inspiration. They had been in the dining room, manuscript pages covering most of the cherry wood table. Virginia was vacillating between three or four different titles, her frustration mounting. Nellie poured her a cup of tea to relax her.

"Don't worry about it, Mrs. W, you'll find a title, I'm sure. After your tea, just go back to your room and think about it. It will come to you, I'm sure." Nellie thought out loud. "Maybe that's why you're having trouble. Because you're here in the dining room, instead of being in your own room. You know what you say in the book, ma'am, a woman needs a room of one's own."

Virginia choked on the tea she was sipping. "That is it! That is the exact title. It is perfect." She slammed her hand on the table; the cup overturned, and the tea spread like wildfire on the lace tablecloth. Virginia jumped back, and Nellie sprang into action while Virginia muttered an apology. Nellie waved it away.

"Don't give it a second thought, ma'am. I have it covered."

Virginia felt terrible. "I'm so sorry, Nellie. I really don't know what comes over me sometimes. Perhaps I ought to ask Dr. Savage—heaven knows he should be good for something."

Nellie waved her hand as though she were shooing a pesky fly.

"No, no, Mrs. W, no need to bring the doctor into this now, silly man that he is. You just get overexcited about things, especially your books. That's why you are such a great writer."

Virginia blushed at the compliment. With her all books and articles still in print, she still found it hard to hear someone say she was even a mediocre writer, much less a great one. She always received criticism much easier.

Sitting on the grass, both women felt exhausted. Virginia's state stemmed from the meticulous line-by-line reading of the proof pages. Nothing was overlooked; every letter was read, and every punctuation mark dutifully noticed. The work was essential but oh so dreadfully tedious. There was no task in the world Virginia despised more. As for Nellie, her exhaustion was from the endless struggle to keep the pages safe from the spring winds, which threatened to carry them off and dump them unceremoniously into the Thames River. Virginia noticed and appreciated Nellie's efforts. The sight made her start thinking. She began to think aloud.

"You know, Nellie, I probably don't ever say this, but the truth is I would *never* be able to do what I do were it not for you and Lottie."

Now it was Nellie's turn to blush. "Aw, Mrs. W, that's very sweet of you to say but—"

"Rubbish! Sweet has nothing to do with it. How could I possibly write books if I had to go grocery shopping, prepare the meals, scour the pots, tend to the house, and wash the laundry? It would be impossible to write even the roughest draft of a novel, much less one suitable for publication. It is no wonder one never hears of a laundress writing the next great English novel, or even a mediocre one for that matter. She simply has no time to write it. She would probably count herself lucky if she could salvage from her day time to scribble a few lines of the occasional poem."

Nellie reflected on what Virginia said and began to slowly nod her head.

"Now that you mention it, ma'am, I sure wouldn't have the time to go writing any books, not with the schedule I have to keep. 'Course, I don't worry about that since I've got no talent anyway."

Virginia patted Nellie's hand in a way that the cook would generally have considered patronizing but now read as caring.

"Don't you worry about a thing, Nellie. You have talents, albeit not literary ones. By Christ, I'd wager your talents are more practical than mine!"

Nellie smiled. "I do think you're right. No servant could do what you do, there wouldn't be enough time in the day. But then, I suppose that is why you someone like you has servants in the first place. You don't have to do those things because you have people to do them for you. And it's a good life all in all, no matter how much me and Lottie complain, but Lord if I don't sometimes want others to wait on me for a change." Nellie could not have known, when she made that statement, that if she waited long enough, she would be in apposition where just that would occur; people would wait on her, and only down the block from where she sat at that very moment.

Virginia stood upright and kicked her shoes off. Her stockings felt damp (Leonard felt it was too warm as of yet for her to go without stockings) as she stood on her tippy toes, reaching her fullest height as she stretched her arms out toward the sky. She wordlessly began to walk, paying careful attention to the colors of the flowers she was passing by. She adored gardens and loved flowers. She had written that one short story about a garden and wanted to write an entire novel about a garden, perhaps a woman tending a garden. A woman very much like Katherine's Ms. Brill, though not too much like her. Virginia's ego wouldn't allow for too many parallels to be drawn between her work and the work of another, even if the "other" was ostensibly a friend. Even if it was Vita. Walking like this, with the cool breeze on her shoulders and the earth at her feet, was exhilarating. The walk reinvigorated her; she walked the entire length of the park and back again. Usually, she could walk for hours, but lately, she tired easily. She worried that she was getting too little exercise, causing her recent fatigue.

Remaining on the grass, Nellie also worried. She worried that they would get back to the house too late for her to get an even decent dinner on the table by seven. And she wondered exactly how long she would be able to keep these pages from flying away.

*****

After the success of *A Room of One's Own,* the women in the house were on a special high. Virginia was certain she now knew how Mary Wollstonecraft must have felt when her *Vindication of the Rights of Women* first made it to the streets of London and was immediately gobbled up by every Victorian woman who could read. Invitations for Virginia to read and speak poured in from every bookstore in London. New York stores offered to fly her across the Atlantic to speak at several events. Nellie felt the effect as well. She traveled with Mrs. W to all her speaking engagements. Lottie could have gone but declined. They had been at Hatchard's. Virginia was speaking about the importance of a woman to have a room of her own and her own income in order to write fiction or, for that matter, to do almost anything creative. She talked about Professor X and speculated, publicly, as she had done privately with Nellie, that one day a woman could be Professor X. When that day came, Woolf promised, things would change for women.

Nellie reveled in her boss's success; it made her feel successful herself, the same way a father who could never play ball gets a vicarious thrill every time he sees his son running on a field with a ball. Lottie did not share in the excitement. When people came over to them—for Virginia graciously never failed to acknowledge them in her speeches, the women who, as she put it, "made her work possible" by keeping everything in order—Nellie would beam, and Lottie would fume.

"Who the fuck does she think she's kidding, talking about us like we're so fucking important to her?" Lottie would whisper to Nellie in their back row aisles, with just enough of an edge to her voice to be irritatingly audible to whatever poor chap had the misfortune of sitting next to them.

"That's why she is saying them, Lottie love. To show us that we *are* important to her, even if sometimes she doesn't say so. It's her way of making up for some of the other things."

"Fey! I don't believe a word of it. She is flinging this bullshit for her 'fans,' whoever they are. It's a joke. Half the people that come to these things are over sixty, and most of them don't even buy a book at the end. They just come for the novelty of it, and to have something to do."

"Now, now, you know that isn't true. She wouldn't be getting offers to fly across the continent and to the States if she were nobody special. She is a genius. Even you, Lottie Hope, can see that."

"Well, I'll admit she's no dummy, that's for sure. But I refuse to see her as this literary genius, not that I'm much of a critic."

"And at this point, I'd like to ask the women I could never do without, Lottie Hope and Nellie Boxall, to stand up and be recognized." Virginia smiled and lifted her right hand up. Nellie heard the comment only by chance and rose quickly, patting Lottie on the hip She got up too, and both of them put on big grins. The people sitting around them had pleased looks on their faces, the same looks one might have when seeing a delightful family of penguins at the zoo. Nellie didn't notice; she delighted in the recognition. Lottie understood. She burned with rage.

When the speech was over, the crowd got up to stretch their legs and help themselves to the wine and cheese offered, compliments of the bookstore. A cash box was conveniently set up right next to where the wine was being poured. Extra copies of the book were placed on either side of the box. To the farthest left side of the table sat some spare copies of *Jacob's Room*, *Mrs. Dalloway*, and *To the Lighthouse*, in case there was a reader new to Woolf who wanted to explore her fiction (or a reader too drunk from the free wine to recall whether or not he already owned copies). At a side table on the front right side of the room, Virginia sat patiently, nibbling on a plate of assorted cheeses and a few crackers, thoughtfully prepared for her by the store manager before the masses were served. Her wineglass was filled to the rim with some second-rate red wine (as usual, no one bothered to ask for her preference; the choice was made for her). She took the occasional sip out of pure thirst (she did not care for water and, in any event, had had quite enough of it while she was speaking) but left most of the beverage untouched.

Nellie and Lottie stayed toward the back of the room, not used to standing or sitting idle while people were eating and drinking. Lottie several times had to fight the instinct to clear people's places or to tend to the trash. They were hoping to chat among themselves, snack a little, but otherwise stay off the radar. It was not to be.

"Yourrr'e the womeeen who she was talkkking about, aren't you?" A fortyish woman with blond hair streaked with gray who wore too much heavy makeup and fake jewelry asked them as she wobbled up close to them. "You're the ones who work for the laaady?"

"Yes, yes, we are," Nellie responded quietly. The smell of cheap wine mixed with scotch on the woman's breath combined with the odor of cheap perfume made Nellie want to get sick. "Well, if you'll excuse us, I think Mrs. Woolf needs us." She turned to Lottie. "Come with me, please, Lottie."

As soon as they were out of earshot of the drunken woman, Lottie began to laugh uncontrollably. Nellie nudged her to keep her voice down. Nellie did not find the incident funny in the slightest. Instead, she thought it was quite annoying, and a bit pathetic at that. They walked across the room, headed toward the table where the missus was patiently signing books. An old man wearing a checkered sport jacket accosted them.

"So what's it like working for such a grand lady as this? Must be real fun, heh?"

"It is quite an experience, thank you. It is certainly never dull in our household, that is for sure," Lottie answered while Nellie looked the other way. The man reeked from body odor with the effects of very cheap cologne. Nellie began to wonder if every older person in all of London was in this very room.

"I should imagine not." The man, suddenly full of savoir faire, turned to Nellie and placed a hand on her shoulder to get her attention. She instinctively recoiled from his touch.

"I didn't notice a man with her, Virginia Woolf, I mean." He lowered his voice to the point that it was quite raspy. "Does that mean she is single?" He asked, a hopeful edge attached to the end of the sentence. Nellie wanted to vomit on the floor.

"No, as a matter of fact, she isn't. She is married, quite happily I might add. Now if you'll excuse me I—"

"How about you then?" He gave her a sideways glance. "I don't notice a ring on your finger. Maybe we can go for a drink, either right now or sometime soon."

If Nellie wanted to vomit before, now it was for certain. She faced him full-front, flashed her brightest smile, and said matter-of-factly, "Thank you, but I doubt I could ever be that thirsty." She place her glass and plate on a nearby table and walked away from him. Lottie followed in suit behind her.

They went outside for some air.

"Can you believe the nerve of that man? Asking if the missus was married and then asking me out in the next breath? Aggh!"

"He probably can't help himself, Nellie. You are very attractive, you know. Besides, poor thing, he probably hasn't had so much as a cup of coffee with a woman in ages."

"With a personality and a come-in like that, I know why, believe me." Both women laughed. "Besides, you didn't get the pleasure of smelling him. Disgusting! I can't imagine any woman on earth would want to get within ten meters of him unless she absolutely had to, unless she were some missionary angel doing God's work maybe."

At this they guffawed. They were so lost in their conversation that neither of them noticed Virginia standing right outside the bookstore door, looking obviously weary. She joined them, eager for some levity, after enduring such a long night.

"What is so funny, ladies?"

"Oh, missus, there were these people, a woman who had had too much to—"Nellie stopped abruptly when Lottie poked her in her ribs.

"It is really nothing, Mrs. Woolf. You had to be there to appreciate it," Lottie offered.

"Well, I may not have been there to appreciate whatever it was that was said, but I do appreciate you, both of you," she said, emphasizing the *both*. "I would not be who I am if I did not have you. I know it, Leonard knows it, and you both know it."

Nellie was overcome. "Aw, you don't have to worry about that, Mrs. W. We'll always be here for you."

When they got back to the house, Leonard was nursing a cup of herbal tea to calm his sour stomach, a consequence of too much acid. Virginia was forever scolding him for the amount of oranges he ate every day and the lemons that he would suck the juice right out of; she found it nauseating, and it was murder on the lining of the stomach. But as usual, he thought he knew best; on nights like this, he paid the price for his obstinacy.

"How was it?" Leonard called out as he heard the women come in through the front door, talking in hushed tones for fear of waking him.

"I had a perfectly darling time. I think we sold out every copy. Even some of my novels sold. Several people said they had read one of them but had never bought it. Since I was there and offering to sign whatever they bought, they said they would buy it."

"That is absolutely wonderful to hear," Leonard responded as he smiled from ear to ear. Nothing made Leonard giddier than the thought of big checks coming in his direction. "I am very proud of you, Ginia."

"Thank you, dearest." She pointed to the servants. "Unfortunately, Nellie and Lottie did not have as grand a grand time of it."

"Oh, what happened?" Leonard tried to feign interest.

"Nothing much really, Mr. Woolf. Just a couple of drunken fools trying to make small talk. One of them was a man with terrible breath. I think he was trying to pick up Nellie."

"He was not, Lottie, don't tell tales." A disgusting image flashed through Nellie's brain. "He drank so much, he probably couldn't get it up no matter how hard he tried."

All three women laughed at the coarse humor. Virginia, always having a wicked imagination and a penchant for bawdy humor, laughed the hardest. Leonard was not amused. The women ceased laughing when they noticed.

"In any event, Mr. Woolf, nothing serious happened, and they did serve good cheese and some mediocre wine," Nellie offered as a final comment.

"Well, that is just fine. I'm glad you found the experience satisfactory, and I don't have to tell you that I appreciate your both being able to make it, especially since I was unable to go myself."

"But of course they went," Virginia interjected. "We may all have our petty differences from time to time, but at the end of the day, they would do anything for me, and I for them." She extended her left arm and draped it around Lottie's shoulder, Nellie squeezed in with them. They stayed that way for a moment, smiling as though a photographer were there waiting to take their picture.

When they broke apart, Nellie made one final comment to Leonard before she proceeded to go with Lottie downstairs. "It's like we were saying to Mrs. Woolf earlier, 'We'll always be there for you and the missus. We're a family, no matter what. We'll always be together.'"

*****

Richmond
15 October 1936

But it was not to be.

Nellie and Lottie believed they would be in their positions forever, but Fate had other plans. Fall had arrived in England, bringing with it cool daytime breezes and nights just chilly enough that you needed a sweater or light jacket. Everywhere you looked, the leaves on the trees were bright orange, as if purposely done in time for Halloween. Everyone was in a good mood, perhaps because of the weather, perhaps because of the approaching holiday season, or maybe just for no reason at all.

It was shortly after dinner when things changed. The last of the dishes had been dried and put away. Lottie was waiting for Nellie to finish closing up the kitchen for the night so they could retire to the basement. Just as they were about to head down, Leonard popped his head in through the sliding door and asked both the women to join him and Mrs. Woolf in the living room for a few minutes. They complied without question or suspicion. It was not uncommon for

Leonard to call an impromptu meeting to discuss an issue of some importance. Once they were seated, the somber ambience of the room was lost on them. They sat on the couch, Leonard sat in his recliner facing them, and Virginia was on the love seat on far right side of the room near the bay window. She did not acknowledge the women's presence. She would not even look at them, choosing instead to gaze out the window at the foliage. She nibbled on some candy corn lying in a candy dish on the end table next to the love seat. The candy corn was Virginia's only concession to Halloween (she had a distaste for anything deliberately scary; she felt life was scary enough). Leonard cleared his throat and began the meeting.

"Ladies, this is uncomfortable, so I wish to get it over with quickly. Times have been tough for us lately, especially with the Depression upon us and war on the horizon. We have all felt the need to tighten our belts." He sat straight back in his chair before continuing. "Mrs. Woolf and I have figured out some ways to economize. As part of that," he paused for what seemed like hours, "I'm afraid we are going to have to let one of you go."

Nellie and Lottie gasped simultaneously. They could not believe what they had just heard. They looked to Virginia. She refused to return their glance for fear she might fall apart. Meanwhile, Leonard continued.

"We value you both, as human beings and as employees, and we sorely regret having to choose between you. But circumstances have made it impossible to continue the status quo. The one of you who is being dismissed will have until the end of the month to find a new position. Of course, if you find a position before the end of the month, you are certainly free to accept and begin it whenever is necessary. For the person staying, you will take on some extra duties, at an increased salary, of course."

Both women numbly nodded their understanding. Nellie was unsure if she could stand up if she were asked to. They waited for the moment of truth.

Leonard's face turned sour. He had given them to digest the information; now he had to finish the announcement.

"Well, we might as well get on with it. The person whom we have decided has to go is ... Lottie."

Nellie broke into tears; Lottie sat poker-faced, and Virginia rushed out of the room. Leonard resumed speaking again, not wanting to give Lottie a chance to respond. He was not sure if he could bear hearing what she might have to say.

"Lottie, I cannot tell you how sorry Mrs. Woolf and I are. It was an impossible decision, but all things considered, I think we made the right one. Of course, it goes without saying that we will give you excellent references. In fact," he reached into his left jacket pocket and pulled out a cream-colored envelope, "Mrs. Woolf has already prepared a letter for you, typewritten, and you know how much she detests using a typewriter." His eyes began to well; he was more affected than he expected to be. He extended his hand to her hoping to make the mood more businesslike, thereby keeping his emotions in check. But the maid would not cooperate. She took his hand for a second, then pulled his body toward her in a full-fledged embrace. The tears flowed from her eyes unabated and started to spill from his eyes as well. He patted her back several times in an awkward attempt to comfort her. Eventually, she pulled away, and they both wiped their eyes, trying to regain their composure.

"Where will Lottie live?" Nellie could always be counted on to be the voice of pragmatism. She had not moved from her spot the entire time.

Leonard was taken aback by the question. "Why, with her new employer, of course," he answered plainly as if to indicate that the answer were perfectly obvious.

"But why, if you'll pardon me for asking, Mr. Woolf? I mean, if you're not replacing her, then you don't need the room for someone else. Why should she have to uproot herself entirely? She already has to find a new job, does she really need to have to find a new *home* as well. Besides, I don't mind saying that I'd rather not be separated from her. We've kind of gotten used to each other." Nellie grinned. "I go to sleep at night by the sound of her snoring." She winked at her companion, who gave half a smile.

Leonard considered the idea. "I suppose it is a possibility. It's unconventional, but then, when has anything been conventional around here anyway?" It was supposed to be funny; it wasn't.

"So then Lottie can stay here?" Nellie ventured. Leonard was not taking the bait.

"I think that we might be able to work something out, but I also think that it's been a long day and a very difficult few minutes. We're all tired and on edge. Why don't we get a good night's sleep and discuss it again in a couple of days. Good night, ladies."

The servants were for the time being satisfied with his answer. They made their way down to the basement, eager anyway to be able to talk to each other freely, in private. Once they got down there, however, they found themselves simply staring, at each other and into space, too stunned to say anything.

"Maybe they'll change their minds," Nellie offered then immediately regretted the unintentional insult to Lottie's intelligence. They both knew the Woolfs too well to think they would waver on something as important as this. They had obviously thought it out, plotted a course of action, and were determined to see it through. Yet still she had hope. It did seem suspicious that Mrs. W did not say anything during the meeting and ran out before her opinion could be requested. But still they made their decisions together; of that she was certain. Which meant there was no hope for redress.

After the initial shock wore off, Lottie's anger took over.

"She did this, I'm sure of it. She did this to me because I've never liked her. I don't kiss her arse like everyone else does." *Like you do*, she wanted to say but didn't. "She likes people around her who praise her and make her feel wonderful. That's not me."

Nellie tried to smooth things over. "Now, Nellie, you know that's not true, not a word of it. In the first place, you do too like her, otherwise you wouldn't have helped her as many times as you have." Lottie was about to open her mouth in rebuttal when Nellie waved at her to stay silent. "But all that said, I know in my heart that Mrs. Woolf would never make a business decision based on personal feelings. She wouldn't be like that."

"Then why, Nellie Boxall, you tell me, why me and not you. What's so goddamned special about you!" She grew red-faced.

"I'm sorry, I didn't mean that the way it came out. You are special, I know that, and I love you for it. I just don't understand what makes you essential and me dispensable."

Nellie was hurt but stoic. "Well, I can cook a lot of different dishes. Cooking has never really been your specialty, you know, my dear. You have been known to burn oatmeal." She slapped Lottie lightly on her arm, and Lottie broke into a grin.

"But still, I work so hard, I really do everything they ask me to, without complaint most of the time. Even though some of the things they want are ridiculous. Why do they have to get rid of me? Let them stop smoking, if they want to save expense."

"I know it's hard, but you have to look at the bright side of it. This could open up all new opportunities for you. This may be all part of a plan."

"Easy for you to say!" Lottie answered back. "You have a job, you have security. The rug hasn't been pulled out from under *your* life. It's been pulled out from under mine."

"But that's just the thing, Lottie dear. You are not entirely displaced. The rug hasn't been totally pulled out from under you. Mr. Woolf as much as said as he will let you still live here. As long as you live here, not much will change. We will still see each other."

"Yeah, in the morning, as I'm hurrying to get dressed to go to work, and at night, when we're both too exhausted to even carry on a decent conversation. What rot!"

Nellie was more optimistic. "It won't be that bad. Well, maybe it will be at first, actually, but once we get used to it and into a routine, it will be just as it is now, except that we won't fight as much."

"That is true. We will have very little time to get on each other's nerves, I'll wager, and we won't be fighting about *her* anymore, since I won't be working for her."

"You see, there is something positive in everything," Nellie said with an optimism in her voice that belied the feeling of despair nestled in her heart.

Lottie was not fooled by her housemate's show of bravura, but she appreciated the effort and let herself by comforted by it. She would have to find another job; it was as simple as that. And when you thought about it, how many times had she thought or talked about doing precisely that. The only difference was that had been talk; this was now necessary action.

Two weeks flew by. Before Nellie knew it, she was working alone. Lottie found a job right away, working in a bed-and-breakfast. The pay was good, and Leonard charged her practically nothing in rent, so most of the money stayed in her pocket. She had little to do in comparison with the amount of work she had with the Woolfs. In her new position, she cleaned the guest rooms and made the beds in the morning and cleaned the common areas. Once that was done, she was pretty much done for the day, except for cleaning up after the meals. The place was never filled to capacity, and the empty rooms did not have to have the beds made obviously. They were not really cleaned either, just a light dusting. When a guest left, the room was scrubbed down, eradicating all traces of the person ever being there. The extra money went into the bank, and Lottie spent a lot of her downtime walking, either on the property of the bed-and-breakfast, or through London when she would hop on the train. All in all, it was not a bad life. In fact, Lottie began to think Mr. Woolf had done her a favor.

It was Nellie who got the short end of the stick. Her workload nearly double, yet her salary increased by not even 5 percent. Lottie came home from work every day, bubbling with energy and enthusiasm, while Nellie suffered from near exhaustion. Nellie was overworked and felt less appreciated than ever before. Even the comfort of having Lottie beside her in bed at night was often not enough to offset the feeling of being slighted.

Much to her own surprise, Virginia missed having Lottie around during the day. She had been very upset when Leonard let her go, though they had made the decision together, but it was simply because she disliked confrontation and hated to see people hurt. She and Lottie had never liked each other, not one bit. Yet in spite of herself, the writer felt a profound sense of loss. Seeing Nellie dusting the rooms that Lottie had once dusted, it was as though things were out of place. The house felt different, like it was out of harmony. Of course, in time, she would adjust; they all would. One always learned to adjust to new circumstances, no matter how good or bad they might be. There was no other choice really, except one. You had to go on living, unless of course you didn't. Life would get back into some type of normal routine, but Virginia doubted very much if the house would ever have the same feel to it again, or the same vibes.

Katherine Mansfield dropped over, unannounced as usual, the day after Lottie started her new job. Nellie had to prepare the tea for her and serve it. She wanted desperately to take the kettle and pour every last drop into Katherine's lap. Just seeing the look on that self-righteous bitch's face would make whatever consequences Nellie suffered worth it.

The comments began right away. "Whatever happened to the other girl you had here, Virginia? The one who served the tea and cleaned up everything so nicely?"

"We had to let her go, it was too expensive to keep two servants," Virginia explained to Katherine in a very low voice, as if keeping her voice down would spare Nellie's feelings on the subject. Nellie was grateful for the gesture, futile as it was, and just as angry at the guest for bringing it up. Katherine had to have already known Lottie was gone. Nellie was sure employers discussed such things with each other. She must; after all, servants had such discussions all the time. Ask any servant in all of England, and you could find out who paid the most money, who paid least, and who was a slave driver. There was no way Katherine did not already know about Lottie before stepping foot into the house. That made her question an act of deliberate cruelty, which, as Blanche Dubois would later say, was the one unforgiveable sin.

"It's too bad. I rather liked her," Katherine murmured, trying to sound convincing. She didn't convince Nellie.

"It's a lie! You never liked her at all. You hardly like yourself, which fits since almost nobody likes you either."

Katherine stood in a state of stunned disbelief. Virginia was horrified and sat spellbound in her chair.

"Well, I don't know about that," Katherine responded. "Like everyone, I have those who find my distasteful, but I most assuredly *do* have friends and people who love me." She tilted her head toward where Virginia was sitting.

"Bullshit! They all despise you and laugh and you, just like they laugh at fucking Ms. Brill, your favorite character, and no wonder. She is a loser, just like you."

Nellie stormed out of the room and out the front door, slamming it with a thud behind her. She was seething with anger, to the point that she was trembling. She knew in an instant that she was dead wrong but had too much rage at that very moment to either do anything about it or even care. She stomped her way out, through the azalea bushes and into the rose garden. She took up the hedge clippers the gardener had left lying on the grass and began to chop the weeds overgrowing on the fence. She chopped furiously, tenaciously, until every drop of rage was channeled and the tension released.

Back at the house, Virginia was apologizing profusely.

"Really, Katherine, I can't imagine what came over Nellie. She is not usually so ill-tempered and so abrupt." She said this knowing it was not entirely true and hoping Katherine would forget another time Nellie had behaved badly toward her.

"Now, now, Virginia, one mustn't make apologies or excuses for one's servants. It really is unbecoming a woman of our station."

"It's just that I feel ghastly, treating you the way she did. It's simply vile."

"Never mind now. I am sure she had her reasons. She was probably very upset about her friend, and something I said struck a nerve for some reason."

"You are very kind to make excuses, Katherine, but really, that sort of behavior is unacceptable. Imagine if every time we had a bad day we went off like that on our servants. They would call the constable on us." Even as she said the words, they both knew well that there were stories of servants treated abominably. How Christian people could go to church on Sunday praising God and singing of His mercy while treating their employees so shabbily Monday through Friday, she would never understand. Did they not remember that

Jesus was a working man? It was this hypocrisy that Virginia hated about religion, not religion itself, contrary to the reports of many posthumous biographers.

"Well, I don't know how kind I am, but I do know when someone has a bad day. It really was no big deal, Ginia. I was just startled. I'll not mention it again."

Nellie returned to the house an hour and a half later, breathing less deeply and possessed over all with a feeling of calm. She let herself in through the kitchen entrance and closed the door gently behind her. She didn't want anyone to hear her come in, because she did not want to be told what she had to do. She thought about everything while she was out, and having released her aggression, she realized that she had been terribly wrong.

When she walked into the living room, the women's backs were turned to her. Nellie meekly approached the guest and cleared her throat. Katherine turned around in surprise.

"Mrs. Mansfield, I want to apologize for how I acted and spoke before. You didn't deserve it, and I didn't mean any of what I said."

Katherine winked at the cook, causing her to crack a smile.

"It's fine, Nellie, I was just saying to Virginia a little while ago that you were obviously tense. I could tell something was wrong."

"Well, that is true, I've been a bit upset with Lottie gone."

"But she is still living here, I understand. Surely that must make things better."

Nellie tried quite hard to keep her tone in check. Having already eaten crow, she did not care to do it again. "Yes, it does make it somewhat better, but by the time she gets home, we're both half-asleep. We don't exactly get a lot of quality time together."

Katherine nodded slowly, to show sympathy.

"I can certainly see where this would create a real strain on you. Definitely enough to make anyone want to lash out at the nearest person, especially a pesky guest who shows up uninvited!"

Both women smiled, the incident now resolved. In different circumstances, they would have hugged and exchanged perfunctory pecks on the cheeks, but there was no question of that in the current situation.

Virginia beamed from ear to ear. The whole situation resolved itself without her having to do a blessed thing.

*****

London
April 1938

The Woolfs moved to London as soon as winter began to recede. Virginia's health had begun to show signs of improvement, and the doctors believed her when she said that being in the city would be good for her psyche. She felt that the country air was stifling her creativity. "If I look at one more blade of grass or farm animal, I shall slit my wrists, by Christ!" she had written in her journal some months back, then ripped the page out and set it afire in the sink, for fear someone might come upon it and find her in need of a rest cure. The house at Richmond was closed up; the family home, which had been rented out for the past couple of years, was vacated, and the Woolfs moved in, for an indeterminate amount of time.

Nellie was thrilled beyond belief to be in the greatest of all cities. She adored London; it was one of the things that had created an indelible bond Nellie with Virginia. Nellie most admired the enduring quality of the Great City. Even in the dark days of Depression, somehow, the museums, art galleries, and theatres managed to stay open. This puzzled Nellie, who could only surmise that not everyone was equally depressed.

The Woolfs were hit hard. Virginia's book sales took a serious dip, while the sales of Katherine's and EM's books, the major output of the Hogarth Press, came to a grinding halt. Why spend precious money on books when the British Library offered them all for the price of the ride on the Tube, or a brisk walk for those who could not afford the modest train fare? It was only some people, the rare birds and bibliophiles, who purchased books rather than borrowing them from the library. Nellie guessed that these were the same people who populated the art galleries while their neighbors hoboed or sold day-old apples for pennies on Oxford Street. Culture was vibrant in this magical city, despite all economic hardship. Was it any wonder that Nellie loved it so?

Nellie still loved the Woolfs, especially Virginia. But she felt out of place with them now, as if she had outgrown her usefulness to them, or they to her. She desired change on many levels. But change, no matter how simple, was at best difficult for Nellie and at worst nearly impossible.

But things had changed over the years. With Lottie working somewhere else, the happy rhythm of the household was irrevocably lost. Lottie was making considerably more money (most of it she was able to keep thanks to the ridiculously low rent Leonard charged her), Nellie was making some more money, but her workload doubled in turn.

Nellie was no longer happy but didn't know what she could do, except for one thing, and she doubted she had the guts.

It was a simple argument over pot roast that made all the difference. Virginia was expecting to have roast beef for dinner; instead, she saw a pot roast being prepared in the kitchen.

"Why are we preparing a pot roast when we already decided upon roast beef?"

"We made no such decision, Mrs. W. I don't know what you're referring to at all."

Virginia always grew indignant when she was contradicted.

"I distinctly remember discussing this last night before you went downstairs for the evening. We said that we were going to have roast beef. I believe you were going to make some of your famous garlic mashed potatoes with it as well, and broccoli on the side."

Nellie laughed. "Oh, ma'am, you're only remember half the story. Yes, we did indeed have that conversation last night, but we weren't talking about dinner for tonight. Today is Wednesday, we were discussing dinner for Sunday."

Virginia pursed her lips, like she had just tasted a sour lemon.

"There is no way I could get that wrong. I would not have wanted pot roast tonight. Pot roast is a Sunday dinner, not a Wednesday dinner, everyone knows that. I was looking forward to roast beef all day long."

Nellie roared. "If that don't beat all, dinners have designated days now. What rot! That is the most fuckin' ridiculous thing I've ever heard of."

"I'll thank you to watch your tongue in front of me, madam. Do not presume to forget that it is to your employer that you are speaking."

"Yes, my employer. A dried-up novelist who is so involved in her own imaginary world that she can't remember what she wants for dinner on what night. Some employer."

Virginia's face inflamed. "Who the hell do you think you are talking to like that? And in my own home no less. I'll have your guts for garters."

Nellie was not nearly as angry but decided to seize the opportunity.

"You'll have nothing of mine, you fool. I'm done here! I'm giving you my two weeks' notice, effective right now. And as for that fucking shit hole that you laughingly call a basement, I will be out of it by the end of the month, Lottie too."

"Bloody hell, we'll be well rid of you." Virginia stormed out of the room, went back to her study, and slammed the door so hard that two books toppled off the top shelf.

Nellie was angry yet relieved. Now she needed to keep her resolve.

The women never formally reconciled; they just ceased to be angry after a day or two and by Saturday were talking normally. Virginia thought everything was back to normal. Since she never visited the basement, she had no way of knowing that Nellie and Lottie were packing it up. The things they threw out were packaged neatly, so as not to make their intentions obvious. By the end of the two weeks, everything they owned was packed away, and they were ready to go.

The moment of truth came. The night before what was to be Nellie's last night, she walked out onto the terrace where Virginia and Leonard were sitting and cleared her throat. Virginia had been reading an article, Leonard smoking a cigar, nursing a brandy.

"Excuse me, ma'am, Mr. Woolf, but seeing as tomorrow will be my last day here, I was wondering what you would like for dinner."

Leonard choked on his brandy, and Virginia dropped the article she was reading to the floor.

"What do you mean, your last day?" Leonard asked. "Surely you wouldn't just leave without giving any notice. That isn't right, especially not after all this time."

"Of course I wouldn't do that. I gave notice, two weeks ago, didn't I, ma'am?" She looked to Virginia for confirmation, but Virginia was too stunned to even think straight.

"Why, yes, you did, I suppose, when we had that row, but I didn't take it seriously. We made up, as we always do, and you've given notice plenty of times—you've never left."

"Right, ma'am, because I always took my notice back. If you notice, this time I didn't take it back."

Virginia was incredulous. "I can't believe you are going to let a silly row get in the way here. It's not like we haven't—"

"It has nothing to do with that, Mrs. W … oolf," she added the full name, reminded of Leonard's presence. "Truthfully, I've been wanting to go for a while but couldn't find the way to tell you, is all. I sort of used our row as an excuse."

By now, Virginia was dissolved into tears. She opened her mouth to speak but could not. Nellie did it for her.

"Oh, Mrs. W." She no longer cared who was in the room. "You know I love you more than just about anything else on this earth. But I've got to move on now, Lottie too. We've got a chance to work together again, both of us at the B and B she is at. They're giving us one of the rooms. It's a bit smaller than the basement, but its fine."

"But why?" Virginia managed to croak out.

"For me, ma'am. I love you, I told you that, but this is your life, and your house. Before the good lord calls me home, I want a chance at my own life. I gotta take a chance."

And that, as they say, was that.

Leonard spoke. "Well, Nellie, Mrs. Woolf and I wish you the best. You always have friends here, and if need be, you always have a home here. Both of you."

"Thank you, Mr. Woolf, I appreciate that, and everything else you've done over the years. Lottie appreciates it too, not that she'd likely ever tell you so herself, but I know she does."

"But you're leaving," Virginia stated dumbly, as if still looking for confirmation.

"Yes, I am," Nellie responded quietly, her cheeks streaked with tears. "But I am going to be living on Piccadilly, not the moon! We can see each other when we wish, write letters, even ring each other up occasionally once I know I can afford a telly. Everything will be okay, Mrs. W, we're a family, and we always will be, we just are a family going our separate ways."

The next day, Nellie and Lottie moved their things out of the house amidst tears, sniffles, mumbled congratulations, and well-wishing. The women were panting, carrying boxes up and down the stairs for hours, right after the breakfast dishes were cleared away and Nellie had taken off her apron for the last time. Lottie mopped the floors and cleaned out the cabinets. Finally, everything was cleaned out, and the car (Leonard's contribution was letting them borrow his car) was loaded. It was time to go.

Leonard and Virginia stood outside the entire time, ostensibly watching the car with its doors wide open (this was London after all). They stood transfixed, as if unable comprehend what was playing out before their eyes. Leonard admired the women's tenacity; Virginia had this feeling of dread that was spreading across her stomach, rising up her throat. Finally, Lottie, recognizing the tension of the moment, announced, "It's time to go." Nellie went to Virginia and embraced her tightly for several minutes. Lottie went to Leonard, who gave her a perfunctory peck on the cheek and a tap on the back. Virginia and Lottie embraced, but for less time than Nellie and Virginia had. The women got into the car; Lottie promised to return it in a few hours when they were finished using it. Nellie didn't have a driver's license; having failed her driving test four times, she took it as a sign that God didn't want her to drive. Never was she more grateful for that fact than at the present moment. She could not bear it if she had to come back to this house today and relive the scene they had just participated in. They got into the car, and Lottie began to drive off.

Nellie had promised herself she would sit forward in the car only, never turning to look back. She was briefly reminded of Lot's wife, being turned into a pillar of salt for looking back.

It was about a ten-minute drive to the bed and breakfast. Their room was off to the side on the second floor. It was a large bedroom with a small sitting room. The sitting room had linoleum, and the bedroom was carpeted. The bedroom furniture was knotty pine, and the mattresses for the two twin beds provided were lumpy, but the women were pleased enough with the accommodations. The drawback was that it had no kitchen in it. The women were expected to take their meals in the kitchen. Private meals in a kitchen of their own were a thing of the past. They would miss that, but the workload was less, and they were no longer living in a basement. They had a room, like everyone else's, even if it was off to the side.

Nellie cooked breakfast for everyone, then lunch and dinner for the family. She did the shopping for the house, and kept the inventory. Lottie took care of the guest rooms and the common areas of the house. During her free time, Nellie spent a lot time in the library. She noticed right away that the room was stocked with every book Virginia Woolf ever wrote. Talk about Fate rubbing salt on wounds. It had been Nellie's decision to leave, and she wanted to, but she could not help feeling homesick for the Woolf's home and for them.

The women had the next two days to themselves. Lottie had gotten the days off, and Nellie had negotiated her starting date to coincide with Lottie's next day back to work. They spent many of those hours in their bedroom, talking, lovemaking, decorating, making the place their own. When they ventured out of the room, they went for long walks. They ate lunches in the street and had tea in outdoor cafes. Slowly but surely, they acclimated themselves to their new life.

Virginia and Leonard puttered around the house for a day or two, hiring a day maid to keep the place clean and eating out for a couple of days after the leftovers ran out. (Nellie had thoughtfully prepared three days of meals in advance. The Woolfs had been surprised to find the leftovers in the icebox.) They put an ad for a cook in *The Sun* the day the leftovers ran out. The cook was not a live-in either; they refused to have live ins anymore.

Virginia and Nellie began meeting regularly for lunch or tea once or twice a week, for several weeks. Eventually, time took hold of their lives again. Virginia got busy with new book ideas and social engagements; Nellie felt like she was constantly shopping when she wasn't cooking. The lunches dwindled until they stopped. The women wrote brief letters to each other, and there was the occasional telephone call, but otherwise, they drifted apart.

Epilogue

I am an old woman. My whole right side seems filled with arthritis. My right knee is so stiff most of the time that I can hardly bend it. My right arm throbs in pain, and the joints in my fingers ache so that nothing soothes them except soaking them in warm water. I add salt to the water; I don't know if that actually helps, but it's what my mamma always did. If it was good enough for her, it's good enough for me.

As you can imagine, stairs are just about impossible for me these days. About a year or so ago, I think, I had to give up my flat because of the stairs. I moved to a walk-in flat. Maybe not as safe, but then what have I got to steal? And one look at this sagging old body would be enough to scare off any man who might want to violate me. The rent is cheaper than in my old place, and I was damned lucky to get it, yet still … When I left my old place, I cried for three days. It was the last place I lived in with Lottie. When I left there, I felt like I was leaving her behind. You can go ahead and call it stupid, 'cause I know it is, but it is how I felt, stupid or not. But feelings don't use logic, that's for sure (which is probably why divorce rates are so high).

Anyhow, I sure didn't want to leave, but I couldn't be a prisoner in my own home either. When I told Adelaide I was moving, she was upset. She thought I'd reconsider; foolish, since she walks almost as badly as I do and is a bit hunched over. The day I moved, lordy, you should have seen the scene she put on. She wailed so loudly, up and down the hall, you'd have thought she was giving birth or getting murdered (funny how the sounds of both are the same). I tried to explain to her that I wasn't moving to Mars, just a few blocks down, but she said that at our age, a few blocks down might as well be

Mars. I saw her point and hated her for it, but only for that moment, and only because she made me feel even guiltier than I already did. Adelaide is a really good woman. I'd even consider … but never mind, I'm too old for that now.

This flat is nice enough, a bit damp for my tastes, but for the rent I pay, I can't complain. I just wear layers and have a lot of bulky sweaters. I decorated with all my little knickknacks and pictures, but it still doesn't feel like home, not really. Adelaide comes over once a week, sometimes more, so she and I still see each other, but it really isn't the same. Now, when she comes, she *visits*; before she came over whenever the hell she felt like it, sometimes just for a cup of coffee in the morning. Sometimes we'd be in and out of each other's flats three or four times a day. We can't do that anymore; that's what hurts Adelaide. It hurts me just as much, though I don't dare show it since I'm the one who caused it. I didn't have a choice, but she won't see it that way. We still have each other's key, but neither one of us has ever used it since I moved. We just have it for emergencies. Thank God there haven't been any emergencies. Life goes on. It's not quite the ideal, but it's living, which is better than the alternative, I suppose.

Thomas did really nicely with his book. He sold it to a publisher not even six months after he finished it. I read several drafts—he wanted my approval before it went to typesetting—and then he gave me one of his author's copies, signed. He dedicated it:

> To Nellie Boxall, without whose kind assistance
> this book would never have been possible.
>
> With love and gratitude always,
> Thomas

I cried when I read the dedication; it made me think of my copy of *The Voyage Out* and when it was signed, at that interview so long ago.

The book was a real success. The publisher paid him a nice advance, and he earned it out within the first few months that it was on the shelves. In case you don't know what that means (I sure didn't), when a book "earns out" an advance, it means that the book has sold enough copies that the publisher made back the money they advanced the writer. After that, the writer receives a check, called a royalty, for any future book sales. The check comes every six months, based on the number of books sold.

Thomas is so sweet. Every time he gets a royalty check, he sends me a check, saying that I should get some of whatever he gets, since I lived the story. It is really nice of him, and I do appreciate it.

Funny thing about Thomas. The whole time I was meeting with him and even afterward when he had finished a polished draft of the book and wanted me to read it before he sent it off to a publisher, he was not with anyone. It was like after his wife comm … died, he wanted to be alone forever, like some sort of monk.

After the book came out, he asked me to go with him on a couple of speaking engagements, but I said no. I am no speaker, especially when it comes to folks I don't know. We lost touch soon after that. No offense involved; there just didn't seem to be a reason for us to talk anymore. All that held us together were the ghosts of the past. Anyway, it was funny.

I got a letter from him yesterday. He is married! Her name is Rachel. Ironically, he met her at his own book signing—so you might say that in a way, Mrs. W and I brought them together. The shock came when I saw her photograph. She looks to be almost my age, and I'm … we'll never mind about that. Maybe I wasn't imagining things when I thought for a while that … well, no matter. He is a good man, and I enjoyed our time together while it lasted. I hope he has found happiness. He deserves it after what he's been through. He says that she had never been with a man before him. I find that an odd statement to put in a letter. What is he trying to tell me? That she is an old maid he rescued from spinsterhood or that she was like me until he "converted" her? That don't make her sound so attractive to me. But, no matter. If his letter is any indication, they are genuinely fond of each other, and Thomas exudes happiness on the page. After all he went through, I think he's earned the right to be happy. He says she would love to meet me, but even if he means it, I doubt she does. I'm part of his past; we were thrown together to complete a project, and we did. There is no reason for us to see each other anymore, and certainly no reason for his new wife to want to see me. All the same, I know how sensitive he is, so I wrote back that I'd love to have them over sometime for tea, seeing as I almost never get out anymore. I told him to ring me up anytime they can make it, and I'll make sure I'm presentable for company. I doubt they'll come, and I'm not sure I want them to. What for? Memories are better; memories are sweet—especially since, over time, memories often change from what happened to what you *wish would have* happened.

Another letter came a few days ago. Elsie, Lottie's last sister, died a few weeks ago. She was seventy-two. Seems like everyone I know is dropping like flies. I suppose soon I'll be next. I am up there in years (you don't need to know exactly how far up there). I was always a vain woman, for my sins. Funny thing, at my age, I don't have anything left to be vain about except my age. So I try to keep 'em guessing. Even Adelaide doesn't know my exact age.

Thank God I have what I need—more than I need unless I live to 120—and my body is telling me pretty clearly that I don't have to worry about that. What worries me about money is who I can leave it to when I'm dead. I got no family to speak of, and Adelaide ain't likely to live much longer than me, so it don't make any sense to leave my money to her. I have cash in the house and a bit in the bank. Not that it's much by most people's standards, but I ain't nobody special, and I never had one of these great jobs that paid people real well. So whatever I have is hard-earned, and I'm real proud that at this age, I have anything at all. And what's mine was earned by me not the government. I sure don't want the government to take it when I'm gone. Lottie has a nephew who comes around once or twice, if he remembers, but I hardly see the need to leave him anything. Adelaide's got a grandson who don't hardly come to see her either, but he is around more often than Lottie's nephew. At least he shows up if Adelaide needs something. Truth be told, he's helped me out quite a few times too, more than I can say for Lottie's nephew. Besides, Lottie's family never did recognize me as being anything to Lottie. To them, I was no one in particular, just a coworker and a roommate. They used to treat me like I was a group of flies circling their family picnic; a nuisance to be gotten rid of, if possible, but likely best tolerated. Why should my money go to anyone in that family? If anything, there's always charity. It seems like every day there is a new letter in the post begging for donations for this cause, that research, those animals, etc. Maybe I'll give to one of them. Otherwise, Adelaide's grandson is the one, I guess. I'd leave it to Adelaide in a heartbeat, but she's the same age as me, so it don't make any sense.

Well, I suppose I should tell more about what happened back then. Lottie and I worked for the bed and breakfast the whole time after I left the Woolfs, until the missus killed herself. We were both devastated, not that Lottie would admit it. To Lottie, Mrs. W was like that annoying relative who you find it so difficult to deal with; you might have rows, you might wish they would go away or not love the idea of spending time together, but at the end of the day, they're still family. When the newspapers first broke the story that she was missing, Lottie and I went right over there to keep Mr. Woolf company during the long vigil while we waited for her safe return or … confirmation of the other. Within two days, the newspaper headlines had changed from "missing" to "presumed dead." They finally found her body, at the bottom of the Danube River. All three of us went to the medical examiner to identify her; Mr. Woolf nearly collapsed when he saw her lifeless body. Lottie and I struggled to keep it together but managed, aside from a lot of tears.

Vita Sackville-West lived out her days, the manly looking thing, but she was never the same after Mrs. W died. As for Mrs. Woolf, may she rest in peace. She thought of me right up until the end. Shortly after all the London papers announced that Virginia Woolf was missing and presumed dead, I received a letter from her solicitor. Apparently, before she died, she tied up some of the loose ends that had been bothering her. I was one of them, I suppose, since the solicitor's letter said I was to report to his office five days hence. I was a bit nervous actually, at first not being able to imagine what it was Virginia Woolf's solicitor could want with the likes of me. I was real nervous at first, until I found out why I was there. Then I was just plain surprised. *I was in the will.* Mrs. W had left me an annuity. I felt so dumb; I didn't even know what an annuity was, sounded like a disease. The solicitor explained it to me like I was seven. Two hundred pounds a year, for the rest of my life. The solicitor himself was in charge of the finances; he handed me a check for the first installment and said that every year on that date, I would get another check. When he handed me the check, it was like a river inside me broke loose. I cried so hard that he took the check out of my hands, so I wouldn't damage it. I never had to work full-time again. I could do the odd catering job, once or twice a month, and still be able to live exactly as I always had. If I consented to working a bit more than that, I could live in pretty nice comfort.

When I recounted the story about the annuity to Thomas, right before our meetings were done and over with, he confessed to me that he knew about it already; it was the main reason he had decided to contact me for information. He said that he figured that any cook important enough to V. Woolf to be left that size of an annuity was someone who was much more than just a cook in this woman's life. Even Sophie Farrell (the family cook for the Duckworth/Woolf family) had not received such an extravagant sum, for all her years of unwavering service and support to the family. So he figured I was special. I guess I was that after all, at least to Mrs. W.

*****

I don't have much time left. I can feel my body starting to shut down. I've always been in tune with my body, and its messages are getting through to me quite clearly. I have hardly any appetite left, I am almost never thirsty, and I rarely need to go to the loo anymore. There was a time, not that long ago, that it seemed I couldn't be somewhere for more than ten minutes *without* having to use the loo.

It is the beginning of winter; the air gets colder by the day, and even the most stubborn leaves are off the trees now. The feel of snow is constantly in the air, although not a snowflake has fallen yet. I don't usually enjoy the winter; I stay inside most of the time since the cold is murder on my old bones. But this winter, I've made it a point to go out every day. I go out in the morning and suck in as much air as they old lungs will take. Breathing in that crisp cold air makes me sure I'm alive. And it's important I do all this now; I, sure as anything, won't be around next winter.

I've been thinking a lot about my life, especially my life with the Woolfs. For all my complaining and bellyaching about different things (and I ain't saying my complaining wasn't justified; it's hard running a kitchen when the missus cared more about books than meat), I have to say that those years were the best and happiest years of my life. Sure, I lived with kin and all. Between all the siblings I lived with and the people I worked with, I sure had enough people around me all the time. I was never alone. Sometimes I only wished that I *could* be alone. But in all those households, even with my own kin, my blood, we always felt like people who just happened to be living together. There never felt like there was a connection between us. It was different with the Woolfs. Come what may, we were a family. Mrs. W and I might be hollering at each other, telling each other where to go and how to get there, but the second one of us was in trouble, the other was there all the way. We'd have died for each other.

And even Lottie, well, it was no secret that she and the missus didn't care for one another so great, yet still, when Lottie was sick, Mrs. W was there, and whenever there was a problem with Mrs. W, Lottie did whatever she had to do to make sure everything was okay. Sure, she made it seem like she was being nice to the missus simply for me, that she didn't give a fuck about her any other way, but I knew her too well. I knew that was all bunk, but I never dared say so.

And Mrs. W had dozens of opportunities and reasons to give Lottie the sack—me too, for that matter. But for years, she didn't. And she looked out for us even in death. After getting the annuity, Lottie and I decided to keep working at the B and B (though we no longer needed to) but moved into a flat of our own instead of living there. We found a place nearby work. It was the place I lived in when Thomas was coming to see me. Adelaide moved in a few months after we did, and she and I clicked right away. Lottie was never crazy about her, but then we never did have the same taste in friends. She always welcomed Adelaide though and tolerated what she perceived as her "intrusions." Lottie loved me more than anything and knew how important it was to me to have friends. We loved that flat. Lottie got sick in that flat and should have died there but … well, you already know all about that. I wish I could do that over again, but life's too short for regrets, especially since mine is almost over; if she's cross with me, she'll be able to tell me so herself real soon.

Me, I don't care where I am when I die. I never wanted to die alone, but that don't matter to me anymore now. Good thing too, seeing as how there is no one left to be with me when that time comes. I mean, sure, there is Adelaide, but at her age, and given the fact that she isn't next door anymore, I don't think she'll be there.

Anyway, as I said, those things don't concern me anymore. I'll die here or in hospital, most likely here since I don't really like going to hospital, and someone will find me, or they won't. Sooner or later, though, I'm sure someone will discover my body, if only for the smell. I could care less what they do with my body. I don't care where it ends up. I'll be with Lottie in the way that matters—in the spirit. As for my body, whoever it is that decides can do whatever they decide.

All things being said, I've had a good life. I'm tired now. I'm ready to go Home whenever the good Lord is ready to welcome me. May the angels guide me, and may Lottie and Mrs. W be waiting for me at the door.

About the Author

Michael DiSchiavi is an educator turned entrepreneur born and raised in Brooklyn, New York, where he still resides. A voracious reader, Michael has always been interested in the private lives of the lesser known "unsung heroes" of history. He has published numerous articles and book reviews on literary criticism and educational issues. This is his first published novel; he is currently in the final editing stages of a novel on Caroline of Brunswick.

CPSIA information can be obtained
at www.ICGtesting.com
Printed in the USA
FFHW022253020219
50378181-55513FF